Sing
TO MY HEART

NEW YORK TIMES AND USA TODAY BESTSELLING AUTHOR

FRANCIS RAY

ESSENCE BESTSELLING AUTHOR

JACQUELIN THOMAS

FELICIA MASON

Sing

TO MY HEART

This work was first published as
HOW SWEET THE SOUND
by Harlequin Enterprises Limited in 2005

HARLEQUIN®

entertain, enrich, inspire™

SING TO MY HEART

ISBN-13: 978-0-373-53459-3

First published in 2005 by
Harlequin Enterprises Limited
under the title HOW SWEET THE SOUND

Copyright © 2012 by Harlequin Books S.A.

This edition published July 2012

The publisher acknowledges the copyright holders
of the individual works as follows:

THEN SINGS MY SOUL
Copyright © 2005 by Francis Ray

MAKE A JOYFUL NOISE
Copyright © 2005 by Jacquelin Thomas

HEART SONGS
Copyright © 2005 by Felicia L. Mason

Recycling programs
for this product may
not exist in your area.

CONTENTS

Acknowledgments

Special thanks to my parents,
Mrs. Venora Radford and the late Mr. Clinton Radford,
who always believed in me and taught me to
always trust and believe in God.
—F.M.

THEN SINGS MY SOUL

Francis Ray

Chapter One

"Caleb and Grace, I have wonderful news. Summerset's city council wants you to work together to put on a gospel concert for Summerset's Annual Harvest Celebration," Harold Jenkins announced with a broad grin on his angular face.

Caleb Jackson barely kept his jaw from dropping at the Summerset Junior College president's announcement. He didn't have to look at Grace Thompson sitting stiff-backed beside him to know she was experiencing the same difficulty. For some reason she was the only professor in his music department who hadn't immediately supported him during his first year as chair. From the polite but distant way she'd treated him since the beginning of the fall semester three weeks ago, the rest of the year didn't promise to be any better. However, she was one of the best and most conscientious teachers he had.

"Took you by surprise," President Jenkins continued jovially, his hands loosely clasped on top of the polished oval conference table. "I don't mind telling you that the Board of Regents and I were very pleased and honored that the city council chose to recognize two of our teachers for their talent. You two continue to make us proud and put Summerset Junior College on the map. I can't wait to see what you come up with."

Murmurs of agreement and approval came from around the oblong table where the dean and the chairs of the other fine arts department were seated. Caleb tugged at the knot in the black tie he kept in his office for "official" meetings. With President Jenkins smiling like a proud parent and knowing he had heeded Caleb's advice and helped push through the increase for Caleb's department's budget for the current school year, Caleb was trapped. There was no way he could say he'd rather walk barefoot through a briar patch than work with Grace, and the feeling was mutual. "We'll do our best," he finally managed to reply.

"This is an undeserved honor," Grace mumbled.

Caleb's head snapped around to stare at her sharply. Was she taking a swipe at his musical talent?

"Well, I better let you two get to it. The celebration is less than two months away." Standing, President Jenkins shook their hands. "As I said, I know, as always, you'll make Summerset Junior College proud."

"Yes, sir," Grace said, another of those polite but strained smiles on her heart-shaped, cinnamon-hued face.

"Thank you," Caleb felt obligated to add as the other people in the room crowded around to offer their own congratulations.

Trying to keep his own smile in place, he opened the

conference room's door. Grace shot him a narrow look as she passed. She must really be aggravated. No matter how much he'd sensed she was annoyed with him in the past, she'd never let it show, keeping her emotions under tight control.

"Professor Jackson, I think we should discuss this," she told him as soon as he closed the door, the usual soft cadence of her East Texas drawl sharp with disapproval.

"Let's talk about it without an audience," he said, glancing around the busy hallway as staff, faculty and students passed them in the administration building. He'd ceased trying to get her to call him by his first name as everyone else at the school did when they were not around the students. But in that, at least, she wasn't singling him out. "Room C should be available."

Nodding curtly, she headed down the hallway toward the exit to the fine arts complex, her back straight and her head high, disapproval in every line of her slim body. A body that Caleb had thought on more than one occasion was put together rather nicely. Repressing another sigh, Caleb shoved his hands into the pockets of his well-worn jeans. Grace probably hadn't liked it that he had shown up in jeans for the meeting instead of a suit. Letting him dress casually was another concession by the president and the Board of Regents.

He'd always been the laid-back, casual type. On the other hand, he'd never seen Grace wearing anything except a suit or a dress with a jacket. The suit she wore today was navy blue and white with a straight skirt. He felt hot just looking at her.

The temperatures during summers in East Texas could easily reach a hundred degrees. Grace never seemed bothered by the heat. She'd never been anything but perfectly dressed and she was usually perturbed that he wasn't. They were direct opposites in too many ways to count. He wasn't looking forward to their conversation, but there was no way around it. *Lord, give me strength,* he thought as he followed her toward the Meadow Fine Arts Building.

Arms crossed, Grace waited for Caleb in the sound-proof music room, the toe of her low-heeled navy-blue pump tapping out an irritated rhythm. *That man is as slow as molasses,* she thought. The only time she'd seen him move with any degree of speed was when he was directing Revelation, the school's nine-member Christian ensemble. And in her opinion, he showed too much enthusiasm. She was pleased for the college to finally receive statewide recognition for its music department, but she was troubled by the music's upbeat tempo.

Caleb apparently had the ability to inspire and galvanize his young students, but he didn't have to do it with that finger-popping, earsplitting music or by trying to dress hip and act like them. He refused to lead by example, something she had always been taught by the teachings of the Word.

She could hardly believe her eyes when she'd met him at the reception to introduce him to the faculty last summer. He'd worn jeans and a tan, raw-silk sport coat like some rock star and had been unapologetic for doing so. He was nothing like his predecessor, Dr. Abbot, a kindly man whose demeanor and dress were always respectful and above reproach. Just as important, Dr. Abbot had been as dependable as the sunrise and as steady as a rock. You never knew what Caleb would do or suggest.

Summerset Junior College had lost a wonderful teacher when Dr. Abbot retired after forty-five years of teaching. He'd been with Summerset since its beginning thirty-five years ago. He'd worked tirelessly to build and increase the prestige of the music department. It seemed almost unfair that an arrogant man like Caleb was able to do in a year what Dr. Abbot had never accomplished.

The door opened. For an endless moment she and Caleb stared across the room at each other. She attributed her increased heart rate to her growing annoyance. Her gaze lowered to his long legs disgracefully encased in revealing blue jeans. Dr. Abbot always wore a bow tie and a suit. That it was a bit rumpled was endearing. He wouldn't have dreamed of meeting with the president in his shirtsleeves.

You'd think Caleb could dig up a jacket and a pair of dress slacks from wherever he'd gotten that pitiful black tie. She'd learned early that he didn't defer to anyone. "I've been waiting five minutes. I have class in thirty minutes."

Releasing the door, he let it swing shut. "Since as chair of the department, I help make and approve the schedule, I'm well aware of yours, Grace."

Her lips pressed together for the briefest second, then she forced herself to relax. She would not allow Caleb to upset her. She'd get this over with, then do what she had done in the past, stay out of his way unless absolutely necessary. "Knowing how busy you are as chair, I'll be happy to take on the entire gospel concert by myself."

Caleb folded his arms across his wide, white-shirted chest. "No way."

"If you're worried about me taking all the credit, I assure you that wouldn't be the case," she told him. She'd always thought he liked being in the limelight.

"You mean you'd lie?"

Grace gasped. She was so shocked, so incensed that for a moment she couldn't speak. "Of course not!" she retorted. No one had ever questioned her integrity, but then she'd never met a person who provoked her as much as Caleb Jackson.

His long arms slowly dropped to his sides. "Then how do you plan to explain my absence at the practices if President Jenkins or one of the regents or city council members just happens to stop by?"

She didn't have an answer, but she wasn't ready to concede defeat. "Perhaps you could come to a few."

"No dice." He came to stand within a foot of her. "You're not jeopardizing my job or my reputation because you and I disagree on how the music department should be run. You're not a band director and you would be lost trying to fill in for me. The only musical instruments you can play are the piano and the organ. I play several others."

Her mouth firmed. He would have to bring that up.

"Get used to it, Grace. We're stuck with each other until this is over."

Her worst nightmare. Her dark head fell forward. "Please, Lord, give me strength."

"Same thing I asked."

Her head snapped up. She couldn't decide if he was teasing her or being sincere.

Dimples winked in his handsome nut-brown face as he grinned down at her. "Thought I was a heathen?"

She thought of Caleb as little as possible. "I have to go or I'll be late."

"That would be a first," he said. "Revelation has practice tonight at seven. You can come before we get started and we can tell them together. Then, if it's all right with you, I'll drop in on your choir practice tomorrow night and we can tell them."

Her eyes widened in surprise. "You know my gospel choir has practice on Tuesdays?"

His expression held a hint of long-suffering. "The schedule again. You weren't able to teach classes at night last year or this because of your obligations at church. You're doing the early evening classes instead."

Caleb had taken up the slack both times. It was unusual for the chair of the department to have night classes even at a small junior college. She'd thanked him, but she didn't like being obligated to him. She hadn't felt the same way when Dr. Alton had allowed her to not teach night classes. "I'm still trying to see if another teacher will take the class. In the meantime, I appreciate your sensitivity. My church means a lot to me."

He looked at her strangely. "Church means a great deal to a lot of us. I'll see you tonight."

Grace frowned. She almost felt that he was taking her to task in some strange way. "I'll be there."

"Good." He stepped aside. "Who knows, we might find it's not as bad as we think."

"Or worse," Grace grumbled softly as she left for her class.

Caleb shook his dark head as the door swung shut. "Why me?"

Why not you?

Caleb's mouth twitched. He could practically hear his mother's voice as clearly as if she were standing there with him. Growing up with his sisters in Dallas he'd asked that question a hundred, a thousand times when he didn't want to do some chore around the house or one he thought Heather and Cynthia, his older and younger

sisters, should do. He couldn't recall a time when com-
plaining had helped. Now they were both married and
living in Dallas with families of their own.

When they'd all been together last month for his
mother's birthday, his family had wanted to know when
he was finally going to marry and have a family. He
had given them his usual answer: he was in no hurry.
He figured when God wanted him to get married, He'd
send the perfect woman to Caleb. Until then, Caleb
would continue making a name for himself in the music
industry.

Going over to the baby grand in the corner, he began
to play "How Great Thou Art," a song that had always
soothed and helped him to take himself out of the equa-
tion and let God lead him in the direction He wanted
Caleb to go. Caleb's mouth twitched again. God had
surprised him when He sent him to Summerset. Other
jobs kept falling through or just didn't seem right. But
from the time he'd dropped over the hill in his vintage
Corvette and seen Summerset in a little valley, he'd
felt this was where God had been leading him…for
the time being.

He'd tried to fight it, of course. He was a city boy,
born and bred in Dallas where there was always something happening. In Summerset, the biggest industry
outside ranching and farming was the tire factory. But
God had never promised following Him would be easy.

Yet, Caleb felt that there was something else God
wanted him to do here. Caleb just hadn't figured out
what it was yet. He had thought it was helping to bring
young people to the Lord through his music ministry,
just as Frank Hemphill, the youth pastor at his church,
had helped him. And although there was a definite increase in attendance on the two Sundays a month Rev-

elation performed at chapel services, he still felt that he was missing something right before his eyes.

Shrugging, Caleb continued to play. He'd learned through the years that God had His own time schedule. In the meantime, Caleb would use the newest opportunity to tell of God's unconditional love and redemption through music.

Done right, and Caleb didn't intend otherwise, the gospel musical would mark another milestone in his career that would lead him to his next position. He enjoyed teaching and the students at Summerset, but he knew in his heart that he wouldn't stay. He would continue to work with young people and help as Pastor Hemphill had helped him, but Caleb had always felt that his destiny was in a larger venue where he could reach the masses and where the sidewalks didn't roll up at ten.

He'd lost count of the times he'd been busy with his music or preparing lessons and let time slip away and hadn't been able to find anyplace open late to eat. He would sure be happy when he returned to a city with all-night restaurants and more than one movie theater.

Until then, he'd do the work the Lord had set before him. He was going to put on a gospel musical that would bring people to their feet in praise...with or without Grace's help.

Chapter Two

Grace saw Pastor French's older-model truck and Alton's car parked in front of Peaceful Rest Church the moment she turned the corner off Collins onto North Fourth Street. She smiled in anticipation of the meeting. She'd called them the second she'd gotten out of class and told them that it was extremely important they meet as soon as possible. Luckily Alton owned his own business in town, House of Music, and was able to leave a sales clerk in charge and meet with them. In consideration of Pastor French's job as a supervisor at the bottling plant, she'd set the meeting up at five-thirty.

Pulling up into the gravel parking lot of the seventy-year-old church, Grace cut the motor and got out. Her six-year-old Taurus looked rather dowdy next to Alton's new silver luxury car, but as she'd told her older brother, Reginald, when he suggested she get a sportier one, she preferred dependability to flash. He, of all people, had understood her reasoning.

Grace closed the car door and stared at the white, steepled wooden church that she had attended since she was in the ninth grade. She could greet every one of the four-hundred-plus members by their first name. She belonged.

Instead of going up the seven steep steps leading into the main sanctuary, she followed the curved brick walkway around the side of the single-story structure to the pastor's study and knocked. The door opened almost immediately. Alton Stone, the choir pianist-organist, smiled down at her.

"Hi, Grace. What's so important we have to meet now? What's the big news you have to tell us?"

Warm laughter sounded from behind him. "Let her get in first, Alton."

Smiling, she entered the small study that held a desk, a small love seat and two straight chairs. Pastor French, tall and imposing despite his sixty-three years, stuck his callused hand out in greeting, a warm smile on his dark face. "Hello, Grace. How are your parents?"

"Fine, thank you, Pastor, and Mrs. French?"

He chuckled. "Probably as anxious as Alton here to find out why you had us meet. She's holding supper."

"So don't keep us waiting. Talk," Alton said, his eyes sparkling in a light brown face sprinkled with freckles over his nose.

"Summerset city council has asked that our gospel choir under my direction and Revelation directed by Dr. Caleb Jackson at the junior college put on a gospel concert jointly to celebrate the city's Annual Harvest Celebration."

Alton's dark eyes widened. Grace waited for him to

object to the arrangement. With them on her side, she'd have a greater chance of getting Caleb to reconsider.

"This is wonderful!"

"What?" Grace said, unable to believe the grin on his face.

"Caleb Jackson is quickly gaining a reputation in gospel music. Benton University hasn't placed in competition since he left to come here. At the Gospel Music Association last year, I heard his name over and over as someone to watch," Alton said, as happy as a schoolboy with an extended recess. "I can't wait to work with him."

She couldn't believe her ears. "His contemporary gospel pop is nothing like the traditional music our choir sings."

Alton, always the peacemaker, tried to reassure her. "It won't hurt the choir to get some oomph in their songs."

Grace felt a twinge of hurt. "You haven't been pleased with the way I've conducted the choir?"

Surprise widened Alton's dark eyes. "How could you think that? Under your leadership for the past four years, Peaceful Rest has won top honors at the choir competition for two years running. When we win this year, we'll tie the record." His grin broadened. "Caleb wasn't the only one whose name was mentioned at the GMA."

Grace's pleasure was tempered by Alton's mention of Caleb's name again. "Then we don't need Caleb with all that hip-hop music he's bound to want to perform," she said with a brisk nod of her head. "Together we should be able to convince him to let us lead the musical."

"Whoa." Alton held up both hands. "Caleb is no slouch in the music department. He led Revelation to statewide honors his first year here. The first in Summerset's thirty-five year history. The man knows his music."

The town's newspaper had run a full-page spread. They'd even had a parade. "But it's not our music."

"Now, Grace." Pastor French spoke for the first time since her announcement. "Just because it's different from what we're used to and enjoy doesn't mean it's not pleasing to God. Our church has an older membership who like the more traditional form of praising the Lord, but I've been concerned lately that the attendance of the teenagers and young adults has dropped off. The right music might bring them back."

"The pastor is right," Alton said. "A lot of churches are leaning toward praise worship with a lot more body movement and beats in the music in an attempt to bring younger people to the services."

"In my opinion, it's gone too far," Grace said tightly. "I won't let Caleb turn this into something that is more fitting for a nightclub than a worship service."

"Has he indicated that's what he plans?" Pastor French asked, twin furrows across his dark brow.

She faltered. "We haven't discussed the music yet, but in the assembly at the opening of school Revelation performed and everyone in the auditorium was on their feet as if it were a rap concert."

"But were they reacting to the beat or to the stirring of their hearts?" Pastor French asked.

Grace didn't know the answer and barely kept from squirming under Pastor French's intense regard. "I'm not sure," she finally conceded.

Pastor French rested his hand on her shoulder. "I can tell you have some reservations about working with

Caleb, but I think you should look at it as an opportunity."

She frowned. "Opportunity?"

"To learn from him and let him learn from you," he explained.

"Maybe he could give us some hints on how to bring in more young people," Alton said. "Nothing we've tried has worked."

Grace tried to hide the hurt she felt. The night of board games she'd suggested had been the most poorly attended of all the activities the church held. And now the two people she expected would be on her side weren't. "He's coming tomorrow night for us to tell the choir. Perhaps you can ask him yourself."

Alton frowned at her.

"Grace," Pastor French said, obviously concerned and noting her displeasure. "We're not belittling your contribution to the church." He glanced at the two trophies on his desk. "You've brought distinction and honor to Peaceful Rest. The gospel choir had a handful of members before you took over. Now it's thirty-two people strong and more would join if we could afford to buy the robes. No one could take your place."

"You should know that," Alton added.

She felt ashamed. "I didn't do it for glory."

"We know that, but you're human and, like the rest of us, you like to know you're appreciated," Pastor French told her kindly. "I've been married too long and preached even longer not to have learned that lesson."

Grace accepted the gracious out he had given her. Whatever happened, she never wanted to jeopardize the love and respect she had worked so hard to earn with these two men. She'd just have to circumvent Caleb another way. "Thanks for meeting with me."

"Thank you for once again bringing honor and recognition to God's house and providing an opportunity to speak of God's love," Pastor French told her.

She turned to Alton. "Thank you, too. Sorry if I got a bit testy."

"That's mild compared to Nina," he said with a shake of his dark head.

Grace smiled. Nina Warner, Grace's friend and a solo soprano in the choir, had been going steady with Alton for the past five years. Nina was trying to get Alton to the altar, but he was being stubborn. "She's blessed to have a dependable, stable man like you."

"That's what I tell her," he said with a shy smile.

They all laughed.

During the six-minute drive to her house, Grace's mind was busy trying to think of a way to get out of working with Caleb. However, seeing the dark blue truck in front of her house pushed thoughts of Caleb from her mind. Unconsciously her hands tightened on the steering wheel even as her foot lifted off the gas pedal. This was a surprise. Her father was always gone when she came home in the evening. She preferred it that way.

Just then a car turned onto her street from the opposite end and parked behind the truck. Relief swept through her. The door on the driver's side opened and her mother emerged. The gentle evening breeze whipped her floral cotton sundress around her. She was still shapely and pretty at fifty-nine years of age. Opening the back door, she lifted out a stockpot.

Around the small frame house came a tall, well-built man in jeans and a sweat-dampened chambray shirt. His walk was self-assured, his posture erect. He quickly crossed the tiny patch of grass Grace called her yard and went to take the pot from her mother.

Seeing no way out of doing so, Grace pulled up in the driveway and got out, dragging her briefcase and purse with her. "Hi, Mama. Daddy. I didn't expect you."

Her father looked at her a long time as if trying to figure out if there was any hidden meaning behind her statement. "Hello, Grace. I wanted to finish the floors before I left today."

She nodded, her hands clamped around the briefcase. Sweat trickled down her back.

"You two are certainly turning this house into a showcase," her mother said into the heavy silence. "I can't wait to see those floors."

"Grace has good ideas and instincts," her father said. "I'm just the muscle."

Her mother waved his words aside. "Nonsense. It's your skill that transforms her ideas into something tangible. Isn't that right, Grace?"

"Yes," Grace felt obliged to say, and thought again that she should have never agreed to let her father do the remodeling in her house. But it had been important to her mother, and somehow Grace hadn't been able to turn her back on the man who had turned his back on her for so many years.

"Grace, get the door." Once again her mother started the conversation. "Oscar, you bring those chicken and dumplings inside. Grace, I made enough for you to have some for two days."

"Yes, ma'am." Grace went up the short walk in a single step and opened the door. Leaded glass sparkled in the top panel. The polished sheen of hardwood floor stretched from the living room to the kitchen-dining area beyond. Four days ago it had been gold shag carpeting.

"It's beautiful," she murmured, and just the way she had envisioned. She turned to her father as he and her mother came in behind her. "You even put the furniture back in place."

"I know how much you like things in order," he told her. "I still need to put the molding around the baseboards, but I figured I could do that later this week. I wanted to get this finished."

She glanced back at the new floor, then to him. No one had to tell her he had worked like crazy to get this done. This morning, as he had for the past month while working on her house, he'd been waiting in his truck when she came outside at seven-thirty. He was trying so hard to please her; she just wished he had been as concerned with pleasing her when she was growing up.

"I appreciate what you've done. It's lovely," she said finally.

He nodded. "I'll put this down and finish cleaning up the backyard. I plan to start on that deck you wanted next."

She noticed as he passed that he looked tired. She recalled the man who always wore a smile and who liked to tease, but these days the easy smile and glib words were gone…at least with her. It was as uncomfortable for him to be around her as it was for her to be around him.

Once she had loved him more than anyone, but that was before he'd decided what he wanted far outweighed his responsibilities as a husband and father. She'd grown up not being able to depend on him to be there for her. Broken promises littered her childhood. Now, he was ready to settle down and be a father and husband, but it was too late as far as she was concerned. As painful as it was to admit, she couldn't put her faith or trust in him.

Both of them would probably have stopped subjecting themselves to this awkwardness if not for her mother, a tenderhearted woman who loved them both and whom they loved.

"Daddy, did you eat lunch?" she asked as he started to open the glass door to the music room.

Surprise widened his eyes as he glanced back over his shoulder. "I don't like stopping."

"I've been living here for two years and saving to have the repairs done. They can wait a little longer." Her mother's life had been disrupted enough. Placing her things on the kitchen island, Grace went to the oak cabinet. "I'll fix you a plate while Mama and I look at the floor and I can show her the plans for my office."

"Why don't you both sit down at the table and eat?" her mother said. "I'll go get the string beans and corn bread out of the car." Not waiting for an answer, her mother practically ran out of the house.

Slow steps brought her father back into the room. "I'll wash up in the bathroom."

Grace plucked two more plates from the cabinet. Her mother would have to be the buffer as usual. Her father's leaving had always hurt her so badly. She had depended on and loved him so much and he had let her down. It was difficult for her to completely forget.

"I'm back," her mother called as she reentered the house. Seeing the three plates in Grace's hands, she didn't comment, just put the chicken and dumplings in a serving dish and helped set the table.

They were seated across from each other when her father returned. Taking a seat at the small dining table, he blessed the food in his deep baritone voice that he had once thought was his ticket to fame and fortune.

"How was work today, Grace?" Once again her mother had to initiate conversation.

Grace passed the bowl of garden-fresh snap beans. "Fine, until I had a meeting with the president."

"Everything's all right, isn't it?" her father asked.

The concern in his voice was evident and, she had to admit, not surprising. "Yes."

"Then what's the problem?" he asked, accepting the chicken and dumplings from her mother, but making no move to serve himself.

Grace was still so annoyed about working with Caleb, she answered without her usual caution. She ended by saying she had just informed Pastor French and Alton.

"Why, Grace, that's wonderful!" Her mother beamed as she served her husband herself. "What an honor."

Grace wrinkled her mouth and accepted the dish from her mother. "It would be if I didn't have to work with Caleb Jackson."

"What's wrong with him?" her mother wanted to know.

"Too many things to number," Grace told her. The serving spoon clinked against the dish betraying her irritation. "He's a wild card and likes his way too much. You never know what's going to come out of his mouth. Dresses like some rock star, but the worse thing is that ungodly music his group has received such recognition for is more suitable for the unsaved. Close your eyes and you'd think you were in some club."

The dish plopped on the table with a thud. "I can't stand that kind of music and can't see how anyone else who claims to know the Lord can, either."

Her mother's sharp intake of breath made Grace realize what she'd said. Slowly she turned to look at her father. She might as well have been talking about him instead of Caleb.

Head bowed, he continued eating his food. Remorse swept through Grace. She hadn't meant to hurt him. "I'm sorry."

His head came up. She saw pain and sorrow in his dark eyes. "Never regret saying what's in your heart. You can't help how you feel."

Grace's throat stung. Mutely she stared at her mother, hoping she would save them both as she had so many times during the past two years since her father's permanent return home.

Her mother swallowed before she spoke. "The Lord looks at the hearts of men. Who are we to do any less?"

Grace wasn't sure if she had been saved or reprimanded; she only knew that her day had been going downhill since meeting with the president, and it wasn't likely to get any better before the day was over.

Chapter Three

Grace arrived at Room C where Revelation practiced promptly at seven. She planned to be in and out in five minutes. She had papers to grade, lessons to prepare. Besides, she didn't want to spend any more time with Caleb than absolutely necessary.

Pushing the door open, she wasn't surprised to find Caleb surrounded by the nine people who made up Revelation. He leaned negligently against the baby grand in the same jeans and shirt he'd worn earlier, only now his shirttail was hanging out. He looked as slovenly as the other male students who also favored jeans and untucked shirts. The entire group appeared engrossed in conversation with him. She was trying to think of a way to announce her presence when Caleb turned his head and looked directly at her.

The funny sensation happened again in her stomach.

She made a mental note to stay away from the cafeteria's lasagna.

"Hello, Professor Thompson." Caleb straightened.

The other students turned toward her and spoke. She returned the warm—if a bit puzzled—greeting and, realizing she was still standing by the door, she walked farther into the room. "Hello, everyone."

Caleb quickly made the introductions of the two female and two male singers, and the five members of the band that played bass, lead guitar, keyboard, drums and piano, then came to stand by her to face the students. "I know you're wondering why Professor Thompson is here and I won't keep you in suspense. Summerset's city council, with the approval and best wishes of President Jenkins and the Board of Regents, would like Revelation and Professor Thompson's church gospel choir to perform together at this year's Harvest Celebration."

The young people looked as stunned as Grace had been when she heard President Jenkins make the announcement that morning.

"Don't all of you tell me how excited you are at once," Caleb said, a teasing smile tugging the corners of his mouth.

David, the keyboardist, folded his lanky arms across his oversize, gray Summerset sweatshirt. He'd been in Grace's Music Theory class last year. "No offense, Professor Thompson, but I don't think your choir can keep up with us."

"David's right, Professor Thompson," Carolyn, the lead soprano added with a wide smile at Caleb. "Dr. Jackson lets us really get down."

"Professor Thompson's gospel choir can hold its own," Caleb said, before Grace could defend her choir and their music. "They're good. They've won top competition two years in a row. We still have to prove we can win the state competition two years in a row. I'd say we're the ones who had better worry about keeping up."

Grace could only stare at Caleb in surprise. Of course she'd seen him when he visited her church, but he had always been gone when she came outside. She wasn't aware that he thought so highly of her choir and knew of their recognition.

"Never forget that the main purpose of Revelation is to glorify God just as Professor Thompson is doing with her gospel choir," Caleb said. He turned slightly to stare down at her. "Isn't that right?"

"Yes," Grace agreed, aware that he had given her the perfect opportunity to present her platform for more traditional songs. "That's why the music for the Harvest Celebration should convey respect and reverence." She ignored the few groans. "We have to be very careful with our selections."

Caleb's dark brow lifted. "Why don't we talk about the music selection after we meet with your choir tomorrow night? What time should I plan to be there?"

Grace realized Caleb had dismissed her idea. She wanted to call him on it, but not in front of the students. "Around this same time should be fine."

"Great. I'll see you out or would you like to stay and listen to us practice?" he asked.

"No, thank you. I have lessons to plan." She turned to the students. "I look forward to teaching you a new way of praise."

There wasn't a smile to be seen at her announcement.

"I'll be back in a minute. Start the warm-up exercise." Taking her arm, Caleb ushered Grace out the door.

She pulled her arm free as soon as the door swung shut. "I can walk without your help."

"You can also mess this up."

She didn't have to be a mind reader to know what he was talking about. "It won't hurt for them to look at music a different way."

"It wouldn't hurt you, either," he returned.

Grace didn't like her words tossed back at her. Her chin went up a fraction. "I'm older and can understand better."

"Twenty-seven does not make you Mother Wisdom. You can still make mistakes," he said.

One mistake in particular she didn't want to think about. "Is that your way of saying I'm making one now?" she asked.

"My students learn and listen because the music speaks to them. They aren't interested in the traditional music you and I grew up with." His face lowered to within inches of hers. "Times have changed, Grace, and unless we change we're going to lose a lot of young people who think anyone over twenty-five doesn't understand them."

"That may be right, but it doesn't mean they can't appreciate the traditional music, as well," she said, her hands on her hips.

"The same can be said for you with contemporary pop." His hands rested on his hips.

"My choir is not going to sing with music better suited for a dance club."

His face inched closer. "We'll just see about that."

"We certainly will." Her chin jutted up higher.

Caleb stared down into her mutinous, pretty face and somehow his gaze was caught by the curve of her mouth and refused to budge. A woman with a mouth so tempting shouldn't be so argumentative. He blinked as the thought jumped into his head. Appalled, he straightened and took a step back.

Feeling off balance, he rubbed his hand over his face. "Grace," he began then stopped because he had no idea what he was about to say.

"Yes?" she said, staring at him strangely.

Caleb tried to get it together. "If we can't get along, how do we expect Revelation and your choir to? And no matter what either of us wants, we have to work together. We're doing this for a purpose much bigger than either of us."

The fight went out of her. He was right. Again. She'd always prided herself on being reasonable and in control. Caleb seemed to bring out the worst in her. "I just have strong convictions."

He smiled and dimples winked in his face. "Tell me something I don't know."

For a moment she saw the winsome handsomeness that drew young and old, women and men, and felt drawn to it just as so many others were. She caught the answering smile before it could fully form. Lowell had been a charmer as well, but he had only wanted to use her. "Good night, Professor Jackson. I'll see you tomorrow night."

"Good night, Grace." Caleb watched Grace until she disappeared through the double glass doors leading to the parking lot. He had no idea what had happened earlier or why. The only thing he knew was that he had no business thinking about one of his teachers in that way, especially Grace, a woman who tried his patience every time they were together. Determined to put the incident out of his mind and assured he wouldn't let it happen again, he reentered the music room.

* * *

Back home Grace went to her bedroom and stared at her reflection in the mirror on the triple dresser. Her face was flushed, her eyes bright, her breathing erratic.

Her eyes clamped shut. How could this have happened to her? How could she be attracted to a man like Caleb? Hadn't Lowell taught her about handsome, charming men you couldn't trust or depend on? If he hadn't, her father certainly had.

Opening her eyes, she turned away and sat on the edge of the queen-size bed. She hadn't missed the way Caleb had been staring at her mouth. She wasn't going to delude herself into thinking he might be interested in her. Women on and off campus were vying for his attention. As far as she knew, he wasn't dating anyone steadily. In a town as small as Summerset she would have heard. His girlfriend was probably in another city. This time she wouldn't let herself be made a fool of again and have people look at her with pity.

Rising, she went to the second bedroom, which she'd turned into an office and went over her lesson plans for the next day. Finished, she prepared for bed. After reading her Bible, she got on her knees and said her prayers. She ended them by asking, "Please, Lord, help me to be strong and stay in Thy perfect will and lead me not into temptation, but deliver me from evil and evildoers. Amen."

Climbing into bed, she pulled the covers over her shoulders. She might not be able to handle Caleb, but God could.

Grace knew the exact second Caleb entered the sanctuary of Peaceful Rest Church. Every single female and most of the married ones stopped talking and stared.

Grace could have shaken each and every one of them. Caleb Jackson's head was big enough.

She turned and watched him continue down the center aisle, his strides long and self-assured. Nothing had probably ever deterred him from doing what he wanted. As he rounded the podium and stepped up on the platform, the whispers became louder. She couldn't keep the frown off her face. You'd think they'd never seen a handsome man before—the thought registered a second later. Her own eyes narrowed in annoyance at the both of them.

"Good evening, Grace," he greeted.

"Hello, Professor Jackson."

His head turned to one side. "Don't you think under the circumstances and to foster better relations it should be Caleb?"

She didn't, but with Alton a few feet away and practically vibrating to meet Caleb, it wasn't the time to say so. She turned to Alton, already grinning and eager to meet Caleb. "Caleb Jackson, Alton Stone, the pianist and organist for Peaceful Rest."

"Pleased to meet you," Alton greeted as the two men shook hands warmly.

"The same here," Caleb said. "You can make that piano and organ talk."

Alton smile broadened. "Thank you."

Caleb turned to Grace. "You're ready?"

No, but I don't have a choice, she thought, and from the twinkle in Caleb's chocolate-brown eyes he knew what she was thinking. Resolutely, she faced the twenty-seven members, sure the five absent would regret they'd missed choir practice, and motioned everyone to come to attention.

"I'm sure many of you have heard of Professor Caleb

Jackson, the chair of the music department at Summerset. Under Professor Jackson's leadership, the group known as Revelation won state honors last year for the first time in Summerset's history."

Applause sounded and she had to wait for it to die down. Caleb inclined his head in acknowledgment and appreciation. Nina was among the last to stop applauding. Grace cut a glance at Alton to see if he minded, but he wore the same easygoing smile he always did. Nothing much got to Alton.

"Peaceful Rest has also gained recognition with two competition wins and we will tie the record for number three the end of November," Grace said.

Caleb began the applause, which was picked up by the choir. "Way to go!" he shouted.

Grace lifted a brow. She could well imagine the revelry that went on during his practices. "Because of the success and recognition of Revelation and the gospel choir, Summerset's city council has asked that both groups work together to present a gospel musical for the Harvest Celebration."

Shouts and applause filled the sanctuary. To Grace it was similar to the night they'd won the competition. "It will mean extra time at practice, of course, but we can do it, and the music ministry will reach people we might not otherwise reach."

"We're behind you, Grace and Caleb," Alton said, then faced the choir. "Isn't that right?"

Applause erupted again.

Caleb chuckled and inclined his head to Grace. After only a moment's hesitation, Grace did the same. Perhaps this was the beginning of a better working relationship.

"Do we start practice tonight?" Nina asked, a wide, excited smile on her pretty face.

"No. We have to decide on the music first," Grace said, not looking forward to that discussion one bit.

"Which we better do soon." Caleb turned to her. "If you're free tomorrow night we can meet for dinner at six at the Sirloin Grill."

Out of the corner of her eye, she saw several female members elbowing each other and grinning. Grace's mouth tightened in annoyance. She didn't want anyone to be under the mistaken illusion that there might be anything remotely going on between them.

"That gives you enough time before prayer service, doesn't it?" Caleb asked, his brows furrowed when she remained silent.

Once again he had surprised her by remembering her schedule. She wondered if he was that well acquainted with everyone's agenda, but didn't have time to think about it with him waiting for an answer. "Yes, thank you. I'll be there."

Dimples winked in his handsome face as he flashed her a smile. "Great. My schedule is hectic tomorrow, so if I don't see you on campus I'll see you at the restaurant. If I'm running late, save us a booth." Oozing with charm and good cheer, he faced the choir. "I'm looking forward to working with you. Good night, everyone." With a friendly wave, he turned to leave.

He hadn't made it off the pulpit before she heard, "As the president of the choir, I think I should go with you, Grace."

"No. Me."

There was some good-natured arguing among the women. Grace gritted a smile and busied herself selecting the song they were to sing for Sunday service. Caleb was not going to disrupt the well-ordered life she had made for herself.

Chapter Four

She expected him to be late. He didn't disappoint her.

Through the plate-glass window of the Sirloin Grill she saw Caleb whip his Corvette into the narrow parking space between a battered truck and her car. As usual, the top was down. He hopped out and started for the entrance. Since she had just glanced at her watch, she knew he was nine minutes late. She liked punctuality. Working with him was going to be impossible.

When time passed and he didn't come inside, she began to wonder why. Her fingers drumming on the table, she debated if she should go see what was keeping him. A woman most likely, she thought with renewed aggravation. Just then, the door opened and two elderly, white-haired women slowly entered. One used a walking stick. Caleb, who had been holding the door, came in after them. Taking their arms, he escorted them to a table near the buffet line and seated them.

"Thank you, young man," they said almost in unison with wide smiles.

"It's always a pleasure to help beautiful women," he said, tipping his baseball cap with the insignia of Summerset Junior College on the bill.

Grace, who had begun to think there was hope for Caleb, quickly adjusted her opinion. He couldn't open his mouth without flirting.

Turning away from the women, his searching gaze locked on her almost at once. With a wave, he started toward her. "Hi, Grace," he greeted and pulled out a chair at the table for four. "Booths all taken?"

Since she didn't want to tell him that she had chosen a table because the booths somehow seemed too intimate, she answered by saying, "The light seems better here."

He glanced at the booth with the individual lights shining over the table, then back at her. There was no light over their table. "Whatever you say."

A waitress in jeans and a Western-style red shirt with black stitching approached their table with two plastic menus. "Good evening, folks. You gonna order off the menu or have the buffet?"

"Just sweetened iced tea for me, please," Grace said.

Caleb paused in taking the menu. "You're not eating?"

"I've eaten."

"Give us a few minutes," he told the waitress, then turned to pin her with his penetrating gaze. "How? Your last class is over at five-thirty."

That schedule again. "Do you keep up with all the teachers in your department?" she asked before she could stop herself.

"I try."

The answer should have pleased her that he took no more interest in her than in any of the other members of the faculty in his department. "You need not concern yourself with me." She opened the black zip folder on the table. "Please order and while we're waiting, we can go over the songs."

As if on cue, the waitress reappeared. "You ready?"

"Two sweetened iced teas, Texas-size chicken fried steak with mashed potatoes and whatever the vegetable of the day is with the salad bar."

The waitress grinned. "Got a good appetite, have you?"

"Yes, ma'am, I sure do."

Collecting the menu, the woman left with a smile.

"If you're finished, we can discuss the songs?" she said. Did he have to flirt with every female he met?

Caleb frowned across the table at her. "What did I do now?"

Grace realized she had done it again. Let Caleb get to her. She forced herself to relax. "I've just had a long day. Forgive me if I sounded curt."

He tilted his head to one side. "Do my ears deceive me or did you just apologize?"

Since he was smiling and they did have to work together and they had yet to select the songs, she smiled in return. "I did." She handed him her selections. "I think we should keep it to five numbers. Start out with a hymn like 'Precious Lord' and end with one of my favorites, 'Blessed Assurance.' The other three songs can be any of the old hymns. Once we decide, I can order the music if Alton doesn't have it in stock."

Caleb leaned back in the wooden chair. "I suppose you want us to follow the music as written."

She couldn't believe he understood. He'd been so

adamant before about the type of music he wanted. "I went by Alton's music store on my lunch break and purchased enough sheet music for Revelation to begin practice at least on the two songs I mentioned."

"Here's your tea. Your food will be out in a bit." The waitress set the oversize clear plastic glasses on the table then left.

"Thank you," Caleb and Grace murmured, but neither looked away from the other.

"This is going to be so wonderful," Grace said, excitement creeping into her voice. "I can feel it."

Caleb braced both arms on the table. "You actually want my students to learn new music and not do one song they're familiar with?"

Just because Caleb's voice was quiet didn't fool Grace. She straightened. "All of your students read music. They'd have to to be music majors."

"True, but I require that they fully learn each selection we perform," he explained, then went on to say, "every member of Revelation is a full-time student with at least fifteen hours of credit. I can't ask them to take that much time away from their studies."

Since Grace had two of those students and was aware of how much work she gave her students to do, she understood his concern. "Perhaps for this one time you could let them read the music and we could do one song they're familiar with within our five."

"How magnanimous of you."

"Hot rolls and chicken fried steak with mashed potatoes and mixed vegetables." The waitress set the platter in front of Caleb. The batter-fried meat nearly hung off the plate. "Yell if you need anything."

"Thanks," Caleb said, then bowed his head to say

grace. Finished, he picked up his flatware and began to eat.

Grace watched him fork in three bites before her stomach reminded her that she'd eaten a candy bar for lunch because she had used her lunch break to buy the sheet music, music that might not be used. Hoping Caleb hadn't heard her stomach growl, she forged ahead. "I'm not trying to be difficult."

His head lifted abruptly. The arched brow said he didn't believe her. With a grunt, he cut into his steak.

Grace licked her lips. He would have to be eating one of her favorites. "This gospel concert is for the glory of God and as such the music has to reflect dignity and decorum."

Up came his head again. "You show me in the Bible where it says that and I'll say no more on the issue."

Grace blinked. "Well, it doesn't actually say that, but it implies—"

"Show me where it implies," he told her.

Once again she was stumped and from his direct gaze he knew it.

"I'll help you out, Grace. It says 'Make a joyful noise unto the Lord.'"

"Hip-hop and pop is not joyful unto the Lord," she said, sure in that at least.

"And how do you know what's pleasing to Him?" Caleb asked. "There's no one way to serve the Lord or please Him except through righteousness. Who are you to say there is only one right way to worship Him with our music?"

Grace became aware of two things: the waitress was standing there and the people sitting at the table next to them were staring at them. Heat washed over her face. They'd all heard Caleb reprimand her.

"I—I have to go." She grabbed the case and stood.

Caleb came to his feet as well, and reached for her. "Grace."

She stepped back. "Good night." She didn't run from the restaurant, but she wanted to.

Caleb watched Grace hurry from the restaurant and had to fight the urge to go after her and apologize. He hadn't meant to come down on her so hard. But he thought a great deal of his students and the hard work they did. He wanted her to understand what she was asking of them. She might love the Lord, but she was also rather rigid in her music.

"If you need a shoulder to cry on, mine's available," the waitress said.

Caleb looked at her and saw by her expression that she had been trying to tease him, not come on to him. "Thanks for the offer." He took his seat and picked up his knife and fork.

He had been busy with meetings or counseling with students all day and all he'd had was a quick cup of coffee and a soft drink. He was about to take a bite of meat when he recalled the growl of Grace's stomach and her saying she had used her lunch break to buy the sheet music. Putting down the utensils, he picked up the music.

No one had to tell him Grace was doing what she felt was right. She believed in her heart what she said. He felt just as strongly she was wrong. The joy, the inner peace and closeness he experienced when Revelation played could only come from a higher power. Perhaps he could use a little understanding himself.

He motioned the waitress over. "Can I please have one of these to go with a garden salad?"

The woman folded her arms and gave him a slow grin. "Trying to soften her up with food, huh?"

"It can't hurt."

Chapter Five

Grace was intentionally late to prayer service. She didn't want her mother to see her until she was more composed. They always sat together. Her mother knew she was meeting Caleb and would immediately guess things hadn't gone well and ask questions. Questions Grace didn't want to answer.

Waiting in the foyer with three other late arrivals, she tried to pay attention to Brother Samuel's heartfelt prayer, but she was unable to push Caleb's hurtful accusations from her mind. He had no right to say those things about her. He was just being his arrogant, dictatorial self. He refused to see that there should be a definite distinction between worldly-sounding music that had an emphasis on self and music in the church with an emphasis on God.

The door to the sanctuary opened and Sister Mason bid them enter. Instead of going to the front, Grace slipped into a seat halfway down the aisle. Nodding to the people seated on the row with her, she opened her well-read Bible and prepared to be fed by the Word as Pastor French came to stand in front of the wooden podium.

She tried to listen to his sermon, but her mind kept veering back to Caleb, the anger in his face and voice. No one had ever spoken to her that way. Everyone knew she loved the Lord and tried to live the kind of life where others would see that love. She volunteered with the young people. On the Sundays her choir didn't sing, she worked in the church's nursery. He had no right to say those things about her.

"Please come to the altar."

Grace came out of her musing when the people next to her stood and realized Pastor French had given the altar call. Embarrassed to have missed his entire message, she quickly rose and joined her fellow parishioners.

Head bowed, hands clasped as she knelt at the altar, she asked for guidance and strength. God demanded order in all things. He would show her how to deal with Caleb. Feeling immensely better, she returned to her seat.

Her conviction remained strong as prayer services closed… until people started congratulating her on the honor she had brought the church. She barely kept the smile on her face. Smiling proudly, her mother joined them.

"Hi, Grace. You and Caleb must have gotten a lot done since you were late."

Her smile felt stiff as she tried to think of a way to

answer without telling a lie. She was saved by an unexpected source.

"They must have. Grace didn't even get a chance to
eat her supper."

Grace's head whipped around to see Sister Johnson,
a robust, friendly woman she had known and admired
since her high school days. All Grace could think of was
that someone from the church had overheard her conversation with Caleb. She tucked her head in shame...
and then she saw the plastic bag the other woman held.

Sister Johnson noticed the direction of Grace's gaze.
The older woman's broad face widened in a grin. "I
promised Professor Jackson I'd give this to you."

Grace still couldn't take it all in. "Caleb left that
for me?"

She chuckled. "He sure did. Said he would have
stayed, but he had another meeting at eight. He told
me to make sure you got your food since you were getting music for the gospel musical during your lunch
break." She beamed at Grace. "Doesn't surprise me
none, I told him. You've always thought of others before you thought of yourself."

Grace felt like a fraud. She'd bought the music to
circumvent anything Caleb might bring and he must
know it.

"He sounds like a wonderful man," her mother said.
"I've been praying about the musical. Why don't you
invite him for Sunday dinner?"

Grace's eyes widened even more. She wasn't sure
if her mother was just being friendly or trying to do
a little matchmaking, but there were too many people
standing around to let it go any further. "I'm sure Professor Jackson has other plans. I know I do." She took

her mother's arm. "Good night, everyone. Come on, Mama, I'll walk you to your car."

"You're the one who should be getting home." Her mother steered Grace to her car. "You go on home, and eat every bite of whatever is in there."

Grace didn't plan to eat any of the food, but it was a good excuse to leave. She kissed her mother on the cheek. "Good night, Mama. I'll call tomorrow."

Opening the car door, she got in and drove home. In her kitchen, she set the plastic bag on the yellow Formica counter. The savory aroma of the food drifted out, causing her stomach to growl. It wouldn't hurt to see what was inside.

She began pulling out the containers. Beneath the last one was a folded sheet of notebook paper.

Please accept my apology. Only God knows what's in our hearts. I hope you can forgive me and we can set up another meeting. I truly believe we've been given a unique and wonderful opportunity to minister to others through our music. I'm trusting in Him to lead us in the right direction. Caleb.

The annoyance she had felt earlier faded. Caleb was right. The opportunity to spread the gospel was too important for either of them to let their personal feelings interfere. The next time they met, she'd do her best to remember their higher purpose and trust in Him that Caleb would be convicted to do the same.

Now, the only remaining problem was to decide when and where to meet. She opened one of the boxes and munched on a cucumber from the salad. She certainly didn't want it to be any place public. Just the thought of her embarrassing experience at the Sirloin Grill made her cringe. They both might want the same thing, but coming up with musical selections they both could agree on wasn't going to be easy.

Her stomach growled, reminding her of her pitiful lunch. Her gaze went again to the other two containers. It would be ridiculously immature not to eat the food when she was hungry. Besides, there had been times, not many, but those few had stuck with her, when she was growing up and her father had been out chasing his dream of becoming a star in the music industry and the family he'd left behind had fallen on lean times. Her mother had always said that God would make a way. And He always had.

Grace had never understood why her mother hadn't put her foot down and insisted her father stay home and take care of his responsibilities. Grace would never marry a man whom she couldn't depend on and trust to put the needs of his family above his own. Lowell's deceit had hurt her badly at the time, but she had accepted that it had been for the best.

Not wanting to think about Lowell, she lifted the lid of the largest container. Her mouth watered at the sight of the golden-brown chicken-fried steak covered in cream gravy. Opening the package of plastic utensils, she began to eat. She didn't stop until she had finished the steak, vegetables, salad and dinner rolls.

While cleaning up the kitchen, she decided where they'd meet. Swiping the counter with the damp dishcloth one last time, she hung it over the faucet to dry. She could be just as hospitable and giving as Caleb. Picking up the phone, she dialed the direct phone number to his office at the college. After the fifth ring, she heard the recording of his richly textured voice.

"This is Professor Jackson, please leave a message and remember, a day without God and music is a day you haven't lived to the fullest."

His words exactly mirrored her own sentiment. Her growing certainty that they could work through their differences came through clearly in her sparkling voice. "Professor Jackson, I accept your apology and thank you for the food. If you have no other plans, I think we should meet at my house Saturday afternoon at five. You have my number if this is inconvenient. Goodbye."

Grace hung up the phone, turned off the light and went to her room. It was just as her mother had always said.

God would make a way.

Caleb was determined not to be late. He often became engrossed in doing class work or writing music and lost track of time. He'd set his alarm clock and the timer on the oven just to make sure he didn't give Grace a reason to be annoyed with him. Not that she seemed to need any, he thought as he turned into her driveway and cut the motor. A quick glance at the stainless steel watch on his arm put a smile on his face. It was 4:51.

Reaching over he picked up the leather zipper folder and got out. The little white frame house was as neat as the owner. So were the begonia flower beds that ringed around the single maple tree and clustered on either side of the short walk. Two strawberry jars of sprouting flowers were on the edge of the porch. An old-fashioned glider painted the same bright yellow as the shutters was pushed against the single railing at the end of the porch. On the other side were more plants.

Her place was as inviting and charming as his was messy. Good thing she hadn't wanted to meet at his house. That she suggested they meet at her place was a good sign and he better get to it if he intended to start off on the right foot. Quickly going up the single step, he rang the doorbell. It opened before the chime ended.

"Good evening, Professor Jackson," Grace greeted as she pushed open the screen door.

They'd work on her calling him Caleb later. "Good evening, Grace. Thanks for opening your home." They hadn't talked since Wednesday night. Like her, he'd left a message on her machine. It was as if each was afraid of making another misstep with the other.

He entered and found the inside as welcoming as the outside. The light blue traditional sofa with yellow piping dominated the room painted a warm eggshell color. A beautiful double-matted picture of a woman in a long white dress standing beside a mounted buffalo soldier going off to war hung on the far wall. Tied to the soldier's saddle horn was a bugle. "Your home is as beautiful on the outside as it is on the inside."

"Thank you," she said, a pleased smile on her face as she closed the door. "I thought we'd work on the dining room table where we'll have more room to spread out."

"Sounds good." He followed behind her and noticed she wore a starched, long-sleeved white blouse and tailored black slacks. Did she ever dress for comfort?

Stepping into the adjoining kitchen-dining room he got another surprise. The area was twice the size of the cozy living area. The white-and-yellow kitchen was spotless, with a breakfast island and two high-backed stools to his right. To his left was a beautifully carved buffet with a silver tea service on top. Over the single pedestal dining table was a six-globe pewter chandelier. Through a double-glassed doorway straight ahead he saw a thriving tropical palm and the rounded curve of a black baby grand.

"This place is great. It's nothing like my rental."

"I'm not renting. This is my home," she said, taking a seat in one of the side chairs on the other side of the table.

Unsure if he had detected a bit of frost in her voice, he chose to think positively. "You certainly have a beautiful one. You put my place to shame." Taking a seat across from her to give her the space she obviously wanted, he looked around again at the crown molding, hardwood floors and textured walls. "Maybe I can talk my landlord into doing a few things to my place. Did you have a contractor?"

Her face instantly closed. "Yes. Would you like some lemonade or iced tea before we get started?"

So, they were back to square one. There was definitely a chill in her voice this time. "No, thank you." Placing his case on the polished cherry surface, he unzipped it and drew out several sheets of paper. "I decided to ask the members of Revelation what they thought of the songs you selected."

"Yes?" she said, leaning toward him to place her hands on the table beside a stack of sheet music and a tablet.

For a moment, Caleb was captured by how the light overhead touched the gentle curve of her face. He cleared his throat. "I'm afraid they weren't that taken with your selections." And that was putting it politely. They'd complained for ten minutes.

She took it better than he expected. "The music is a departure from what they're used to."

"Exactly." Caleb leaned closer to show her the sheet

music in his hand. "I thought we'd compromise on one selection so we could at least get started next week. How about 'Stand'? It has a traditional beat, but with enough tempo in the chorus to appeal to everyone."

Grace slowly nodded. "It's a good song. I think it will speak to a great many people."

"And 'Stomp' is a selection they've done with great success." "Stomp" lived up to its name with a fast, hand-clapping, foot-stomping beat that got people out of their seats from the first note and didn't let them sit down until the music was over...if then.

Even before he'd finished, she'd straightened, her mouth compressed in a narrow line. "I thought I had made it clear that my choir won't sing a song better suited for a nightclub."

He barely refrained from telling her that as the music director she did not own the choir. Instead he showed her another piece of paper. "This is the list of the top gospel albums and songs in the country. I grant you there are also the traditional songs within the Southern gospel and gospel music, but the ones that are getting the most attention are the ones that have more of a beat, which, I think and most people agree, is why they speak to the people where they are."

"I'm sure they played music in Sodom and Gomorrah, too," Grace said, her chin tilted, her arms folded.

Caleb mentally counted to ten and tried again. "Just because gospel music makes you want to get up and clap your hands doesn't mean it has suggestive words the way some of the secular music has. We have to reach people where they are."

"We don't have to stoop to what the world is doing to do it." She unfolded her arms. "I will not compromise my principles."

He rolled his eyes heavenward and asked for patience. "Making music that causes people to lift their hands in worship and praise won't hurt our principles."

"Perhaps not yours," she snapped.

He straightened. "What do you mean by that?"

She shoved her hand toward him in obvious disgust. "Just look at you. You're supposed to be an example for your students. Instead you act like one of them with the way you wear those tight jeans and run around in that sports car. You should act your age. You're disgraceful."

That ripped it. "Coming from you I take that as a compliment. God wants His children to have joy in all things. You're so uptight and sanctimonious you've forgotten that as well as how to have any fun."

Her eyes widened in outrage. "How dare you say those things to me!"

"It's no more than the truth. If you'd stop looking down your nose at everyone else you'd see as much."

Glaring at him she came to her feet and planted her hands on the table. "I do not look down my nose."

He stood as well and copied her pose. "Yes, you do. There's no bend in you, no give. The only way is your way. If you don't change, you'll wind up a never-been-kissed old maid."

Hurt darkened her eyes.

Instantly contrite, Caleb reached his hand toward her to apologize. "Grace, I'm—"

She jerked upright. "Leave and don't come back."

Seeing her eyes blink, hearing her unsteady voice, he feared she was near tears. He gathered up his papers and turned to go. He wasn't sure he could handle tears, especially knowing he had caused them. Opening the door, he glanced over his shoulder, felt his gut twist. He hadn't meant to hurt her and felt compelled to apologize. "I'm sorrier than you'll ever know."

She looked away from him and didn't say anything. He hadn't really expected her to.

Outside he slowly walked to his car. Instead of getting in, he glanced back at the front door, hoping against hope that Grace wasn't inside crying. If she was, it would be his fault...again, and this time he wasn't sure any amount of food or apology would get her to talk to him again. His position as chair of her department certainly wouldn't do it. Some of the worst underhanded backstabbing was done in academia. The corporate world had nothing on them.

It would take God to make this work.

He glanced skyward. "As always, it's in Your hands."

Caleb was reaching for the door handle when a late-model truck parked in front of the house. A tall, middle-aged man in knife-edge-creased jeans and a blue-plaid shirt climbed out. His dark eyes narrowed as he studied Caleb. His light-brown face didn't curve into a smile nor did he nod his graying head as most people in the small town did when Caleb met them. Reaching back inside the cab, he pulled out a tool belt and strapped it around his trim waist.

The contractor. Caleb glanced back toward the house. Somehow he knew Grace wouldn't want anyone to see her while she was upset. Tossing the notebook into the passenger's seat, he moved to intercept the man. "Good evening. Does Grace expect you?"

The man folded his arms across his impressive chest. "And who might you be?"

A reasonable question. "Caleb Jackson. And you?"

"Oscar Thompson. Grace's father."

Chapter Six

Caleb closed his eyes. When he opened them Mr. Thompson's hands rested on his waist, much too close to his tool belt, which held an assortment of sharp and very lethal-looking items.

"You look rather worried, son," Mr. Thompson said in a voice as slow as molasses in the winter, but his eyes were as sharp as glass. "Should I be?"

"I made her cry," Caleb confessed, swiping his hand across his face. "It's not the first time. I don't mean to. I'm sorry, sir."

Surprisingly, Mr. Thompson's hands moved away from the tool belt. He leaned casually against the side of the truck. "You're that professor at the college who plays that music she doesn't like, aren't you?"

Caleb wasn't sure if he should breathe easier or not. "Yes, sir."

Mr. Thompson glanced toward the house. "I might be the one that owes you an apology."

"What?" Caleb's brows bunched in confusion. "I don't understand."

Grace's father's troubled gaze slowly came back to Caleb. He turned and removed a toolbox from a locked compartment in the truck's bed. "I better go in. Meet me at the city park on the north side in thirty minutes. We'll talk."

"All right," Caleb agreed, but Mr. Thompson had already moved on. Puzzled, Caleb got in the car and started the motor. He didn't back out, however, until the front door opened. As much as he strained to see Grace, he only caught a glimpse of her white blouse before Mr. Thompson went inside and the door closed.

Putting the 'Vette in Reverse, Caleb backed and headed toward the park. Another appointment he didn't plan to be late for.

"What were you and Caleb talking about?" Grace had tried to work on her lesson plans in the music room while her father put in baseboard molding in the dining room, but had only lasted five minutes. Her father certainly hadn't volunteered anything.

"Nothing much." Down on his knees, he nailed the molding in place to match the new hardwood floors. "Seemed like a nice young man."

Grace tsked, then came down beside him to hand him the nail he was reaching for. "You wouldn't think so if you knew what he said to me."

Taking the nail, he faced her and asked, "Did he get out of line?"

Grace blinked. Her father stared back at her. It didn't take much to recall the fiasco with Lowell and how afterward every time he saw her, he'd run in the opposite direction. When she'd mentioned it to her mother, she'd said the "men" had had a talk with him. "No. No, sir."

Nodding, he moved and tapped the nail into the wood.

Grace moved with him, assisting as needed until they were finished. Closing his toolbox he came easily to his feet and waited until Grace was upright before he spoke. "I'll come by next week to start on the deck in the back."

"Thank you, Daddy," she said, feeling awkward as she always did when they were alone.

Picking up the toolbox, he went to the door and opened it. "If you ever want to talk about anything, you call."

"Yes, sir," she replied dutifully, but they both knew she wouldn't. She couldn't forget that there were too many times in the past that she had wanted to talk to him and he wasn't there. "If you'll wait, I'll write you out a check."

"It'll keep." His expression sadder than she had ever seen it, he quietly left.

Grace felt tears prick her eyes. She didn't know if she was crying for herself or her father.

"Grace doesn't like your music because that's the kind of music that took me away from her and my family." Mr. Thompson explained as he and Caleb leaned against the hood of his truck. In front of them the three-acre city park was alive with a Little League softball game, children playing on the swings and late-afternoon joggers.

Caleb heard the roar of the crowd watching the game, but his attention never wavered from Mr. Thompson.

The older man stared at the children yelling and playing on the swing sets and crossbars. Caleb noticed the sadness in his face, which was strongly reflected in his eyes.

"I was the lead singer in a group called the Mystics. Man, we thought we were the best. The Miracles didn't have anything on us. I would have put my pipes up against Smokey Robinson any day. We were going to the top." He shook his head and took a drink from the can of cola in his callused hand.

"We never even made it close, but we chased that dream all over the country for fifteen long years and my family suffered because of it. Every time we'd get a gig, off I'd go, hoping this time it would lead us to the top. It never did. We moved so many times I lost count. By the time I accepted it never would, Grace was a junior in college and she and I were almost strangers."

"I'm sorry," Caleb said. He knew what it was like to chase a dream.

"Yeah, me too." Mr. Thompson's sigh of regret came from deep in his chest. "Deloris, her mother, wanted to stop the moving when Grace's older brother got in high school. After seeing how drugs and gangs were destroying so many young people in the cities, she wanted to move to Summerset when our son was in the tenth grade. I did what she wanted, but I kept trying to catch that elusive star."

The crowd at the softball field roared. Neither Caleb or Mr. Thompson noticed.

"Because of those uncertain days, Grace doesn't like change or the unexpected. Like her mother, she can pinch a penny until it screams. She saved and bought the house two years ago and started fixing it up. She craves stability more than anything in this world and that house gives it to her."

Now Caleb understood why she didn't like change. "You've done a good job remodeling."

He stared off into the distance. "She doesn't know I know, but her mother had to practically beg her to let me do the job. I've always been able to fix things. That's how I was able to get work when we moved so much. Her mother thought it would bring us closer, plus save Grace some money. It did neither. Grace makes any excuse not to be in the room while I'm working and she pays me by the hour, just like I charge other people."

Caleb heard the loneliness and remorse in his voice. "Perhaps one day she'll be ready to move on."

"I pray she will every night." He faced Caleb. "Today, for the first time, she helped me like she used to as a little girl. I have you to thank for that."

"Me?"

"She wanted to know what we had talked about. Of course I didn't tell her, but she stayed and helped me anyway. Felt good having her give that much of herself." His face saddened. "She's forgiven me, but she can't forget that I wasn't there for her. She won't let herself need me again."

"Since I seem to upset her every time we're together more than five minutes, she may be helping you a lot in the coming weeks," Caleb said with a wry twist of his mouth.

"Grace is doing what she believes," her father defended.

"I know, but I happen to think she's wrong." Caleb's hand fisted on the can of soda he'd accepted from Mr. Thompson earlier. It was still full.

"You ever think it might be you?" Grace's father asked.

Caleb's head drew back in surprise. "I beg your pardon?"

"One of you is going to have to meet the other halfway. You ever sat down with one of her suggestions and tried to increase the tempo? Maybe start off slow then take it up a notch or two?"

He hadn't. "My students vetoed every one of her suggestions."

Mr. Thompson looked Caleb directly into the eyes. "Seems Grace might not be the only one set in her ways. If you're the hotshot music man I read and heard you are, it shouldn't be anything for you to take those songs and rearrange them."

"Grace will scream bloody murder if I change one note into what she calls 'music better suited to a club,'" Caleb said.

"She might, but there are two things in both of our favor. Grace loves the Lord and she has a good heart. She wants the gospel concert to be a success," Mr. Thompson said. "Today is not the first time I saw the longing in her face when she looks at me. Maybe she's getting there."

Caleb said nothing, just took a drink of his cola. If Grace hadn't been able to get over her conflicted feelings about her father for these many years, what chance did he have for her to get over her anger with him in time to prepare for the gospel musical in less than two months?

If one choir member asked her at church when they were going to start practicing for the concert, twenty of them did. She'd given them all the same pat answer of "Soon" and hoped they didn't see the worry in her face. Caleb, with his unacceptable demands and unfounded accusations, had put her in a terrible position. After prayer service she hurried through the side door to the nursery, but she wasn't fast enough.

"Grace, I need to talk with you."

Trying not to groan, she turned to see the president of the gospel choir, Roxie Sims, hurry to catch up with her. Dressed in one of her trademark wide-brimmed hats that exactly matched her lavender suit and shoes, she came to a halt in front of Grace. "I'm glad I caught you. The choir members are anxious to get started."

"Yes, ma'am, I realize that, but Caleb and I are still working on the music," Grace told her, wondering how many more times she'd have to repeat that.

The older woman's arched brow shot up. "It's taking a long time, isn't it? You didn't have that much trouble with the songs for the gospel competition."

"No, ma'am, but there are extenuating circumstances."

Mrs. Sims drew herself up straighter. "Then as president, perhaps I should know."

Grace considered telling the retired schoolteacher that she was no longer a student in her English class, but some habits you didn't outgrow. Besides, Mrs. Sims had never been one to gossip. "We're having a difference of opinion on what to sing. He wants some of that finger-popping music, but I insist it be traditional music."

Just then the voice of the youth choir drifted through the sliding doors. From the sounds of it, there were fewer this Sunday than the last four Sundays when they had sang. "It's a shame their parents can't get them to practice. I bet they know the lyrics to every secular, scandalous song on the radio. They need to be in church learning about Christian values."

"True, but as the grandmother of one of those missing young people, I can tell you we won't get them singing 'What a Friend We Have In Jesus' the way we did when we were growing up."

Caught between being offended and disbelieving, Grace whipped her head around. As the music director of the church, all music had to be cleared through her. "There's nothing wrong with that song."

"For us, no." Mrs. Sims put her gloved hand on Grace's shoulder. "We're in competition with the devil, Grace. We have to reach the young people where they are."

Grace recalled that Caleb had said the same thing. "But we shouldn't be confused with him."

"The young people hear secular music each day the Lord brings. They dance to it, sing to it, talk on the phone to it. Then they come to church and hear music that, in their opinion, is old-fashioned and 'old-fogy' and tune us—and with that the Word—out." Mrs. Sims removed her hand. "If you've been around any teenagers or young people, you know they're masters at tuning us out."

"You think Caleb is right?" Grace whispered softly.

"I'm afraid I do," she said gently. "I've been meaning to discuss the same thing with you, but I didn't know how."

"You think I'm rigid."

"I think you're a wonderful, loving young woman who has very definite ideas on what is right." Her shoulders heaved with her indrawn breath. "I wish more young women had your principles and your unshakable belief in God."

Grace wrapped her arms around herself. All this time she had thought she was doing what the Lord wanted, what the church wanted. "Perhaps I should resign."

"Grace Ann Thompson, if you say something so idiotic again I'm not sure what I'll do to you," Mrs. Sims said, the brim of her hat bobbing in agitation. "That kind of talk is one reason I hesitated in speaking to you. You're the best music director this church has ever had. We're blessed and proud to have you. We would be lost without you. Don't make me lose my religion."

Grace found herself smiling at the affronted expression on the other woman's face. "I wouldn't dream of it."

"Well." Mrs. Sims pulled her lavender gloves snugger on her hands. "I've had my say and expect you'll be able to give us a report at choir practice Tuesday night."

Grace didn't look forward to facing Caleb, but she didn't see how she had a choice. "Yes, ma'am."

"Good. I better get back out there. Goodbye, Grace." She turned to go.

"Mrs. Sims, if you can make sure Terry is at our practice and his Thursday night, I think he'll be surprised," Grace said.

Understanding and appreciation lit the older woman's eyes. "He'll be there and so will his friends if they want to have that pool party he planned at my house for Saturday," Mrs. Sims told her and reentered the sanctuary.

Grace continued to the nursery. She had a lot to think about. One thing she didn't want to dwell on was facing Caleb.

Later that afternoon, Grace found herself unable to settle. Since talking with Mrs. Sims, Grace had thought back over the past years and remembered her vetoing any programs that had any inkling of secular in them.

Even the music for the kids' lock-in party she reluctantly agreed to were songs she picked out. In the past year the youth choir had gone from thirty to eleven, and they were children or grandchildren of the members of the deacon board.

Grace stared out the window in the music room to the stakes in the backyard for her deck. If her father worked on this as quickly as he did on the other projects, he'd be finished in a week. She might not have counted on him while she was growing up, but as a contractor, he was the best.

He just wasn't the best father. He loved his music and his dream too much. He'd always been singing, trying out new songs, trying to get just the right sound to take the Mystics to the top. Because it had taken her father away from her she'd gotten to the point where she hated that type of upbeat music.

And she had let that hatred close her mind to anything remotely similar.

The stinging reality of what she had done hit her. Hard. She was as sanctimonious as Caleb had accused. She had judged him on superficial issues. God looked at the heart, not what a person wore. Who was she to say what type of music to worship Him was acceptable and what was not? All she could do was make sure her heart and reasons were in order.

She hadn't done that.

Dropping to her knees, Grace bowed her head in prayer. *Lord, forgive me for my transgressions. Thank You for opening my eyes and my heart. Please give me the strength and the courage to stay in Thy perfect will and not my own. Amen.*

She came to her feet. Tomorrow wouldn't be easy, but her heart felt lighter than it had in a long time.

* * *

Just open the door and do it, Grace admonished herself as she stood outside Music Room C on Monday afternoon. Caleb's secretary had said he was there working on the gospel musical. Obviously he was going ahead with his selections. It still rankled that none of her selections were acceptable, but she just had to accept it.

Taking a deep breath, she opened the door and stopped. Her mouth gaped as much from Caleb's deep, rich voice as from what he was playing. "Blessed Assurance." Only it wasn't the slow, soulful music she was familiar with, but with a faster, upbeat tempo. She wasn't aware she had made a sound, but she must have because he glanced up. Their eyes met.

Again she felt the strange sensation in her stomach. Nerves. She let the door swing shut and walked farther into the room. "Your secretary told me where to find you."

"Hello, Grace." Caleb came to his feet. "I'm glad she did. We need to talk."

"That's why I'm here." Grace glanced away from him to the sheet music on the baby grand. "That's one of my selections."

"I know what you're going to say, but I just want you to listen to it first. I've been working on it all weekend." He picked up several sheets of music from atop the piano and came to her. "I haven't been able to get anywhere with any of the rest. Revelation will just have to use sheet music."

Grace was a bit stunned. "You're willing to use some of my selections?"

"Yes. I was so busy talking about you being rigid that I wasn't looking at myself being the same way. I was wrong and I apologize."

She hadn't expected this turn of events. "I'll accept yours if you'll accept mine."

"Done. Now, what do you think of what you heard?"

"It's different," Grace said slowly.

"At least you didn't slam the piano top down on my fingers," Caleb said, his mouth curving into a smile.

Before she knew how it happened, Grace smiled back. "I think I was too stunned."

"Come on. Sit down and I'll give you another chance." Taking her by the arm he sat her on the bench, joined her, then began to play and sing.

Grace found herself clapping her hands. Her eyes widened as she realized what she was doing. She tucked her head and placed her hands in her lap.

Caleb stopped playing. "If the tempo makes you uncomfortable, we won't do it. Revelation can accompany your gospel choir on 'Stand,' and then bow out and your choir can do the rest."

Her head came up. "That isn't fair. They were so excited. Nor is it what the city council had in mind."

"They'll have to accept what they get," he said firmly.

He was serious. He'd give in to her rather than make her uncomfortable. President Jenkins would be disappointed, but he'd accept Caleb's decision. He respected him too highly not to. Grace thought of all the times she'd had such very uncharitable thoughts about Caleb and realized she had been wrong about him and a lot of other things. "We'll do the concert together or not at all." Opening her purse, she drew out new sheet music to "Stomp." "The president of the choir convinced me that it might not be a bad idea to have some of your songs."

"Thank you." His hand closed around the pages.

With him sitting so close to her and staring at her, she felt a bit nervous and rose to her feet. "I recall Revelation also did 'We Fall Down' and I think that should be included."

"They'd like that," Caleb told her.

"The choir has wanted to sing that song for a long time." She adjusted her purse strap over on her shoulder. "Well, I should go. I have a class."

Caleb went with her to the door. "Did you skip lunch again?"

"I wanted to get the music." She reached for the door handle.

"There's one thing I need to say before you go."

"I thought Revelation and the choir could practice together Tuesday night at the church," Grace said.

"That wasn't it," he said. "I needed to apologize for that remark I made. Any man would count himself lucky if you allowed him to kiss you."

Grace felt heat suffuse her face. Her lashes swept over her eyes in an unconscious flirtatious gesture. Not knowing how to answer, she slipped out the door, but she was smiling before she went two steps.

Chapter Seven

When Grace arrived home that afternoon her parents were waiting for her just as she had requested. She watched them holding hands as they sat side by side on the portion of the deck her father had already finished. She'd known they would be together.

Opening the half-glass door, she stepped onto the stone path that led to the deck. They stood together, their hands still locked. Grace had never understood her mother's unconditional devotion to a man who swept in and out of her life so easily. Yet, looking at the lines time and defeat had etched on her father's face, perhaps it hadn't been easy for him, either.

"Thank you for coming, Mama," Grace said, trying to figure out where to begin.

"You said it was important," her mother answered simply.

To her mother it had always been important to see

to the needs of her children…except in one instance. "I really need to talk to you about my feelings toward both of you."

Both parents tensed, but as usual, it was her mother who spoke. "We know, sweetie. We always have."

Grace was shaking her head before her mother finished. "But you don't. Not really."

"You tell us, then. We'll listen," her father said.

Grace swallowed the lump in her throat. "It was important to me that you stay at home, Daddy." She bit her lip before she could continue. "I used to beg both of you, but you always went anyway. Mama, you should have made him stay."

Her mother left her father's side and came to Grace, her eyes softly pleading. "I loved him enough to let him go. Keeping him would have been wrong."

"But we needed him." Grace fought tears that threatened. "I needed him."

"I know that now." Mrs. Thompson's hands were as unsteady as her daughter's when she took them in hers. "You weren't independent and outgoing like your brother. I thought it was because you were a girl and that you would eventually grow out of it. I kept thinking that until…" Her voice trailed off.

"Until I began avoiding him," Grace finished.

Tears pricked her mother's dark brown eyes. "Yes. It hurt him so bad and I hurt for the both of you. He loves you."

And I turned my back on him, Grace thought. She had been so wrong.

Grace finally looked at her father, his hands clenched, his face unbearably sad, and asked the question that had been burning in her heart for years. "Why didn't you sing inspirational songs?"

"Perhaps because I grew up in Memphis and not a day went by that I didn't hear the wail of my daddy's sax or my uncle's guitar. Music was in my blood, but it had a different beat."

Grace recalled the fun visits to her father's parents in Memphis and the wonderful times they'd had together. The rambling house her grandparents lived in would be full of music and the smell of good food. "Why wasn't singing in the church choir enough?"

"I enjoyed some of the songs, but not all. Loving the Lord doesn't mean I can't enjoy other types of music. It does mean that wherever I go, I hold myself in such a way that His light will shine in me."

More than she had done. She might have turned her back on her father, but he had never turned his back on her. "Daddy, I'm sorry."

He met her more than halfway, his strong arms going around her. "It's all right, baby girl."

Her tears fell faster. He used to call her that when she was a little girl. "I was so angry at you for leaving us, for loving your music more than you loved us."

"Never." Stepping back, he palmed her face and stared into her eyes. "Sure I wanted it for myself, but also for my family. I wanted all of you to have the best." He cast a brief glance at his wife. "Your mother has worked ever since we got married until two years ago. I wanted to sit her down, give her a fancy car, diamonds, trips."

"As long as I have you and the children, I'm content." Mrs. Thompson came to stand beside them. "Material possessions don't mean anything if you don't have love. We have love."

With one hand he pulled her to him. "You'll always have that."

Grace brushed the tears away. "Let's go inside and eat. I made your favorite meal."

Caleb almost kept on going when he saw Grace's father's truck parked outside her house, but he was too hyped not to pull into her driveway. Grabbing the black zippered case, he slammed out of the car and bounded up the steps. It took two rings of the doorbell before the door was opened.

Grace's dark eyes widened in surprise on seeing him. "Caleb—Professor Jackson, what are you doing here?"

"You were right the first time. It's Caleb." He lifted his zipped case. "I finally worked out all the music for 'Blessed Assurance.' I wanted to run it by you before I share it with Revelation at tonight's practice."

Her face glowed. "I can't wait. Please come on in."

Caleb entered the house and followed her to the music room. Her father was there with an attractive middle-aged woman who Caleb could tell from the resemblance was Grace's mother even before she introduced them.

"I didn't mean to interfere, but I wanted Grace to see if she approved of the revised music before the students hear it."

"Not at all," her mother said. "We'd love to listen, too, if you don't mind."

Caleb looked from Grace's mother to her father. "I'd like your opinion."

"Daddy used to be a singer with the Mystics," Grace said, lifting the lid of the baby grand.

She didn't see her father's chest swell with pride and love, but Caleb did. It appeared as if Grace had forgiven them both. Another prayer his Heavenly Father had answered. He took a seat on the bench and opened the music. "Grace, sit here where you can see the music and come in where I want the choir to join in." He angled his head over his shoulder. "Feel free to join in, Mr. and Mrs. Thompson."

Caleb began playing. He knew the instant Grace sat beside him. They both knew, and her parents probably did as well, that she didn't need to be beside him to read the music. He liked having her close, even when she was annoyed with him.

Grace joined in and Caleb almost hit the wrong key. He simply stared. She had a clear, soul-stirring voice. She caught him staring, but this time instead of stopping she smiled and kept on singing and clapping her hands.

Caleb returned the smile and they continued singing. Her parents joined in and although her mother's voice was a nice alto, it was her father's moving tenor that reminded Caleb so much of Andrea Crouch's. Caleb could see why he had taken his talent on the road. It always amazed him when some artists made it and others with just as much talent didn't. But the Lord had His reasons and to question Him was to waste a lot of time.

"In my opinion, you've done a fine job, Caleb," Mr. Thompson said when they finished.

"I think so, too." Grace turned to Caleb. "Now, if only your students will agree."

"I'll let you know." Caleb rose to his feet and glanced at his watch. "I better take off. Goodbye, Mr. and Mrs. Thompson, and thanks for joining in."

"Thank you," Grace's father said. "It's been a long time since I heard Grace sing. Isn't she something?"

Caleb stared down at Grace who had come to her feet, a shy smile on her pretty face. He felt a little tug in the region of his heart. "Yes, she is."

Grace blushed. "I'll show you out."

Caleb followed her to the door. "I didn't mean to stare."

Her lashes briefly swept down. "If you can, please call me tonight if you have time and let me know what they thought."

"I'll make time," he told her. "By the way, have you ever thought of doing a solo? You have a beautiful voice."

"I also get nervous singing by myself. I'm more comfortable directing. Good night," Grace said.

"Night, Grace."

Whistling, Caleb bounded down the steps and vaulted into the car without opening the door. He wasn't showing off, he told himself as he pulled out and waved to Grace who was still standing in the doorway. He was just saving time.

It's a go. I'll meet you tomorrow in the cafeteria during your lunch period to discuss the joint practice tomorrow night.

Grace was nervous remembering Caleb's words. She kept looking at the double doors of the college cafeteria to see if Caleb had made it yet. She'd come straight from her class. Hurried, in fact. It was no longer possible to deny that she was attracted to him. And, from the way he looked at her sometimes, he felt the same way.

Picking up her tray with a grilled chicken salad, she headed toward the area designated for the staff. Through the bank of windows in front of her she could see the other white buildings on the rolling hills of the five-acre campus. She loved teaching and she loved her life here, since she and her father had settled their differences. He'd been there that morning before she left. They'd shared a cup of coffee and a hug.

She put her tray on the small table just as Caleb came through the door. As usual her heart did a little dance. As usual, he was surrounded by several students. He was a popular teacher. She didn't have to think long to realize students never crowded around her. It had always been her practice to hold a part of herself back for fear of being hurt. God's children didn't live with fear.

By the time she'd removed her food from the tray and put the tray away, Caleb was there. "Hi. Sorry I'm a bit late."

"That's all right," Grace told him, wishing her nerves would settle and that she didn't want to look around to see if everyone in the cafeteria was watching them. Caleb unloaded his tray and took a seat across from her. She had to smile at the amount of food. "Mrs. Roberts really loaded your tray."

"She says I need to keep up my strength with all the running around I do." Bowing his head, he said grace for both of them.

Grace murmured amen, then picked up her fork. The cafeteria manager was right. "I never thought about it, but besides teaching you're the advisor for two student organizations, on the faculty council, and you teach accredited and noncredited courses at night."

He dug into the mound of buttered mashed potatoes. "You only go through life once, so you might as well fill it with joy."

Grace paused. "I think I forgot that."

"The important thing is that you remembered." He forked meat loaf into his mouth. "Can you call someone to open the church early tonight? The drums and keyboard need to be set up early so we can get started on time. President Jenkins approved the overtime for two men from maintenance to deliver them, then pick them up afterward. Musicians, as you know, like playing on the same instruments or I'd just store them at the church."

"I'll call Deacon Scott. He lives down the street." She took a sip of sweetened iced tea. "Have you thought of any additional songs?"

Caleb stopped eating and leaned back in his seat. "Revelation wants me to sing 'How Great Thou Art.' It's our closing and signature song. If that's all right with you?"

"I have no objections." She was actually looking forward to hearing him do the solo. "We'll begin with 'We Fall Down,' then 'Stand,' 'Blessed Assurance,' 'Stomp' and close out with 'How Great Thou Art.'"

"Well, it's good to see two of my favorite teachers working so closely together," President Jenkins said, stopping by their table.

Grace flushed. She had been so involved with Caleb she hadn't noticed the president approach. From the startled expression on Caleb's face, he hadn't, either. "Good afternoon, President Jenkins. Thank you for having the instruments delivered."

The president's broad grin grew. "Anything for the welfare of Summerset students. Just heard that T. C. Holloway, one of our successful alumni, might be able to attend."

"That's big news. He's a nationally known minister," Caleb said.

"He preached his first sermon at Peaceful Rest," Grace enthused. "He was the pastor of Peaceful Rest before the present pastor."

"He hasn't forgotten that he got his start here. He's been very generous to us," President Jenkins said.

He had also made donations to Peaceful Rest, Grace

thought. He was a much beloved son of the church. "I hope he can come."

"I hope so, too. He can see Summerset Junior College in action. Well, I'll let you two get back to planning. Make us proud. Goodbye."

"You think he told us about Reverend Holloway coming to make us work harder to shine?" Grace leaned over and asked when the president was out of hearing range.

"There's not a doubt in my mind," Caleb answered softly. "But neither is there a doubt that the music is going to be hot."

Grace chuckled. Only Caleb.

Caleb entered the sanctuary with the members of Revelation at four minutes to seven. Grace and Alton were waiting for them in front of the choir stand. It appeared that all the members of the gospel choir had shown up for practice. They were off to a good start.

His gaze unerringly came back to Grace. She'd removed the cropped herringbone jacket she'd worn when they had lunch to reveal a slim-fitted white dress with capped sleeves. She looked fresh and innocent and she was smiling at him. He'd always thought she'd be pretty if she smiled more.

He was wrong. She was beautiful.

He caught the surprise in her face when he stepped out of the aisle and she could see he had changed from the jeans he had worn at lunch to charcoal-gray dress slacks. He winked. Laughing, she covered her face. He caught some of the members of her choir elbowing each other and knew it would be all over town by tomorrow. If things went as he planned tonight, he'd give them something else to talk about.

Going up on the platform, he and Grace completed the introductions. Together they went over the music selections. In a matter of minutes they were hard at work on the first song. As he'd told his students, Grace had a great choir. The lead soprano's voice had a fabulous range. He knew before they had been at it ten minutes that he'd been right this afternoon when he said they'd be hot.

"Looks like we have an audience," Alton said from his seat at the organ.

Caleb turned around to see a few young people, older adults, Grace's parents and President Jenkins and his wife. He looked at Grace. "Looks like we're being sized up."

"At least they're on our side." She waved to her parents. "All right, Caleb, let's give them what they came for."

He grinned like a fool, pleased that she was comfortable enough with the music and at ease enough with him to joke. "After you."

With an uplifted flourish of her slim hands, the choir came to attention. The music was a swell of sound that sent joy straight to the heart. The addition of the choir was beautiful. When they finished "We Fall Down" many of the people in the choir had their hands uplifted in praise.

Grace had tears in her eyes and it tore at Caleb's heart. What had gone wrong?

"Caleb, there was no reason for you to come over after you'd taken the students back to the campus. I told you I'm fine," Grace said as she sat in her living room later that night staring down at her hands in her lap.

"Then why do you look so sad?" he questioned.

"Practice went great. Your parents were pleased. Neither the students nor the gospel choir wanted to go home. President Jenkins wanted an encore. Everyone is happy except you. Are you having second thoughts?"

Her head slowly came up. "No. As you said, everyone is pleased."

"And that makes you question the direction of the music program in the past," he correctly guessed.

She didn't even think about evading the answer. "Tonight I looked at the young people who hadn't been coming to choir practice and thought what might have happened if you hadn't insisted on a different type of music. Tonight they listened and enjoyed themselves. I invited them hoping they would, but I hadn't counted on how it would make me feel like a failure." Her voice trembled. "By holding on to my anger at my father, I failed them."

"No, you didn't." He came off his seat to sit next to her and take her unsteady hands in his. "You did what you believed in your heart was best for them. I don't think your father would mind me telling you that he told me a little bit about what was going on between you two. You dealt with the possibility of being hurt the best way you knew, by controlling your life. And that meant every aspect."

"Not always." She pulled her hands free. "My freshman year in college I met a man. Lowell Goodings. I thought he was a Christian, but he proved to be an unprincipled man who prayed on the naive freshmen. I believed his lies that he came from a poor family and gave him the pitiful little money I earned tutoring. It finally came out when I was bragging about him to another student. I felt so embarrassed and such a fool."

"He made you withdraw and trust even less." He

gently brushed her hair aside. "When you're that young it's difficult to forgive and go on."

"I'm afraid I wasn't very Christian in my thoughts about him at the time," she confessed.

"Also understandable."

She faced him. "Or you."

"I think I'm growing on you now," he said.

She smiled in spite of herself. "Just when I was beginning to think you weren't so conceited after all."

"It's not conceit when a guy likes a special woman and hopes she likes him a little bit, too," he told her, then blinked as if he had been surprised by what he had just said.

Her smile froze. She felt her heart thump in the familiar tempo it always played when he looked at her.

"Sometimes it takes us a little while to see what is right before our eyes." He paused as if unsure of how to proceed, but his sincerity was obvious. "I'd like the chance to get to know you better outside of the college and practicing for the gospel concert. How about it?"

Grace looked away from Caleb's intense gaze as he waited for an answer. They were direct opposites in temperament, but she wanted to go out with him. She wanted to take a chance for the first time in eight years. She took a deep breath, faced him and said, "I'd like that."

Pleasure spread across his handsome face. "Let's see if we'll both like this." He leaned forward and pressed his lips gently against hers.

Grace's toes actually tingled. She blushed, but she didn't look away from the happiness in Caleb's eyes.

"How about dinner tomorrow night before prayer service? I can pick you up at five forty-five."

Mixed with the wild exhilaration was caution. "This

is a small town," Grace reminded him. "People will talk."

Caleb didn't move. "It won't bother me, if it doesn't bother you."

Instead of answering him, she studied him for a long moment. If Caleb had been the womanizer she'd thought, she would have heard. "You haven't dated very much here."

His head twisted to one side. "Never wanted to, and in case you're wondering, there is no one in Dallas."

"The thought had crossed my mind," she said with complete honesty.

"I'll bet." With a teasing smile he pulled her to her feet. "Get some rest and I'll pick you up at five forty-five."

Her eyebrow lifted. "I haven't said yes."

"You hadn't said no, either. Lock up tight." He kissed her on the cheek and then he was out the door.

A bemused smile on her face, Grace went to the window and pulled the sheer curtain aside to watched Caleb pull off, then she did what she hadn't done in too many years to count.

She went to her closet to find something special to wear for a date.

Chapter Eight

Caleb was on time. He'd expected Grace to be ready and she was. But he hadn't counted on her father still being there working on the deck. He followed her out to the back to say goodbye to her father.

"Bye, Daddy," she said over the noise of the buzz saw.

Mr. Thompson cut the power tool and lifted his goggles. "Be careful and have fun."

"Good evening, sir," Caleb said. "I'll take good care of her."

"If I thought otherwise, she wouldn't be going," Grace's father replied.

Caleb blinked.

Grace rolled her eyes, then kissed her father on the cheek. "Now that you've tried to scare Caleb, you can go home and eat your own dinner."

"Good night, Mr. Thompson," Caleb said as they started for his car.

"I've never seen the top up," Grace said as he opened the door and helped her inside.

"With two sisters I know how women are about their hair." Getting in, he buckled his seat belt. "By the way, I like that dress."

"Thank you and may I say you look rather spiffy yourself. Dress slacks two days in a row. I'm flattered."

"You should be," he said, pulling to a stop at a signal light. "I wouldn't make this great sacrifice for just anyone."

She laughed as he'd wanted. "Sorry about Daddy. Mama warned me that he's determined to make up for the time he wasn't here when I was going out on dates."

The light changed and Caleb pulled off. "How do you feel about that?"

She twisted toward him. "Don't tell him, but it's kind of nice. Though I think he went a little overboard tonight."

"When my sisters' dates came to pick them up, my father would always just happen to mention that he was a crack shot. Heather and Cynthia probably had more first and last dates than anyone in our high school." Caleb parked in the front of the restaurant and came around to open her door. "Of course, they're both married now and living in Dallas."

"My brother, Reginald, is married and living here." She stood. "It wouldn't surprise me if he's at the next practice."

They entered the restaurant and were shown to their seats. "Can he sing?"

"About as well as a bullfrog with a cold," Grace said, picking up her menu. "When Desiree comes home and they're both singing, it's an experience, but I love them both."

"Desiree?"

"Desiree Coleman. She, Nina and I went to high school together and were always close. They both grew up here. Desiree now lives in Dallas," Grace explained. "She has the desire to sing, and has a strong voice, but the notes come out wrong."

"That must have been difficult for her when you and Nina sing so well."

"Not at all. Desiree doesn't have a jealous bone in her petite body. She's a wonderful person."

"Maybe she can come to the gospel celebration."

"That's a great idea. I'll call her tomorrow."

"Now that's settled, let's order. I'm starved."

Grace arrived home thirteen minutes before prayer service was to start. "Thanks, Caleb. I had a wonderful time."

"Surprised you, huh?" He grinned, his hand on the door frame above her head.

She quickly learned that, like her father, he liked to tease. "Probably fooled you, too."

"Not at all." His hand lowered to gently cup her cheek. "I have class tomorrow night, but are you free Friday night?"

Grace's knees felt a little shaky with his hand on her. "Yes. Why don't I fix dinner? Daddy's not finished with the deck, but it's still nice out back and I can grill some steaks."

"You got a date. Should I bring anything?"

"No. Can you wait until seven to eat?" she asked. She'd quickly discovered he had an enormous appetite.

His thumb stroked her cheek before he answered.

"Some things are worth waiting for." His head lowered until his mouth, warm and sweet, found hers.

Grace's eyelids fluttered closed. She'd never been kissed as if she were precious.

"Good night, Grace," Caleb murmured against her lips, then he was gone.

Grace opened her eyes to see him pulling out of her driveway. She watched him until he had turned the corner. He certainly knew how to put a smile on woman's face. Humming softly, she went inside to get her car keys to go to prayer meeting.

For once Grace was as anxious to leave as her students on a Friday afternoon. Directly after her last class, she hurried to her car. She pulled out of the staff's parking lot forty minutes past five. She was making good time, she thought as she waited for the light in front of the campus to change. She'd left nothing to chance.

The T-bones were marinating in the refrigerator, and she had bought fresh flowers for the table. She'd made a three-layer coconut cake for dessert. The giant baking potatoes would go in the oven as soon as she got home. She'd even given the house a thorough cleaning. It wasn't lost on her that Caleb would be the first man she had invited to her house. The first man she had cared about since Lowell. She thanked God that she had moved on with her life, in so many ways.

The light changed and she pulled off in a stream of cars, trucks and SUVs. The college had a dormitory, but many of the students left for the weekend. She couldn't understand why. She had lived in Summerset since she was fourteen and in the ninth grade. Even before she and her father had settled their differences, she couldn't imagine living anyplace else. This was her home and she never wanted to live any place else. Everything she wanted was here.

Checking the lane, she pulled into the bakery's parking lot and barely kept from groaning. It was jam-packed. Her idea to get freshly baked bread no longer seemed like a good one. She was considering leaving when a parking space opened up. Seeing it as a good sign, she pulled in.

Ten minutes later she hurried out with her onion bread to discover a truck with a trailer hitch double-parked behind her car and three others. One of the other blocked car owners was angrily denouncing the absent and rude driver. Deciding to act instead of complain, she started back inside to locate the owner.

She had almost reached the door when the angry blast of a car horn on the busy street caused her to glance in that direction. Her body stiffened in shock. Caleb was driving by with an attractive young woman she had never seen before sitting in the passenger's seat.

On the drive home Grace vacillated between warning herself not to jump to conclusions and recalling what a gullible fool she had been with Lowell. Common sense told her that there could be a dozen different reasons for the woman to be in his car; rational thinking went out the window when your emotions were involved. No closer to making up her mind, she pulled into her driveway and got out.

Her father came from around the house at a fast clip. "I was listening for the sound of your car. I was beginning to worry about you. You said you were coming straight…" His voice trailed off when he neared. "What's the matter?"

Until she was sure, she was keeping her own counsel.

"Long day." Reaching back in the car, she pulled out her briefcase and purse, then started to close the door.

"Wait. You're leaving the bread." Opening the door wider, he picked up the clear, handled bag. "Bread's mashed a little."

It was almost flat. She'd mauled it when she'd seen Caleb drive by.

"Sliced, it might not be so bad." He valiantly tried to push the onion loaf back into shape. "What do you think?"

Grace glanced at the pitiful squashed bread, then at her father. She'd tried to push him out of her life, but here he was trying to help her. Just like her Heavenly Father loved her in spite of her sins, in spite of all the times she'd messed up or turned her back on Him. Her earthly father loved her the same unconditional way.

If not for Caleb, she and her father might never have settled their differences. If God had sent Caleb into her life for no other reason, she was grateful. "I love you, and I'm glad you're a part of my life."

Her six-foot-two, 180-pound father stared at her, blinked, then swallowed hard. "No more than I am," he said, his voice rough.

Grace had to swallow herself. She hooked her arm through his. "Come on. I have a guest coming for dinner."

Caleb stuck the bottle of sparkling grape juice under one arm and rang the doorbell. In his other hand was a box of chocolates. He resisted the urge to ring the bell again when it wasn't immediately answered. He'd never been this anxious to see a woman. Grace was an unexpected development. He kept catching himself thinking about her. The realization prompted alternate grins and shakes of his head. Who would have thought it?

The front door finally opened. "Hello, Caleb. Come in."

"Hi, Grace." He stepped inside, intending to kiss her until he realized that the smile on her face didn't light up her dark eyes. "Is everything all right?"

"Of course." She closed the door.

"You're sure nothing is wrong?"

"Absolutely."

Not convinced, he handed her the chocolates and juice. "I know you said not to, but I wanted to bring something." He followed her to the kitchen.

A smile flirted around her soft mouth. "Thank you. That was sweet. Would you like some juice now or iced tea?"

What he'd like was some answers as to what was bothering her. "No thanks."

Turning away, she put the bottle in the refrigerator and set the two-pound box of chocolates on the island. "The steaks and potatoes are almost ready. Come on outside. I don't want them to burn."

His puzzlement growing, Caleb followed her to the backyard. Smoke and the mouthwatering aromas of grilled food wafted from the grill. He didn't feel as if he had a right to pry, but he didn't like seeing her look so sad. "The deck looks great. Your dad is some carpenter."

"Thanks on both accounts." With the prongs of the long-handled meat fork she lifted the edge of the steaks, then nudged over the foil-wrapped potatoes.

So, it wasn't her father, he thought. He took a seat on the deck. "Come sit down."

She hesitated, then placed the fork on a plate. She didn't drag her feet, but she wasn't hurrying, either.

"I like the dress you have on even better than the one you wore Wednesday night," he said.

"Thank you."

He didn't get the same shy, pleased smile she'd given him the other night. Sitting beside him, she folded her hands in the lap of her floral-print sundress. He reached out and took one of her hands in his. He felt her pulse leap, then steady. She didn't pull away, but she didn't seem inclined to talk, either. It was up to him.

"Today started off hectic, with two teachers late and one sick. Then I had your kind of lunch."

She frowned up at him. He smiled.

"Candy bar on the run."

He thought he saw her mouth curve, before she turned away. "Then, this afternoon one of the students I advise couldn't start her car. I had to take her to work at the H-E-B grocery store. Traffic was a mess on Main. I might miss Dallas, but not the bumper-to-bumper rush-hour traffic."

Grace's head whipped around. "A student?"

Encouraged by her interest, he continued. "Macy Peters. She's a transfer from Temple University. I don't think you have her. Nice girl, but she talked my ear off. At least I was able to pick up the juice and chocolates at the grocery store."

Grace shut her eyes, then slowly opened them. "I need to tell you something, but first I better get the food."

"Sure. I'll help." He stood, pulling her up with him.

Grace put the meat and potatoes on a platter then took them inside and set it next to the mangled bread. She picked up the wicker basket holding it and faced

Caleb. "This afternoon I stopped to get this, saw you pass with the student, and this is the result." She returned the mashed bread to the table. "I understand if you don't want to stay for dinner, but I hope you'll forgive me enough to still be able to work with me for the celebration."

"You thought I was dating another woman while I was taking you out?"

"I'm sorry. I should have known better." Regret coated each word.

"Yes, you should have." Caleb folded his arms. "If I hadn't told you about Macy would you have ever told me what was bothering you?"

She couldn't evade the truth. "I'm not sure. I was grateful for you helping to heal the rift between me and my father."

His brows bunched. "Grateful, huh?"

She bit her lips. He didn't seem pleased. "Yes."

"Well, it seems I should have followed my first instinct." Caleb pulled her into his arms and kissed her. "Is there possibly another reason why you're glad I'm around?"

Grace stared up into his face. "Beside making me glad to be alive, I can't think of a single reason."

Caleb's eyes darkened, his head lowered just as the doorbell rang.

"That would be my father." Reluctantly pushing out of his arms, she went to the door and opened it. Not only was her father there, but her mother, as well. Grace looked behind them. "Should I expect Reginald?"

"You're all right?" her mother asked, her dark eyes troubled.

"Wonderful." Grace opened the door wider for them to come in.

"Good evening, Mr. and Mrs. Thompson." Caleb leaned nonchalantly against the entrance leading into the kitchen-dining area.

Mr. Thompson's searching gaze went from one happy face to the other. "We were passing by and I thought you might have cut that cake."

Grace's lips twitched. "Not yet. We were just about to sit down and eat."

"Then we won't keep you." Mrs. Thompson took her husband's arm and sent Grace and Caleb an apologetic smile. "Your father can get some cake tomorrow." The door closed.

Smiling Caleb reached out his hand and this time Grace eagerly took it.

Chapter Nine

Grace woke up with a smile, then bounded from bed to get dressed. She and Caleb were going to play tennis. She hadn't played since her college days and was terrible at it, but that didn't matter. What she was looking forward to was spending more time with Caleb.

When the doorbell rang, she went to answer it. Caleb was there in his tennis whites. She greeted him with a smile, a kiss and a cup of coffee. He accepted all three with heartfelt gratitude.

"Thanks." Caleb sighed and took a seat on the stool at the kitchen island. "How did you know?"

"I noticed you always come to meetings grumpy and out of sorts until after your second or third cup of coffee," she confessed, her hands wrapped around her own steaming mug and took a seat next to him.

"Oh, yeah." He took another sip of the cream-and-sugar-laced brew. "Glad to know I wasn't the only one interested."

"But I fought it," she confessed.

"You didn't stand a chance against us." Before she could comment, he kissed her cheek and she lost her train of thought. "Ready?"

She slid off the stool a bit reluctantly. "I'll warn you again that I'm a terrible player."

He came to his feet and took her hand. "That's all right because you're a fabulous kisser."

Laughing at his audacity, she grabbed her racket and purse and let him lead her outside to his car. "Can you put the top down? I figure playing tennis will do a number on my hair anyway."

"Your hair could never be anything but pretty," he commented as he activated the top.

Grace barely kept from sighing. To think she had almost missed this. *Thank you, Lord.*

Rounding the hood, Caleb opened the door. "Let's go play some tennis."

All three courts at the college were being used, as were the city courts. His hands curled around his racket, Caleb tapped it against the side of his leg. "This wouldn't happen in Dallas."

"You can embarrass me some other time." Grace twirled the racket in her hand.

He glanced at her. "You mind waiting a bit? If the court doesn't clear, we can go have some breakfast."

"Stop pouting. I've always wanted my date to push me on the swing." Looping her hand through his arm, she firmly turned him toward the playground in a nearby crop of trees.

The idea of them sharing something for the first time

appealed to him immensely. "How high do you want to go?"

She cut him a glance. "Probably not as high as you'd like."

He chuckled. "Spoilsport, and I wasn't pouting. I just wanted to show you a good time. It's difficult enough for a guy to impress his date in a town where there's nothing to do."

Clearly taken aback, Grace stopped and stared up at him. "There's lots to do."

"Not compared to Dallas." He took her racket and laid it beside his on the grass. The courts and running trails might be occupied, but the playground was deserted. "Hop on."

Grace sat down and wrapped her hands around the chain. "Roller-skating, movies, football and basketball."

He set the swing in motion. "High school sports are great, but they can't compare to professional games."

She looked at him over her shoulder. "Didn't all the Dallas teams have losing seasons?"

He grimaced. "They're coming back."

"Ah," she said, then continued her list. "Visiting with friends. Church. Dining."

He sent her a little higher. "Name me one restaurant that has a linen tablecloth."

Grace came back in an instant. "The Longhorn at the Holiday Inn."

"One can't compare to the hundreds in the Dallas–Fort Worth area." He shook his dark head. "I miss the city."

"I thought you liked Summerset?" Grace tried to twist around to see his face and almost fell out of her seat.

He grabbed and steadied her. "I do. I just like Dallas

better." He looked toward the court. "It's free. Let's go." Caleb picked up the rackets, caught her hand again and jogged toward the court. He didn't notice the pensive look on Grace's face.

The day was sun-kissed and filled with laughter and fun. Grace didn't mind, at least not much, that she had played tennis abominably. When she finally returned a serve, Caleb had cheered and made a halfhearted attempt to return the ball. Afterward he'd taken her home to shower and change, then picked her up that evening to go to the Longhorn for dinner.

Grace had such a good time, she managed to forget Caleb's comment about missing the big city until she crawled into bed that night. Snuggling deeper under the covers, she dismissed the idea that he might leave. He was the chair of his department—the youngest one on campus. He wouldn't give that up. Assured she was right, she closed her eyes and drifted off to sleep. She had to get up early in the morning for Sunday school.

Grace wasn't surprised to enter the sanctuary ahead of the choir and see Caleb. What did lift her brow was seeing him sitting with her parents. He wore a dark blue suit. His navy-blue-and-red tie looked like silk. If tongues weren't wagging about them already, they certainly would be. Inclining her head in greeting, she called the members to attention to sing their first selection.

After service she knew she was right when she walked out the side door of the church and saw Caleb waiting for her. Usually by this time most of the cars parked along the streets and in the small parking lot in front of the church were gone. Not today. Several members, including her father, were talking to Caleb in front of the church.

As if he had some sixth sense where she was concerned, he looked up. The crazy feeling in her stomach that she had attributed to anything but awareness of Caleb returned full force.

Excusing himself, Caleb came to her. "The choir was filled with the Spirit today. They were great and so were you."

"Thank you." Adding a bit of swaying motion had certainly rejuvenated them. She had decided to incorporate it into the music they were practicing for the gospel competition. "Looks like you attracted a lot of attention," she teased.

"Tell me about it."

Her father joined them. "I'm hungry. You two can talk at the house. Your mother went on to get dinner ready." He held his hands out. "Give me your car keys and I'll drive your car."

She didn't hesitate. "Thanks, Daddy."

"See you at the house. Your brother and his wife are coming," he told them and went to her car.

Taking her arm, Caleb led her to his Corvette. "I guess he couldn't wait."

Caleb and Reginald bonded over football...on television and in his parents' big backyard. The impromptu game of touch football drew several neighborhood men, as well. Their wives joined them and cheered them on. Wearing a pair of jeans and a T-shirt loaned to him by Grace's father, Caleb made two touchdowns. Fortunately, Grace's father and brother were on his winning team. He scored points with Mrs. Thompson as well when the neighbors said they were hungry and he volunteered to pick up a couple of buckets of chicken and the fixings for extra food beyond what she'd made.

Later, sitting on the grass in the backyard with Grace beside him and seeing her contented smile, Caleb felt with growing certainty that he now knew the other reason he had been led to Summerset. A strand of hair blew across Grace's face and she carelessly brushed it behind her ear. She looked carefree and beautiful in a sleeveless blouse and clam diggers.

"You're staring," she whispered.

"You're shouldn't be so beautiful," he said in his normal voice.

Grace hid her hot face behind her hands. The other women there looked expectantly at their husbands. The men good-naturedly teased Caleb, chiding him that beating them at football was bad enough without making them look bad in front of their wives.

Caleb leaned casually back on his elbows and looked at Grace. "Not my fault. Blame her parents."

The men groaned. The women sighed. Mrs. Thompson beamed. Mr. Thompson stuck his chest out with pride. Reginald pulled his own wife closer and nodded his head in approval. Grace openly blushed with pleasure.

It took over a week for the news that Caleb and Grace were dating to spread through Summerset campus. They decided to tell President Jenkins personally. He took the credit for putting them together and sent them off with his blessings.

"That wasn't so bad," Grace said.

"Told you," Caleb said as they started down the hallway. "After rehearsals tonight, want to grab a banana split at the Dairy Queen?"

"Don't you ever think of anything except eating?" She walked through the door he held open for her.

"You mean there are other things out there?" he told her.

She laughed. "Caleb, you're incorrigible."

"No, I'm a man who is enjoying life. I'll pick you up around eight-thirty." Squeezing her hand, he started across the campus with long, ground-eating strides.

Grace watched him go. He occupied her thoughts a great deal, too. But that was to be expected when you loved someone. The truth no longer scared her. Caleb was a man she could trust and depend on. Hugging her notebook to her chest, she continued to the Meadows Fine Art building, already anticipating seeing Caleb again.

Over the next month when Grace and Caleb were not conducting joint practices for the gospel concert, they spent as much time together as their hectic schedules would allow. On those occasions when they didn't go out, they stayed at Grace's house, relaxing on the finished deck or working in the music room on new songs for the church's choir or Revelation.

Grace had just come inside from watering the plants on the deck when she heard the doorbell and saw the familiar shape of Caleb through the half-glass door. They were going to a movie. She hurried the rest of the way and opened the door.

He scooped her up and twirled her around.

She laughed and stared up at him when he finally set her on her feet. "That's some hello."

"You won't believe it." He shook his head and laughed. "I still can't believe it. It's the chance of a lifetime."

"Why don't you tell me so I can decide?"

He shoved the door closed behind him, then took her hands. "Before I do, I think you should know something else that's even more important." He glanced around the room. "The phone call I just received made this more immediate. You deserve to be surrounded by roses, candlelight and soft music when I tell you. We'll have to do it the next time."

She began to shake. "Just say it."

His hands moved to palm her face. "I love you, deeply, irrevocably."

Joy swept through her. "Oh, Caleb!" She launched herself into his arms.

His arms closed tightly around her. "I hope this means you love me back."

Leaning away, she gazed up at him with love shining in her eyes. "So much so that my heart and soul sings with it."

He trembled. Momentarily touched beyond words, he leaned his forehead against hers. "You humble me. I definitely should have stopped for roses."

"Oh, Caleb," she whispered. "I'd rather have your kiss."

His lips touched hers tenderly. "You are so incredible."

"This is incredible."

"I'm blessed beyond measure," Caleb told her. "I can't believe everything is coming together at once. God is good."

"All the time," Grace said.

"Amen. Now for the other news. I've been offered a position at the Northern University in Chicago for the next school year. They're renowned all over the nation for their music department, but not gospel. They want me to start a progr—" He stopped abruptly. "What's the matter?"

Grace felt as if she'd been given something precious and irreplaceable then had it snatched away. "You'd leave Summerset?"

"I never intended to stay here," he told her. "I made it no secret. I thought you knew. I told President Jenkins when he sought me out that I'd be here three years at the most. He said the school wanted me anyway."

"But you're the chair of the department." This wasn't supposed to be happening.

"He probably thought he could keep me by offering me the position, but I always knew Summerset was a way station, not my final destination."

Way station. "I see." In a minute she'd start to breathe again.

"Come on, Grace. Sit down." Caleb urged her onto the sofa and sat beside her. "If you don't want me to go, I won't."

Happiness lasted only seconds, then she saw his face. He wanted to go. Just like her father had wanted to go. "Why can't you be happy here?"

His hand tenderly cupped her face again. "Because it's not where God wants me to stay. I've always been aware of something tugging inside me that guides my steps. I admit I don't always like where He leads, but it's always turned out to be for the best."

"How do you know it's not your own ego that's leading you?" she asked. Then she shook her head in shame and regret at her uncalled-for remark. "Forgive me. I know you better than that. It's just…"

"You see your father in me," he finished softly.

Instead of answering, she withdrew his hand from

her face and held it in hers. "When do they want you to come for the interview?"

"Tuesday."

Her hands jerked. "Will you be back in time for practice that night?"

"Grace, I'm not going to give up one of God's programs to do another." His hand twisted to rest on hers. "If I can get someone to cover my two classes, I can fly up late Monday night and be back in time for the practice. If not, I won't go."

She swallowed the lump in her throat. If this was where God was leading him, he had to go. "I can take the Music Appreciation class at one."

His eyes softened with love. "Thank you."

"You'll go to that interview in a suit and you'll get that job," Grace said firmly.

"But you won't be here waiting for me when I get back." It was a statement not a question.

"I can't." Withdrawing her hands, she rose to her feet. "If you don't mind, can we cancel the movie?"

"Grace—"

"Please, Caleb," she interrupted.

"I'll go, but it's not over." His thumb brushed a tear from her cheek. "Don't cry. He didn't bring us together to tear us apart."

Opening the door, he was gone. He took her dreams and her heart with him.

Chapter Ten

Grace woke up with a splitting headache and red, puffy eyes. She made herself get out of bed when she wanted to linger with the covers over her head. She had to go to church. As miserable as she was, she needed His word to help ease the desolation she felt.

Less than an hour later, she opened the front door and came to a halt. Tears that she had thought were under control slid down her face. She blinked them away to stare down at the immense bouquet of pink and red roses on the porch. He had no right to do this to her. Even as the thought went through her head, she knelt and picked up the roses.

From his vantage point across the street behind a huge oak tree, Caleb watched Grace. He had been waiting for the past hour and was thankful Grace's elderly neighbor was an early riser and thought it was sweet that he wanted to surprise her with flowers. What he was was desperate and in love. He had only wanted to bring Grace happiness with his love, not pain. She'd looked so sad last night and just now as she picked up the flowers and took them back inside.

He had almost been afraid that she'd toss them. He should have known better. She was hurting, not mean-spirited or vindictive. That wasn't the kind of woman God would have chosen for him. And with every breath he knew Grace was God's choice for his wife.

They just had to convince her. His heart ached for her and what she must be going through. She had to let go of her fear and let God guide her. And she had to do it by herself.

Sticking his hands into the pockets of his jeans, Caleb went back to his car, which was parked a block over. He'd considered going to church at Peaceful Rest, but dismissed the idea. He didn't want to embarrass Grace or make this more painful than it already was. But he intended to show her that he loved her and that if she'd trust him, he wouldn't let her down.

He glanced skyward. *Please be her comforter during this difficult time. She'll need it in the days to come.*

For the first time Grace wished she wasn't on a first-name basis with the members of her church. There was no way she could disguise the fact that she had been crying. But at least the children's choir was singing this Sunday, so she could sit in the audience. Her parents had immediately seated themselves on either side of her.

"It'll be all right, Grace," her mother murmured.

Too full of emotion to speak, Grace swallowed and nodded.

As the church service progressed she didn't join in

on one song. She couldn't. Every time she opened her mouth, her throat would clog. Instead she fixed her gaze on the stained-glass angel with outspread arms behind the choir stand. Angels had descended to minister to Jesus. He had promised the same to His children: "I will not leave you comfortless."

The congregation took their seats and Pastor French walked to the wooden podium and began to flip through his Bible. "I want you to turn with me to II Corinthians 5:7. And it reads, 'For we walk by faith, not by sight.'" He stared out at the congregation. "I want to use as my subject this morning, 'Whose steps are you following?'"

An eruption of amens sounded throughout the church. Grace's attention snapped from the angel.

"Watch me now and listen. The devil is a trick-ster. He'll use any means to bind you, and his great-est weapon is fear. If you're a child of God, and have claimed it, act like it. Be bold and step out on His word. Don't cower in fear and let the devil get the glory and the victory."

Grace listened to the message and replayed her de-cisions in the past. Then she asked herself whose steps she was following. Once she had been so certain she was on the right path, but being with Caleb, loving him, had made her take a hard look at the way she believed. She continued to love God, but the narrow confines were gone. Caleb was right. There was more than one way to love and honor God.

"God can't lead you into a blessing He planned if you don't have the faith and courage to follow Him, to reach out and take it." Pastor French straightened and closed his Bible. "I'm claiming mine and the devil bet-ter get out of the way."

Shouts of amen and praise filled the sanctuary as

Pastor French extended the invitation and the children's choir began to sing "How Great Thou Art." This time Grace was able to join in.

The Tuesday morning interview went well, Caleb thought. Yet, more than what the people interviewing him were saying, he was listening to what He said.

Total silence.

The campus was beautiful, the budget wonderful, the salary fabulous. It was the chance of a lifetime.

But there was no joy in Caleb's heart. Walking through the fine arts department with the president of the university and the dean, Caleb reasoned at first it was because he was worried about Grace. He almost convinced himself. It wasn't until he was on his way to the airport in the cab that he recalled Grace asking him if it was his ego that was sending him.

He hadn't thought so until now. He had been so caught up in the great opportunity and the prestige that he hadn't stopped to consider that Northern might not be the place God intended him to go. Hands clasped between his legs, Caleb hung his head. Worse, he hadn't prayed about the decision. He'd just assumed.

"Forgive me."

"You say something, mister?" the cab driver asked as he pulled up in front of the terminal at O'Hare.

"Just talking to God," Caleb answered.

The gray-haired cabbie cut the meter and turned to stare at Caleb. "Do it myself all the time. He's the only one who'll never change on you and who will always tell you the truth even when you don't want to hear it."

Caleb nodded. "Even when you're out of His will there's a comfort in knowing He's there and will lead you back in the right direction." Paying the fare, Caleb entered the terminal. He couldn't wait to tell Grace.

Grace was just finishing her dinner when the doorbell rang. Somehow she knew it was Caleb even before she got up from the table and went to open the door.

"I'm not taking the job," he blurted as he came inside. "I'm staying." He reached for her, but she stepped back. "Grace, don't you understand?"

"I've been doing a lot of praying and thinking about us, Caleb. Please have a seat and I'll try to explain." She waved him to the sofa and took the side chair across from it. If she was to get through this she needed not to be able to touch him.

"I thought you'd be happy," Caleb said, clearly not understanding her reaction.

She folded her hands in her lap. "If God wants this for you, you have to go."

"That's just it." He scooted forward on the seat. "It's not. I can always tell." He faltered for a brief moment. "You were right. I jumped the gun because I was caught up with myself and the prestige of the position."

"At least you're man enough to admit it. Not many would." She drew a deep breath. "But that doesn't change the fact that one day you will leave Summerset."

He made a motion to go to her. She held up her hands to stop him. "No, please. I won't get through this if you don't stay seated."

Caleb settled back. "Okay."

"You know where your destiny lies. I'm just realizing I'm still seeking mine." She glanced around the room. "I made this a home because growing up we moved so much. Even the house my parents live in now, they bought after my father came back."

"Grace, I know you like stability, but life isn't like that all the time."

"I'm not sure I can be happy any other place," she confessed. "Until I'm sure I have that kind of unshakable faith and courage to withstand whatever life throws in my path, I don't think we should see each other."

Misery swept through him, and Grace looked even more miserable. How could he have messed up this badly? "I shouldn't have gotten ahead of God's plan for us. I blew it."

"If it's God's plan, neither you nor I can alter it," she told him, her conviction obvious. "I just need to make sure it is."

This time he went to her and knelt in front of her. "I'll try to be patient. I love you."

"I love you, too." Her unsteady fingers brushed his jacket lapels. She blinked several times before continuing. "Nice suit. I bet you impressed them."

"I'm more concerned with impressing you and getting you to trust me again."

Her hand stilled, then she placed it in her lap. "Would you like some leftover chicken and dressing from Sunday dinner before we go to practice?"

He said he'd try to be patient, but that didn't mean he wasn't above trying to spend as much time with her as possible. "I would if you'll keep me company." He held his breath waiting for her answer.

"All right." Grace stood and went to the kitchen.

Caleb slowly straightened. Following Grace he tried to take comfort that she hadn't sent him packing, but he couldn't quite manage it. She had yet to smile at him. *Please, Lord. Show me the way.*

Caleb's despair was like a weight on his chest. Once again, there was total silence and his joy was gone.

* * *

The choir members' heads were worse than a game of Ping-Pong as they bounced from Grace to Caleb. He could only imagine what Grace had gone through Sunday at church. You couldn't tell it now. She was laughing and acting as if she didn't have a care in the world. It was Caleb who, at first, had difficulty getting it together.

He paid more attention to Grace than what he was doing. He fervently hoped and prayed that he'd never make the mistake of not seeking His guidance in every facet of his life, just as he continued to thank Him for Grace. Despite what he had put her through, she hadn't turned her back on him. Her name said it all. In fact, it was Grace who helped him get back on track.

She motioned the choir to cut, then came to him. "Caleb, while I'm working on increasing my faith and His guidance, don't lose sight of yours." Without waiting for an answer, she went back to where she had been standing.

He didn't make another flub. She was right. Caleb turned his mind to the music and off his own problems. Practice ended on a high note, literally and figuratively. They were ready for the concert Saturday.

"Grace, can you meet me during your lunch hour to prepare a press release?" he asked. The people milling around stopped.

"You can't do that without me?" she asked, probably as aware as he was that people were listening.

"Yes, but I do better with you." He planned to tell her every chance he got that he wanted to be with her.

"I'll be there."

Turning, he herded his students out to the van. While

Grace was working on her faith and courage, perhaps it would be a good idea to take a look at his own.

Summerset's Harvest Celebration was to be the crowning event after months of preparation. George Rutherford Summerset had founded the city when the axle on his horse-drawn wagon had broken down on the way to Shreveport. He'd liked the fertile soil and green valley so much that he'd stayed.

The downtown sported red, white and blue banners and most of the stores were closed to allow their employees to enjoy the all-day celebration. After the parade and the mayor's speech, people were ready to enjoy the traveling carnival until the gospel concert scheduled for the afternoon.

Grace meandered over the grounds enjoying the sights, the laughter of children and adults, and the beautiful fall day. She smiled with the sheer joy of living. She hadn't been able to do that at times during the past week. Prayer and a great deal of soul-searching had helped her reach this point. God would lead her in the right direction. Of that she had been sure. Once she had reached that decision, it would be easy to let go.

Stopping at a food booth, she dug money out of her pants pocket and purchased corn on the cob. Butter and juice ran down her chin as she bit into it. Laughing, she grabbed a napkin, looked up and saw Caleb. Warmth flooded her heart. Whatever happened she'd always love him. She couldn't run away from that fact or change it. Fear would no longer be a part of her life.

A smile still hovering on her lips, she continued toward him. "Hi."

"Hi," Caleb greeted. He hadn't talked to her since their meeting Wednesday. He took it as a good sign that she was smiling. She looked great in a pink-plaid blouse and white pants. "Ridden any rides yet?" he casually asked.

"No." She delicately wiped her mouth. "I thought I'd look around first."

"Care if I walk with you?"

Her dark eyes twinkled mischievously. "I'll think about it if I can have a bite of your smoked turkey leg."

He eyed her corn. "A bite for a bite."

"Deal." She took a hefty bite out of his drumstick, then grinned at the look of surprise on his face.

He bit into her corn with the same gusto. "Now that we've shown people how greedy we are, let's go see what else we can get into." He reached out his free hand and she put hers in his and they set off.

They ended up at the Ferris wheel. "You game?"

Grace stared up at the circle of metal as it revolved high in the sky. "I don't like my feet that high off the ground unless I'm in an airplane."

"I'll be there."

Her gaze came back to him. "I'll probably have a death grip on your neck the entire time and you have to sing later."

"I'll chance it."

Grace was true to her words the first scary seconds of the ride. After she was sure she wasn't going to fall out she relaxed and enjoyed it, enjoying the bird's-eye view and eagerly pointing to the steeple of Peaceful Rest. When her ride was over, her feet firmly planted on the ground, she tried to catch her breath.

"Let's go to the ring toss."

"I don't know, Caleb. That game is hard."

"I'm winning you a stuffed animal."

Ten dollars later, Caleb found himself in an unenviable position. The woman he loved was empty-handed and some of the church members and students from the college had gathered around. Pride warred with common sense. He hadn't even come close to getting a ring over the neck of one bottle.

"You mind if I try?"

He looked at Grace with surprise. She couldn't do any worse than he had. He paid the man.

Three tosses later, Grace handed him a pink panther. "I warned you about pouting."

He kissed her quickly on the lips, squishing the animal between them. "My hero."

People around them applauded. Grace shook her head. "Come on, I want a nutty ice cream bar."

"You lead, I'll follow."

Her eyes darkened for a moment. She stepped back. Caleb could have bitten off his tongue for reminding her they still had problems to work through. "Grace—"

"On second thought, we better get to where they set up for the concert and make sure the instruments and sound equipment are there and working. Dr. Holloway is there with President Jenkins. We have to be at our best." Without waiting for an answer, she turned and walked away.

The sound of the organ drifted out to the crowd standing in front of the raised platform. The stirring sound was joined by the keyboard, bass guitar, drum. The beautiful voice of the lead soprano of Peaceful Rest flowed through the mix seamlessly to a full-blown choral accompaniment with the band and all the singers as they lifted their voices in praise with "We Fall Down."

When the last note was sung, the crowd was on their

feet and Grace had tears in her eyes. Caleb went to her. "Grace?"

She looked at Caleb through her tears and shook her head.

Reluctantly Caleb turned to Revelation who started out alone with "Stand," but were soon accompanied with the choir and most of the crowd. The next songs were just as joyously received, then it was time for the closing number. Caleb went to the mike.

"Thank you. A special thanks to Summerset city council for realizing the importance of recognizing our Creator, and to President Jenkins and the Board of Regents of Summerset Junior College for lending us their unwavering support. My deepest appreciation also goes to Pastor French of Peaceful Rest for allowing us to use his wonderful church to practice." Caleb paused.

"In all things we should give thanks to our Heavenly Father and let Him direct our paths. I forgot that and it may cost me a woman I love very much."

A hush fell over the crowd. People seemed to sway toward the stage.

"But whatever happens, I'll never forget her or believe God won't work things out between us. This song has always brought me peace and I leave you with it and wish you untold blessings."

Caleb looked skyward and began to sing a capella "How Great Thou Art." "'Lord, my God. When I in awesome wonder—'"

"'Consider all the work thy hand hath done.'" The strong clear voice of Grace joined his. She went to stand beside him. Their full-bodied, indelible voices touched the heart and soul and brought another hush to the crowd. The harmony and vocal delivery was superb. When they finished, their hands were linked and uplifted in praise.

They were quickly surrounded by the members of the choir and Revelation, and the audience. When Caleb turned from accepting the congratulations of President Jenkins and Dr. T. C. Holloway, Grace was gone.

He found her sitting on the deck in her yard, her head bowed. He didn't know if she was crying or thinking or praying. "Grace?"

She straightened, then came to her feet. "Caleb."

He felt a deep ache and a deeper emptiness in his heart when he saw the wary look on her face. "I love you. I'll keep on saying it until you trust me enough to marry me."

Her hand threaded through her hair. "I used to think my mother was weak for letting my father walk in and out of our lives and drag us all across the country. I realize now how brave she was and how much she loved all of us." She swallowed. "No one should hold anyone back from their dream, especially if they love that person. Love is unconditional."

He quickly crossed to her. "I wish I could tell you what you want to hear, but I can't. One day I'll leave Summerset. Marry me and go with me. You'll have another home with me."

"My decision came to me while we were singing 'We Fall Down.' No matter how many mistakes we make, God is always there to pick us up and show us the way." She stepped closer to him. "Earlier today when we were at the carnival I was storing up memories for the day you would leave and learning to live without being afraid."

"Trust me. Trust us," Caleb pleaded.

"I do with all my heart." Her smile was tremulous. "You had it wrong. Where you lead, I'll follow."

His breathing quickened. "Are you saying yes?"

"Summerset is safe and I hid behind that safety." Her arms circled his neck. "Believing and trusting in God means living without fear. I'm stepping out on His promises. With you, I truly believe I can live life to the fullest as God intended."

His arms tightened. "You will. I promise."

"There's not a shred of doubt in my mind."

His soul rejoicing, he picked her up, twirled her around and kissed her, thanking God for sending him to Summerset and to the one woman he would always love.

"When the time comes and we have to leave, we'll make a new home," Grace said. "God led us here and He'll lead us to another place full of love and happiness."

Caleb smiled. "He will make a way."

"Always."

* * * * *

MAKE A JOYFUL NOISE

Jacquelin Thomas

To every thing there is a season,
and a time to every purpose under the heaven....
A time to weep, and a time to laugh;
a time to mourn, and a time to dance.
—*Ecclesiastes* 3:1, 4

Prologue

With increasing rage and shock, Bradley stalked into his apartment, slamming the front door in the process. He had just been fired after working with Missionary Christian Church for the past two years.

He wasn't happy at all with this sudden turn of events. Bradley hadn't seen this coming. But perhaps it shouldn't have been so surprising, he admitted. He had never been one to follow church politics and had refused to take part in the plan to oust the previous minister. Instead, Bradley offended more than his share of the so-called know-it-alls in the church with his moody temperament and brash words. They were the ones who sat in the front pews every Sunday looking down their holier-than-thou noses at everyone else.

They were the ones who raised their eyebrows whenever the choir would start to sway to the upbeat music. They were the same ones who didn't like the new contemporary sound of the mass choir. They insisted that it was the devil's music.

The more vocal of this group of "holy warriors" had chastised Bradley on several occasions. They insisted that he stick to more traditional gospel songs but he staunchly refused. When that didn't work, they began putting pressure on the pastor.

"I guess he couldn't take it anymore," Bradley muttered. "I should've known my days were numbered after Pastor Nelson left."

The newly installed preacher didn't like contemporary gospel music or the fact that Bradley had once recorded secular music. He was perfect for Missionary Christian Church because he was a very conservative preacher—something the old folks in the congregation wanted. Bradley just couldn't understand why some people were so resistant to change. As far as he was concerned, the church needed some new music. Something that would minister to the youth, as well.

Bradley strode into his office and turned on the computer. His eyes landed on the pile of unopened mail stacked neatly beside the seventeen-inch flat-screen monitor. He hadn't opened his mail since his return from the annual Ministers and Musicians Conference in Hampton, Virginia, a week ago.

Returning his attention to the computer screen, Bradley opened up his email—another item that had been neglected since his return to Los Angeles. He downloaded 126 messages. Most of it had to be spam, he decided and deleted several without opening them.

When Bradley reached the email from his longtime friend, T. C. Holloway, his anger abated somewhat as he opened it. He had just recently seen him in Hampton but wasn't surprised to find a message waiting from

T.C. He had always been the better of the two of them when it came to staying in touch. He had taken time from his busy schedule to email , telephone and write letters throughout the many years of their friendship.

The great Reverend Doctor Thornton Holloway was a renowned television evangelist now, but he still made time to connect with the people most important to him. T. C. Holloway had always been a good friend.

Better than me, Bradley acknowledged. Unlike T.C., he was more of a loner, preferring his own company to the company of others. Bradley would shut down for months, hiding away from the world when he didn't want to be bothered. T.C. knew this about him and respected his feelings.

He began to read the email from his friend.

Hey, Bradley,
It was great seeing you at the conference. We haven't hung out like that in a long time. I'll be in Los Angeles around the middle of next month and look forward to hanging out again.

The reason for my writing is that I kept thinking about some of the things we talked about in Hampton. My old church in Summerset, Texas, is in desperate need of a music director and when I described you, everyone was enthusiastic and urged me to contact you immediately. Basically, the job is yours for the taking.

Your first major task would be coordinating the gospel competition for the Annual Harvest Celebration, which will take place the first week of November, and the second would be the statewide choir competition, which culminates in February. For the past three years, Peaceful Rest Church has landed first place in the competition. If they win again this year, they will make his-

tory as the only choir in Texas to win for four straight
years in a row.

Bradley had to smile. T.C. had always been competi-
tive. It amazed him to see the strong ties his friend still
had to this church in Summerset. Bradley admired such
loyalty. He continued reading.

You have been very successful with all the churches
you've worked with in the past. It is my prayer that you
will now come to the rescue of Peaceful Rest Church.

They need you, friend, and I hope that you will accept the position of music director after you hear the
praiseful sounds of the adult choir. I've asked someone from the church to send a tape for your review.
You should receive it shortly.

Summerset is a small town about seventy-five miles
from Dallas—not at all like what you're used to; however, I do recall when we talked that you were considering leaving Los Angeles for greener and perhaps
smaller pastures. I think you will find the town and its
friendly folk a pleasant departure from the concrete
streets and impersonal feel of the big city.

I look forward to hearing from you.

Your brother in Christ,

T. C. Holloway

Bradley's eyes scanned the stack of mail once more.
Near the bottom was a thick padded envelope. He
reached for it.

This must be it. The packet had come from Summerset. Bradley tore into it with excitement.

The accompanying note simply stated, "This is the
choir here at Peaceful Rest Church. The soloist is Ve-

ronica Chapman. We look forward to hearing from you. Alton Stone."

After hearing the tape, Bradley smiled. "My mother used to always say that when one door closes, another one opens…." he murmured.

Chapter One

Bradley popped the cassette of the Peaceful Rest Church choir into the car stereo as he drove the rented automobile along Interstate 75. He changed lanes before glancing down at his handwritten directions and exiting onto a road that ran past the tall, faded welcome sign greeting visitors upon their entrance into the close-knit community of Summerset.

"T.C., I don't know about living in this hick town," he muttered. To some, the sight of cotton and wheat fields, lush green pastures dotted with cattle and tall whitewashed fences might be a tantalizing picture but it filled Bradley with disdain. He was definitely not the farm-boy type.

He caught sight of an old rusting, broken-down car sitting in a nearby yard nearly covered in overgrown grass and his mouth took on an unpleasant twist. He turned his nose upward at the putrid fumes emanating from the local tire factory while pushing a button to close the car window. He detested the smell of cattle tinged with burning rubber.

"What am I doing here?" Bradley asked himself.

The melodious sounds coming from the cassette player brought a smile to his face, reminding him of the very reason he'd come to Summerset. Bradley had always been able to pick talent—the only problem was that once he succeeded in making them stars, he was often kicked to the curb without so much as a thank-you. He had a feeling this time would be different, though. His luck was changing—Bradley could feel it.

As he drove deeper into the community, Bradley's opinion changed concerning the town, which transformed before his eyes into a community filled with picturesque large oaks towering over colorful flower beds. Beautiful Colonial-style homes and conservatively painted wood frame homes lined the streets.

Farther down Main Street, Bradley eyed the colorful little boutiques, shops and a couple of restaurants that adorned the downtown district of Summerset. He drove for another ten minutes before pulling into the parking lot of Peaceful Rest Church.

The church, a white structure with two columns in front and stained glass windows depicting several Biblical scenes, sat on the right just as the directions stated. He parked the car and got out, straightening his tie. Staring at his reflection in the car window, he critically inspected his tailored suit and expensive Italian leather shoes.

Adjusting his sunglasses, Bradley made his way toward the concrete steps of the tiny white church. As he neared the porch, he whispered, "Miss Veronica Chapman, I'm going to make all your dreams come true. I'm going to make you a star. In return, you're going to put me back in the game."

She was the real reason Bradley had come to Texas. He couldn't care less about the choir—he had something to prove to the music industry and Veronica was going to help him do it.

The members of the choir gathered in the church foyer fifteen minutes before the service was to begin.

"I still can't believe it. *The* Bradley Rhodes is here at Peaceful Rest Church. I just can't believe it."

Desiree glanced briefly over her shoulder at the young woman gushing on and on about the new music director. Turning her attention back to her friend, she whispered, "Who exactly is this Bradley person? I know he's supposed to be good with choirs but..."

Nina broke into a smile. "I think everyone is excited because he's kind of a celebrity. He used to sing with that group Indigo. You remember them, don't you?"

Nodding, Desiree answered, "Oh, yeah! I used to listen to them back during my high school and college days. Isn't he the one who used to wear the sunglasses all the time and had all that hair hanging down his back? I think his stage name was Brick."

"That's him," Nina confirmed.

"I used to have such a crush on that man." Desiree eased her aching right foot out of her three-and-a-half-inch high-heel shoe. Wiggling her toes, she relished the feel of the soft carpet beneath. She wouldn't have had to wear the fashionable, albeit uncomfortable, shoes if she were taller, Desiree reasoned.

Nina nodded. "I think we all used to be crazy about that man. I used to love listening to him sing 'Love Me.' Girl, that was my song."

With a soft sigh, Desiree wriggled her foot back into the shoe. "Mine, too. I had to sneak and play it whenever my parents were out of the house. You know they didn't allow me to listen to secular music." Desiree ran her fingers through her curls, pushing them away from her face. Standing in the hot June sun caused beads of perspiration to pop out on her face and neck, making her hair damp.

"So Brick is working with church choirs now?" Desiree continued as she lightly patted her face with a tissue.

"Yeah. He's been doing it for a while, from what I understand. I heard that he's a good friend of Reverend T. C. Holloway. I think they went to college together or something like that."

Desiree's eyebrows rose in surprise. "I didn't know that. I really miss Reverend Holloway. He's a good preacher."

"Me, too," Nina agreed. "But I'm glad he's doing so well. I see him all over the television these days." Breaking into a smile, she added, "Alton knows Bradley, too. From the old days—only he doesn't talk much about his past. He simply refers to that time as the days B.B.S.— Before Being Saved. He especially is quiet about his touring days with recording artists."

"That would really make me curious," Desiree admitted.

"It does, but then I don't like reliving the wild days of my past, either."

"I didn't really have any wild days—my life was boring."

"No, it wasn't, Desiree. You had a great life. Your mom and dad were wonderful."

"Don't get me wrong. I love my parents to death

but they were so strict. Girl, you know how they were.
I would've loved to have been able to just let my hair
down every once in a while. They wouldn't let me do
anything."

"You were a bit of a goody-goody," Nina teased.

"You're one to talk," Desiree shot back. "Every time
I tried to be sneaky, you would suddenly become my
conscience. You wouldn't let me stray one bit."

"Because I knew if you got into trouble, then I would,
too. You didn't know how to be sneaky or tell a lie."

The two women shared a laugh.

Nina lowered her voice. "When I went off to college—I really thought I was grown. Humph, couldn't
nobody tell me nothing. I thought I had the world all
figured out." Shaking her head sadly, she uttered, "Girl,
I just didn't know the half of it."

"We've all had moments like that, Nina. I know I
have. Especially when I went to college. I was just like
you. I really thank God for His grace."

"It was God and His loving mercy that kept me out
of some serious situations," Nina stated. "I'm so glad
I had a praying mother. I just know it was her prayers
that helped me through my issues."

Desiree nodded in agreement.

A group of people standing near them began discuss-
ing Bradley Rhodes again. Desiree gave Nina a knowing smile when one of the women posed the question
that was on every single woman's mind.

"Do any of you know if Bradley's married?"

Desiree acknowledged that even she wanted to know
the answer to that question, as well. Summerset was a
small town and the chance of finding a good husband
was slim to none, so anytime a new man blew into town,
his marital status was the first question.

Although she faithfully believed that God would send her a mate, Desiree couldn't deny the loneliness she experienced from time to time. However, she refused to give her impatience rein over her emotions— she'd had more than one bad relationship as a result. It had been her deepest desire to have her lifemate be chosen by God.

The more everyone talked about the new music director, the more her curiosity piqued. Desiree couldn't wait to meet Bradley Rhodes.

Desiree eased into place as the choir members began lining up for their march into the sanctuary. All around her the air was still electrified with the buzz of Bradley Rhodes's stepping in as music director for Peaceful Rest Church. Everyone was hoping that under his tutelage, the choir would be ready to compete in the choir competition held during the Harvest Celebration in November.

"I don't know why they have her up front," someone behind her complained. "If Grace Thompson was still the music director, we wouldn't have no foolishness like this."

"I don't know what she was thinkin' 'bout. That gal know she can't sing a' tall. How she figured on being in this choir I'll never know...."

Another person chuckled.

Desiree's body stiffened but she didn't turn around. There was no need to—she knew the woman was referring to her.

"I think people should be required to audition for the choir," someone else was saying. "Not just walk up in the choir stand like that just because they want to sing.

Grace sho' wouldn't have put up with this. Humph, she sho' wouldn't have."

Nina placed a reassuring hand on her friend's shoulder, the gesture bringing a smile to Desiree's lips.

"Don't you listen to them," Nina whispered. "They don't think anyone can sing except for themselves. Alton told you it was okay to join the choir."

Desiree glanced over her shoulder and whispered back, "I'm really not worried about them, Nina. I'm singing for God—not to please them. He can hear the melody of my singing and He's all I care about." She knew Grace Thompson—had known her since they were in elementary school together. Desiree wished she'd moved back home just a few weeks earlier—just before Grace and her family moved away. She knew that Grace wouldn't have had a problem with her joining the choir.

Someone toward the back of the line said, "Desiree, maybe you should come back here just for today."

"Like that's going to make a difference," another choir member added.

Nina gave the woman a silent lashing with her eyes.

"I'm not trying to be mean but if Grace—"

"Prudence, what do you call it?" Nina cut in. "You couldn't be more rude. Desiree has feelings just like you." Folding her arms across her chest, she added, "I'm sure you wouldn't take it well if someone was talking about your singing or trying to boot you off the first row. If Grace were still here, you know she wouldn't tolerate no mess like this. Is this how we glorify the Lord?"

Giving Nina a sheepish look, Prudence responded, "I'm just saying that maybe we should put our best foot forward. Brick, I mean Bradley, came all the way from Los Angeles to hear us—"

Nina cut her off by saying, "And he will. With Desiree leading the choir like she's been doing since she joined."

"Humph," Prudence snorted. "Whatever."

Nina was about to give the woman another tongue-lashing, but Desiree gave her a gentle nudge on the arm. "It's okay. Like I told you earlier, I'm not worried about these folks. God knows my heart. He knows that I have a fire and passion to sing for His glory."

"Nobody in this choir is a Shirley Caesar or Yolanda Adams, so they just need to shut up."

"Girl, we're about to go into the sanctuary. Take that frown off your face. Alton see you looking like that—he'll get up from that piano so fast and take off running for fear he's done something to make you mad. You know how nervous he can get."

Desiree's comment had the desired effect. Nina burst into laughter.

"That's better."

They heard music drifting from the sanctuary.

"It's time," Nina announced.

Desiree hummed softly to herself. This was her way of warming up. She led the march into the sanctuary and to the choir stand because she sat on the end of the first row. All the sopranos sat in the first row, followed by the alto section. She was also the shortest person in the choir, standing a proud four feet eleven and a half inches, so if she sat anywhere else, no one would be able to see her.

She loved singing and took what the fourth verse of Psalm 98 said to heart: "Make a joyful noise unto the Lord, all the earth: make a loud noise, and rejoice, and sing praises." For as long as she could remember, Desiree longed to be in the choir. Her chance had come when Veronica died suddenly, leaving a slot open. Although this was definitely not the way she would have chosen it to happen, Desiree was thankful for the opportunity.

She was also painfully aware that her singing wasn't anything to brag about. When she was in school, her music teachers would always encourage her to just mouth the words whenever the class was singing. But her mother continued to encourage Desiree, reassuring her that God even loved bad singing when it came from the heart. That was all the encouragement she needed. From then on, Desiree sang as much as she could and as loud as she could manage. She was determined to give God her all.

Chapter Two

The church definitely had a small-town feel to it, Bradley decided. His eyes traveled around the sanctuary, taking in the padded wooden benches, hardwood floors, balcony seats in the back and the huge stained-glass rendition of an angel with arms outstretched that served as the backdrop for the choir.

A thin young man wearing glasses walked up to Bradley and said, "Hello, I'm Alton Stone. I play the piano for the choir. I sent you the tape."

The two men shook hands.

Bradley regarded him with curiosity, trying to place a name with the face. "I've seen you before…."

"We toured together back in '89 or '90," Alton replied. "I played keyboards for Toni Blackman."

"That's right. It's good to see you again." Bradley nodded. "I never would've figured the next time we'd meet would be in Summerset, Texas. Talk about a small world."

Alton laughed. "I left Los Angeles back in '95. This is where I grew up and when my father became ill, I had no choice but to come home. He died six months later…I stayed here for my mom and my girlfriend."

The memory of Bradley's own father's terminal illness rushed to the forefront of his mind. Bradley nodded in understanding. "I lost my dad five years ago and my mother three months after that. She just lost her zest for life when he died."

He listened intently as Alton gave him a brief history of the church and the choirs, then took him to the administrative offices to meet Pastor Simon French and his wife Lilli Belle. Bradley arranged a time during the week to have a one-on-one with Pastor French before he and Alton returned to the sanctuary.

Before they could finish talking, Alton was called away. Bradley took a seat near the front and quietly observed the people moving around the congregation. Every now and then he exchanged a polite, simultaneous smile with one of the members or nodded a nonchalant greeting.

He was well aware of all the whispering around him, although he pretended otherwise. He enjoyed being a celebrity and didn't mind the starstruck stares, the finger pointing or the awed whispers.

Bradley sat there eagerly anticipating the entrance of the Peaceful Rest adult choir. He couldn't wait to hear the sultry voice of Veronica Chapman again. She had the kind of voice that could soothe hurts, give hope and provide a beacon of light for lost souls searching for a way home to Christ.

He believed she could give both Whitney Houston

and Yolanda Adams a run for their money. Hearing her sing this morning was going to be a pleasant change from some of the other vocalists he'd heard recently.

He couldn't get over how many people fooled themselves into believing that they could sing. Bradley cringed just at the memory of the last audition he'd heard. They weren't beyond hope, but he wasn't interested in putting in a lot of effort. The last time he'd invested his time and energy had been a disaster. The singer was now touring all over the place, leaving Bradley empty-handed and at the mercy of his most recent church, which had promptly kicked him to the curb as soon as they were able to secure a minister on their side.

Bradley pushed the bitterness aside for the time being—he didn't want to ruin the moment. This time things would be different, he reasoned. He could feel it in his spirit. He and Veronica would enjoy a long season together. Bradley was so sure of this that he'd sent recording sensation Kandi Tate a copy of the tape. She was looking for the perfect choir to accompany her on her next album.

His last thought before Alton began playing the organ was that Kandi hadn't bothered to return his call. Bradley settled back in his seat on the second pew. He felt the tingling of excitement igniting within.

The double doors swung open slowly and Bradley glimpsed the choir members resplendent in their black robes with gold braided trim. Smiling, he stood up along with everyone else.

The smile on his face disappeared slowly as the choir marched into the sanctuary singing. Bradley's expression was one of horror as he resisted the urge to cover both ears with his hands.

* * *

"Onward Christian soldiers…" Desiree sang loudly. "Marching on to…" Her eyes met those of Bradley Rhodes and her heart dropped at his expression. She had never seen anyone look so appalled.

Desiree didn't think she could possibly sound that bad. Refusing to prolong their eye contact, she gazed straight ahead and continued to sing, although her voice wasn't as loud as it had been. She didn't know why, but the look on Bradley's face wounded her.

You're singing for the Lord, Desiree's heart reminded her. It doesn't matter what that man thinks.

Try as she might, Desiree was having a hard time reclaiming the zest she'd felt earlier. She was grateful when the song ended and the choir members took their seat. I know some of them saw Bradley's expression, Desiree thought as she released a soft sigh. This is all I need. Ever since she'd joined the choir, several members had complained and put pressure on Alton to make her leave. He refused.

Desiree could feel the heat of Bradley's gaze on her and shifted uncomfortably in her chair. She stole a peek at him a few minutes later and was relieved that he seemed to be focused on Pastor French.

Bradley no longer wore his dark hair long; instead it was cropped close to his scalp and lay in glossy waves. His skin was the color of rich dark chocolate and complimented eyes the color of midnight.

Her eyes lingered for a moment on his perfectly shaped full lips.

Bradley turned his attention back to her, causing Desiree to drop her eyes but not before glimpsing the frown that settled into his features. Pulling at her robe, she forced her attention to the pastor standing at the podium.

After the prayer, it was time for the choir to sing another selection. Desiree's eyes traveled to Bradley and found him staring boldly back at her.

She stiffened at the challenge and opened her mouth to sing.

Astonished, Bradley stared at the petite woman on the front row singing as loud as she could. He could look at her and tell that she was truly pouring out the song from her heart—she just sounded like a bird with a cold.

He glanced over at Alton, sending him a sharp glare. Was this some sick joke?

Alton gave him a pleading look, which Bradley ignored. His eyes bounced around at the people sitting around him. Up until now, they had stolen peeks at him, awarded him with tentative smiles. Now they simply stared straight ahead as if afraid to see his reaction.

One of the deacons sitting at the end of the front row bobbed his head to the music and every now and then would throw up a hand. What in the world was he listening to? Bradley could feel the beginning of a headache coming and prayed for the earsplitting sound of that woman's voice to stop.

He nearly jumped to his feet shouting Hallelujah when the choir sat down.

She gave Bradley a smug look as she took her seat. She looked to be around twenty-five, he estimated. He noted the way her brows furrowed when she frowned, but it was her eyes that held him—warm, brown and piercing.

Bradley didn't retain a word of the pastor's sermon, his mind clouded with frustration at having come all the way to Texas for nothing. How could T.C. have even suggested this? He was suddenly grateful that he had not heard from Kandi Tate. At least he would be spared that humiliation.

As soon as the service ended, Bradley eased out of the pew and was looking for the nearest exit to make his escape. Alton's voice halted his steps.

"Hold up, Bradley," he called. "Where you're goin' so fast?"

"How could you do this to me?" Bradley demanded as soon as Alton reached him. He struggled to keep his voice low. "You know, I never figured T.C. would play me—"

Holding up a hand, Alton interrupted him. "It isn't like that. Bradley, just hear me out, please."

"What happened to the woman I heard on the tape? Is she even a member of this church?"

"She was," Alton answered. "She—"

Irked, Bradley cut him off. "What happened? Did she leave Peaceful Rest? Maybe I can still talk to her."

"You can't." Alton took a deep breath before saying, "Veronica died two weeks ago, Bradley. I was going to tell you earlier, but we were interrupted. I tried calling you right after I found out, but your voice mail was full. I know how this looks Bradley, but you can't leave. We really need somebody like you."

"No, you don't," he retorted in cold sarcasm. "Not with that woman I heard this morning."

"She loves being in the choir, Bradley. This is a dream of hers. How can you tell someone that they can't sing for the Lord?"

Bradley shook his head furiously. "I can't deal with that voice. I don't think I've ever heard anyone sing that loud and sound that bad. Where does she keep that voice in that small body?"

"We need you, Bradley. You heard the tape—the choir doesn't sound bad. Veronica was good, but the choir can hold their own. You know it."

"You're right," he admitted after a moment. "The rest of the choir sounds great." They hadn't sounded too bad this morning except for that screeching woman. To Alton, he said, "Get that lady out of the choir and I'll stay."

"Bradley..."

"Those are my terms," he stated flatly. "I won't have it any other way."

"I'm not going anywhere," a voice stated from behind them.

Chapter Three

"I'm not going anywhere," Desiree sputtered again, bristling with indignation.

Breezing toward them, she continued, "I know why you're here, Mr. Rhodes, and while I appreciate your intentions, I really think you need to remember that we are here to glorify God first. Psalm 95:1 says, 'O come, let us sing unto the Lord: let us make a joyful noise to the rock of our salvation.'"

His expression was taut and derisive. "Joyful noise is right. Lady, you can't sing!" Bradley retorted. Seeing the wounded expression on her face, he tried to soften his tone. "I'm not trying to hurt your feelings, but let's be truthful."

The force of his reply caught her off guard. "My name is Desiree," she managed to state in a trembling voice. Tears stung the backs of her eyes, but she wasn't about to let this rude excuse of a man see her cry. Desiree shot him a cold look before adding, "My voice may not be pleasing to you, but God loves the way I sound. I'm in this choir to sing for Him. Not for you."

While this argument had always effectively worked in the past, Desiree knew it hadn't made a dent in Bradley's armor at all. She thought once more about the reason for his being in Summerset and suddenly felt selfish. No matter what she thought of the man, he was there to help the church. She couldn't allow her own personal dreams to interfere with the financial needs of the church. The prize money could pay for some of the church's much-needed repairs.

"If you don't want me to be in the choir, I'll leave," Desiree announced finally. "But I want you to understand something. I'm not doing this for you, Bradley Rhodes. I'm doing this for the church."

Nina joined them. "What's going on?"

Desiree took a deep breath and announced, "I've decided to leave the choir."

Looking straight at Bradley, Nina asked, "Why?"

"I think it'll be better for everyone involved."

Anger lit up Nina's eyes as she turned to face Alton and Bradley. "Uh-huh," she muttered.

Patting Nina gently on the arm, Desiree whispered, "I'll talk to you later. I really need to get out of here. I don't want to show out in church. We've already caused a scene. I don't want to give everyone more to talk about."

She didn't bother to look at Bradley—just brushed past him on her way to the double doors. Desiree wanted to be as far away from him as possible.

Surprised, Bradley stared after her. The tiny woman had an easy grace about her—in contrast to the hardened edge in her demeanor. He really hadn't expected her to back down so easily.

He struggled, trying to recall her name, but couldn't at the moment. However, the delicate features of her face stayed in his mind. Medium-brown eyes framed by perfectly arched brows and short bouncy auburn curls that went everywhere... Bradley couldn't deny that she was a very beautiful woman.

Alton interrupted his thoughts. "Bradley, this is my girlfriend, Nina Warner."

"It's nice to meet you." Wearing a smile, he extended his hand to the tall slender woman.

"I'm very disappointed in you, Mr. Rhodes," Nina said as she shook Bradley's hand. "I know you're behind Desiree's leaving the choir. I don't appreciate the way you treated my friend."

Bradley's smile vanished, wiped away by Nina's tone. "I'm sorry you feel that way," he replied smoothly, keeping his face expressionless. "I am just trying to do what everyone wants—put Peaceful Rest's adult choir on the map. I can only make that happen if I have the right people in the choir." Bradley gave her a slight smile. "I'm really sorry about...eh..." *What is her name?* he wondered to himself.

"Her name is Desiree," Nina interjected.

"Well, when I see Desiree again, I'll apologize to her. How's that?" Bradley didn't want to start off making enemies.

"You have a good day, Mr. Rhodes," Nina responded. She glanced over at Alton and said, "I'll be outside."

Nina walked away, leaving the two men alone to finish their conversation.

"I haven't made any friends so far."

"Nina and Desiree aren't the type of women to hold

grudges," Alton announced. "They'll both be fine after a while." Changing the subject, he said, "Bradley, thanks so much for taking the job. You won't regret it—you'll see."

"You've got some good people in the choir. Nina sounds real good."

"She's our main vocalist now."

"I didn't say it before, but I'm sorry to hear about Veronica. What happened?"

"Car accident," Alton explained. "I still can't believe she's gone. I kept expecting her to walk through those doors last Tuesday night for choir rehearsal."

They slowly made their way to the exit.

"What are you planning to do with the rest of your day?" Alton inquired. "We can grab something to eat and I'll give you a tour of the town."

"I really don't have anything planned. That's fine." Bradley gestured toward the door. "What about Nina? Did you two have plans? 'Cause I'm already on her bad side. I don't want to make matters worse."

"She's probably going to want to spend the day with Desiree. Those two are pretty close and she knows that Desiree is upset right now."

"I have nothing against Desiree. I hope you know that. This is not a personal attack against her."

"I know," Alton confirmed.

"She volunteered to leave the choir."

Alton weighed him with a critical squint before saying, "Only after you insulted her singing. I wouldn't have stayed, either."

"She can't sing," Bradley pointed out. "I wouldn't be able to get this choir invited to the church across town much less a recording studio as long as she was in the choir."

Alton had to agree. "I know. But, Bradley, Peaceful Rest isn't trying to do anything like that. We're just hoping to win the statewide gospel competition."

"Well, before I'm done, I'll have you all doing a lot more than that. Don't be afraid of change. Look at your friend. I really admire her for wanting to sing, but she has to face the truth. She is going to have to try her hand at ushering or something else—I'm sure God has something for her to do."

Desiree cried the entire five minutes it took her to drive home. Usually when it was bright and sunny like today, she walked to church. However, this morning she was running late and had decided to drive. Now she was grateful for that decision.

She parked in front of her house and climbed out of her car. Her mother met her at the front door.

"Mama, what are you doing up? You're supposed to be taking it slow." Three weeks ago, her mother had had to have a lump removed from her right breast. "Where's Daddy?"

"He in thare," Margaret stated. "I think he trying to fix us some dinner. Lawd have mercy on our souls…"

Desiree gave a short laugh. "I guess I'd better hurry up and get changed, so I can help him." Her father had not been gifted with cooking skills.

"How was the church service today?"

"It was good," Desiree replied. "Pastor French showed out this morning."

"I hate I missed it. I wish he'd tape his sermons like some of those big churches in Dallas do."

"We can't afford the equipment right now. Maybe when we're in a better financial situation, Pastor French will consider it."

"We need to replace those pews, too. I told your daddy to mention it to the Pastor and Deacon Stevens."

Desiree nodded in agreement. They talked for a few minutes more before she headed to her bedroom with her mother following slowly behind her.

"What do you think of that man—the new music director everybody in town been making such a fuss about? He was thare, wont he?"

Despite all her many years of living in Texas, her mother still refused to let go of that deep Southern accent, proof of having grown up in Albany, Georgia.

"He was there all right," Desiree stated flatly. She removed her dress and hung it on a hanger and placed it in her closet. "He's practically Grace's polar opposite. She was such a nice person and a wonderful music director. I miss her."

"Okay, what happened between you and this new director?"

Desiree eyed her mother. "Nothing. Why would you ask me that?"

"Because I know you. I knew you before you knew yourself." Margaret eased down on the edge of the queen-size bed. "Now tell Mama the truth. What's got you looking so sad?"

"I left the choir."

Margaret gasped in apparent surprise. "Why'd you do that, Desi Mae? You always wanted to be in the choir. That's all you ever talked about."

She hated when her mother called her that. "It's for the best. Bradley Rhodes thinks that he can really lead the choir to another win. We'd make history, Mama. I don't want to keep them from winning, so I figured it'll be best if I stepped aside."

"What's that got to do with you singing? If you don't

want to sing during the competition, then don't. But I really don't see why you can't sing on Sunday."

"He hates the way I sing, Mama." Folding her arms across her chest, Desiree added, "That Bradley Rhodes is so mean."

Emotion flickered in Margaret's eyes. "He told you that he didn't like your singing?"

Nodding, Desiree replied, "He said that I couldn't sing at all. It's not like I didn't already know it—you'd already told me as much."

"Honey, come sit down here for a minute."

Desiree did as she was told.

"Now you know I didn't mean nothin' by that. I just didn't want you having no false illusions about things, but I never meant to hurt your feelings."

"I know, Mama. You told me that I was singing for God and that He even loved bad singing. You weren't rude to me—just honest."

"Yes, I was, but I should have taken it a step further when I saw how much you wanted this. I should've paid for some singing lessons. Honey, if you want to sing, then you shouldn't give up on your dream. Dreams don't always come easy. If this Bradley person is so good, then why can't he teach you to sing? They way people talk about him around town, you'd think he was some sort of miracle worker."

Desiree's mood brightened. "You're absolutely right, Mama. I don't know why I didn't think about this."

Rising to her feet, Desiree stated, "I'm going to offer a compromise to Bradley Rhodes. I want him to give me three months to improve my singing—with his help, of course. If I still can't cut it at the end of the third month, I'll gladly leave the choir for good. He'll have no choice but to let me stay."

Chapter Four

Tuesday night, Bradley paced back and forth on the hardwood floor in front of the choir stand without saying a word. Every now and then, he would glance up at the members. His actions were slow and deliberate. Finally he spoke, knowing they were anxiously waiting to hear his thoughts on their singing. "That was okay. You need to put more—" Bradley stopped short at the sight of Desiree entering the sanctuary. She was the last person he expected to see come through the double doors.

He waited patiently until she approached him before asking, "What are you doing here?"

"I've changed my mind" came her response.

Bradley's patience was beginning to wear thin. "Miss…."

"Coleman," she finished for him. "My name is Desiree Coleman." She said it slowly, as if talking to a child.

"Miss Coleman, I thought we decided that your talents lie elsewhere."

"No, you decided that," Desiree retorted. She was well aware that everyone was listening to their conversation. "I was going to leave the choir, but then I started thinking."

Bradley frowned, but didn't respond.

"I've always wanted to sing in the choir. It's been a dream of mine."

"I—" he began.

"Let me finish, please," Desiree interrupted. She couldn't allow him to stop her now. She had to finish before she lost her courage.

"I apologize." Bradley pulled at the collar of his shirt. He was uncomfortably aware that all eyes were on them. Even Alton had stopped playing the organ and Nina had eased out of the choir stand and was coming toward them.

"Mr. Rhodes, I don't mean to be pushy or anything. It's just that this is something I really want and I don't believe I should just walk away. I'd like to offer you a compromise."

"Excuse me?"

"A compromise," Desiree repeated. "I would like you to teach me to sing."

"What?" Bradley demanded in a loud voice. Remembering where he was, he immediately changed his tone. "Lady, I don't have time to teach you how to sing. Now I'm sure there are other people in this town who can do that." Pointing to Nina, he asked, "Why haven't you asked your friend to help you?"

Desiree didn't back down. "I want you to do it. The way I see it is that you're the only one who really has a problem with my singing. Everybody in the choir is standing over there so nervouslike because they want to hear your comments. They consider you an expert. So since you're the expert, I figure I can't go wrong if you work with me."

Bradley was dumbfounded.

"Mr. Rhodes, please do this for me," Desiree pleaded. "Just give me a chance. If I'm not ready by the Annual Harvest Celebration—then I'll leave the choir for good."

"Desiree, you don't have to do this," Nina interjected.

"I'm fine with that," she replied. "All I want is a chance to prove myself once and for all."

"I think that's fair," Alton tossed out.

Bradley glanced over at his friend, then back at Desiree. "I don't see how this can work out, but okay. What harm can it do?"

Desiree awarded him a big smile. "Thank you, Mr. Rhodes. You won't regret this."

I already do, Bradley thought to himself. *I already do.*

Desiree wanted to shout for joy, but managed to retain her composure. Smiling, she took a seat on the front pew to watch Bradley work. She didn't miss the look of relief on his face when she didn't stroll up to join the other choir members, but Desiree was too happy to let his reaction get her down. She'd won a small victory and would rejoice.

When he sang the first verse of the song they were rehearsing, Desiree felt a chill race down her spine. Bradley may not be the nicest man she'd ever met, but he sure could sing. She allowed herself to be carried along as she listened to him.

When Bradley finished singing, Desiree applauded along with everyone else.

He gave a slight nod of appreciation and moved on. "Okay, now I want to hear you all sing it just like that."

The choir members were showing signs of frustration after singing the same song five times.

"We can move on once you get it right," Bradley reminded them. "You're almost there."

His comment surprised Desiree because she thought they sounded great. Bradley Rhodes was a perfectionist, she realized.

"Alton, let's make this next song more upbeat," he was saying.

Bradley began swaying to the music.

Desiree noticed that a few of the members were watching him with raised eyebrows and this amused her.

"Feel the music," Bradley encouraged. "Praise God with your entire body and soul."

With the exception of a few choir members who seemed rooted to the floor, everyone began to clap and sway as they sang "I Believe."

By the end of rehearsal, the choir sounded wonderful. Even Bradley was complimentary to the members and seemed like a different person. It was obvious that he worked very hard. He would give them his best.

Nina joined her. "Why didn't you come into the choir? You should be up there singing with us and not down here."

"I'm going to wait until I start my singing lessons, Nina."

"Are you sure you want Bradley to teach you how to sing? I don't mind working with you, Desiree. I never suggested it because I didn't want to offend you in any way."

"I want Bradley to work with me. He's the one everybody is trying to please."

"I hope you know what you're doing."

Desiree smiled at her friend. "Nina, it's going to be fine. You'll see."

"You're still here, Miss Coleman."

It wasn't a question. Desiree glanced up at Bradley. "I wanted to see how well you work with people."

He gave her a tight-lipped smile. "Have a good evening, ladies."

"Bye," Desiree replied. When Bradley disappeared through the doors, she whispered, "He is so good-looking."

"Too bad his attitude stinks."

Desiree couldn't agree more. "I can't believe this is the same man I was so crazy about back in college."

She couldn't keep her mind off Bradley for the rest of the evening. Desiree couldn't help but wonder why someone so handsome seemed to be in a permanent bad mood. He seemed almost bitter about something.

After rehearsal, Alton followed Nina back to her apartment where they snacked on ham sandwiches, potato chips and chocolate chip cookies.

"Alton, I have to tell you something," Nina said in between bites. "I'm not sure I like your friend, Mr. Rhodes. He has a terrible attitude. I especially don't like the way he's treating my girl."

"Nina, he's okay. Bradley and I are not exactly what I'd call friends, but I do know he's been through a lot over the years," Alton explained. "He's a nice guy—just dealing with some things."

"Like what?" Nina reached for her glass of soda. Raising it to her mouth, she took a sip.

"I know that he was fired from the last church."

"I can understand why with that charming personality of his," muttered Nina as she set her glass back down.

"It was more than that. I think he got a raw deal myself."

"Honey, you look at life through rose-colored glasses. You only see the good in everyone—even when it's not there."

"There is good in everyone," Alton countered. "Sometimes you just have to pull it out of them. The Bradley I remember is a real nice guy."

"All I know is that he'd better not hurt Desiree. Because if he does, he'll have to answer to me for sure." Nina pushed away from the table and stood up.

Alton burst into a short laugh. "I know Bradley don't want that."

Placing her hands on her hips, Nina warned, "You better tell him. I mean it. I'll hurt him."

"I know you will, baby." Rising up, Alton moved toward Nina. Placing his arms around her, he bent his head to plant a gentle kiss on her cheek. "Let's change the subject. I don't want you getting all riled up."

Nina wrapped her arms around his waist, and laid her head on his chest. "So what do you want to discuss?"

"How about getting married?"

Stepping away from Alton, Nina met his gaze, her eyebrows rising in surprise. "Alton Stone! Now, I know you're not thinking this is a proposal. If you want me to marry you, you're gonna have to do much better than that. I want romance and everything else that goes with popping the question."

"Come on, baby. I can't believe you're giving me a hard time. You're the one always talking about getting

married. I figured all I had to do was just say the word."
Alton reached out, pulling her back into his arms.

She backed away from him. "I mean it, Alton. I want
you to do it up nice and pretty. This is one of the biggest decisions in my life. I want somethin' to tell my
grandkids one day."

Chapter Five

"What have I gotten myself into?" Bradley muttered the next day while having lunch with Alton. He was conscious of the fact that lately he seemed to be asking himself that question a lot.

"Desiree is a very nice lady." Alton picked up a French fry and stuck it in his mouth. "She's not going to give you any trouble," he said after swallowing.

Bradley glanced over at the man standing beside him. "She's been giving me trouble from the moment I heard her calling people from the grave."

Alton gave him a puzzled look. "Huh?"

"You certainly can't call what she does singing." Bradley picked up his vanilla milk shake and took a long sip. Putting it back down, he said, "That lady doesn't sing—she screams like she's in pain or something. I've never heard nothing like it in my life."

"Bradley, man, why are you so hard on her?"

He couldn't believe Alton had the nerve to ask him something like that. The answer was so obvious. "The woman can't sing. Am I the only one who hears her?"

"With a little training, I think Desiree will improve greatly."

Bradley gave him a crazy expression. "You really think she can be helped with a few singing lessons?"

Alton nodded. "I do."

"I have to confess that I'm not convinced. Obviously you're immune to her screeching." Bradley released a long sigh. "How long has she been in the choir?"

"She just joined a few weeks ago. Right after Veronica died. Desiree only just moved back to Summerset from Dallas."

Bradley couldn't imagine why she'd chosen this town over a city like Dallas. But then he'd left Los Angeles. "I don't know why you let her into the choir in the first place. From now on, people are going to have to audition. They can't just walk up from the congregation like your friend obviously did. I'm not having it."

"Give Desiree a chance, Bradley. I don't think you'll be disappointed."

Bradley chose not to respond. He didn't want to start making waves already. As much as it galled him to admit it, until he found something better, he needed this job.

Normally Desiree's workday moved pretty quickly but not today. It was the longest eight hours she'd ever worked in her life. By the time the clock struck five, she was halfway to her car.

She drove out of the Summerset Trust Bank's parking lot, heading home. Desiree had time to make dinner, eat, take a shower and then rush off to the church.

She was so excited about this evening she could hardly contain herself.

Her father had just arrived home and was climbing out of his truck when she pulled into the driveway.

Desiree got out of her car and greeted him with a kiss. "Hey, Daddy. How was your day?"

"It wasn't too bad. We had an accident at the factory—nothing major, but it set us back a couple of hours."

"What happened?" Desiree questioned as she followed her father into the house.

"Silas French cut his hand. They told me at the hospital he's gonna need some stitches and time for his hand to heal. He's gonna need some therapy, too."

"Does Pastor French know?"

"I called him on the way to the hospital but he said he already knew something had happened. Simon and Silas are so close that when one gets hurt, the other feels the pain. He and Lilli Belle were there when I left."

"I've heard twins sometimes have that type of connection."

"I took some hamburger out to make a meat loaf," Desiree's mother announced as she met them in the living room. "I feel strong enough to make it."

"Mama, the doctor said for you to take it easy. You're still not completely healed, you know. Don't worry, I can make the meat loaf." Putting an impish grin on her face, Desiree added, "I know your secret recipe by heart."

"I never gave you my secret recipe."

Desiree burst into a short laugh. "Mama, I've watched you enough times. You thought I wasn't paying attention, but I was."

An hour later, they were all seated around the dining room table, having meat loaf with mashed potatoes, green beans and hot, buttered corn muffins.

"You did a wonderful job with the meat loaf," Margaret complimented. "I guess you really were watching me while I cooked."

"I love cooking, Mama. I'd rather eat a nice home-cooked meal than go to a restaurant any day." Desiree took another sip of her tea. "Oh, before I forget. I have to go by the real estate agent's tomorrow after work. She needs another check stub before I close on Friday. Buying this town house has been nerve-racking. I'll be so glad once this is over and I'm in my own place." Smiling, she added, "Just think. I'm going to be a home owner."

"You did the smart thing," Barton stated. "I tell the young people that work at the factory this all the time. If you can buy a house or something—do it. Don't throw your money away on rent. God bless the child that's got its own—that's what my dad used to tell me all the time."

"You have everything you need?" Margaret inquired.

Desiree reached for another muffin as she nodded. "Yes, ma'am. I have most everything with me from the apartment in Dallas. I didn't throw away much—I knew I'd be buying a place when I came back home."

"You know a lot of girls wouldn't have moved back to Summerset after living in Dallas."

"I guess I'm just a small-town girl." Desiree sliced off a piece of meat loaf and placed it in her mouth. After a moment, she said, "The main reason I even wanted the promotion to assistant bank manager was because the job was located here in Summerset."

They continued to talk as they finished their dinner.

Barton helped Desiree clean the kitchen while her mother made herself comfortable in the family room.

"So, you're gonna have your first real singing lesson, huh?"

"I sure am."

"You make sure you have some fun with this, Desi," Barton advised.

"I will, Daddy."

When they finished, Barton ambled over to join his wife on the sectional sofa to watch the news while Desiree made her way up the stairs to her bedroom to get ready.

She quickly showered and changed into a pair of jeans and a short-sleeved cotton shirt. After brushing her hair and slipping on high-heeled sandals, Desiree left for the church.

She drove the short distance and parked. Desiree glanced down at her watch before climbing out of her car. She was fifteen minutes early for her singing lesson. There were several other cars parked around the church, she noticed, but had no idea whether Bradley had already arrived.

Desiree half hoped that he hadn't. She wanted some time alone to pull herself together before having to deal with him.

However, when she walked into the church, Desiree found he had beaten her there and was seated in front of the piano playing a soft tune she didn't recognize.

He glanced up at her entrance and nodded a greeting.

"I didn't expect you to be here this early," she stated.

"I don't like to be late."

"Oh" was her soft reply. Although Bradley's face appeared calm, he didn't seem to be in the best of moods. Some of the excitement she initially experienced dissipated. *I'm supposed to have fun with this,* Desiree reminded herself before pasting on a casual smile.

Dropping her purse on the front pew, she said, "I'm ready to get started. Do you want me in the choir stand?"

"Sure. Why not?"

A few minutes later with microphone in hand, Desiree was ready.

"First, we're going to do a warm-up exercise. Listen carefully. Do re mi fa sol la ti do re mi fa sol la ti do…"

Desiree did as she was told. After the fourth time, two octaves lower, she wanted to scream.

"Now let's try it one more time," Bradley directed.

"Why? Am I doing something wrong?"

"Ms. Coleman, we're wasting time."

Desiree chewed on her bottom lip to keep from responding.

"Relax, Ms. Coleman. After this, we will move on to the next part of our lesson."

She took a deep breath and exhaled slowly. "Do re mi fa sol la ti do…"

As soon as she finished the scale, Desiree asked, "Can I sing something now?"

Bradley didn't bother to conceal his amusement. "I'd like for you to sing 'Row, Row, Row Your Boat.'"

I most certainly didn't hear him correctly, she thought. Giving Bradley a questioning look, she murmured, "Excuse me?"

"You do know it, don't you? I thought it was the national anthem for children."

"Yes, I know the song, Mr. Rhodes," she snapped. "I just can't believe you're serious."

He met her gaze. "I am very serious."

He's trying to humiliate me, she kept telling herself. *I am not going to let this man get to me.*

Desiree reluctantly did as he asked. "'Row, row, row your boat…'"

Bradley cut her off before she could get to "gently down the stream." "Eh…Desiree, you don't have to sing so loud. You're pulling up your chest to create sound." He paused and began again. "You're overpowering your singing."

"I want people to hear me."

"Now who's got the ego?"

Rolling her eyes at him, Desiree twisted her mouth into a frown. "You know I didn't mean it that way."

"Let's try it again."

"This is not singing, Mr. Rhodes," Desiree complained. "I want to do some real singing. You are just trying to make me so frustrated that I'll quit."

"I'm not doing anything like that. One thing you need to remember is that you have to crawl before you can walk. It's very important that you understand exactly what your range is—the physical mechanics behind singing and that you know what is happening when you sing. It's the only way to utilize your voice to its full potential."

"Whatever…" Desiree muttered under her breath.

He turned in his seat around to face her. "Did you say something? Ms. Coleman, do you know what I mean when I say sing in your chest voice, your middle voice or your head voice?"

"No."

"If you continue singing the way you do, you're going to experience a tightness in your throat or larynx. You have to do proper warm-ups and warm-downs, Ms. Coleman. I mean if you're not willing to cooperate, we can just forget the lessons. However, you will not be allowed to sing in the choir per our agreement."

She sighed in resignation. "I'm ready. Let's just do it."

Bradley eyed her for a moment.

"Well, what are you waiting for?"

He surprised himself by laughing. This pint-size woman was something else.

By the end of the lesson, Desiree wanted to wrap her hands around Bradley's throat she was so frustrated. Her eyes filled with unshed tears.

"I'll see you on Thursday for your next lesson?"

She could only nod in response. Desiree put away her microphone and rushed out of the choir stand.

"That man is such a hateful person," she muttered as she stormed out of the church. "This is not going to work."

"Desiree…"

She heard him call her name but kept going.

Bradley called her a second time.

Desiree tossed an angry look across her shoulder. "Right now I have nothing to say to you, Mr. Rhodes. I just want to go home."

"You forgot your purse," he announced dryly. Bradley stood near the bottom step and waited for her to walk back.

Desiree took her handbag from him. "Thank you," she acknowledged before turning on her heel.

"Have a good evening," he called out.

This time she didn't bother to respond. Desiree unlocked her car and got in. She drove away from Peaceful Rest Church with a heavy heart.

"Well, Desiree, you certainly messed this one up," she muttered.

She was grateful to find that her parents had already gone to bed because she didn't feel like talking to anyone.

Seated at the breakfast table in the dimly lit kitchen after making a sandwich, she replayed her interaction with Bradley in her mind while she ate.

"When did you get in?" her father inquired from behind her. "I didn't hear you come in."

"Not too long ago. I thought you and Mama were asleep."

"Naw. Just watching some TV."

"Want me to make you a sandwich?" Desiree offered.

Barton shook his head. "I'm going to fix a bowl of ice cream for your Mama."

He removed a bowl from a nearby cabinet and opened the refrigerator. "How did your singing lesson go?"

Desiree glanced up at her father. "Horribly."

Barton sat down across from her. "What happened, sweetie pie?"

She gave him a recap of her evening.

Her father reached over, covering her hand with his large one. "It sounds as if this Bradley Rhodes knows what he's talking 'bout."

"Yeah, he does," she admitted grudgingly. "And I guess he was right." Desiree wiped her mouth with a napkin before saying, "Daddy, I threw a tantrum. I'm so embarrassed."

Barton chuckled. "Sweetie pie, everything will be okay. But I want you to remember something. You have to crawl before you can walk."

"Bradley said as much," she murmured. Desiree

KIMANI ™
ROMANCE

An Important Message from the Publisher

Dear Reader,

Because you've chosen to read one of our fine novels, I'd like to say "thank you"! And, as a special way to say thank you, I'm offering to send you two more Kimani™ Romance novels and two surprise gifts— absolutely FREE! These books will keep it real with true-to-life African American characters that turn up the heat and sizzle with passion.

Please enjoy the free books and gifts with our compliments...

Glenda Howard
For Kimani Press™

Peel off Seal and Place Inside...

EDITOR'S
FREE GIFT
SEAL
THANK YOU

We'd like to send you two free books to introduce you to Kimani™ Romance books. These novels feature strong, sexy women, and African-American heroes that are charming, loving and true. Our authors fill each page with exceptional dialogue, exciting plot twists, and enough sizzling romance to keep you riveted until the very end!

KIMANI ROMANCE...LOVE'S ULTIMATE DESTINATION

Your two books have combined cover price of $12.50 in the U.S. $14.50 in Canada, but are yours **FREE!**

We'll even send you two wonderful surprise gifts. You can't lose!

2 FREE BONUS GIFTS!

absolutely FREE

THE EDITOR'S "THANK YOU" FREE GIFTS INCLUDE:

Two Kimani™ Romance Novels
Two exciting surprise gifts

▶ Detach card and mail today. No stamp needed. ▶

YES! I have placed my Editor's "thank you" Free Gifts seal in the space provided at right. Please send me 2 FREE Books, and my 2 FREE Mystery Gifts. I understand that I am under no obligation to purchase anything further, as explained on the back of this card.

PLACE FREE GIFTS SEAL HERE

168/368 XDL FTF5

Please Print

FIRST NAME

LAST NAME

ADDRESS

APT.#

CITY

STATE/PROV.

ZIP/POSTAL CODE

Thank You!

The Reader Service - Here's How It Works:

Accepting your 2 free books and 2 free gifts (gifts valued at approximately $10.00) places you under no obligation to buy anything. You may keep the books and gifts and return the shipping statement marked "cancel." If you do not cancel, about a month later we'll send you 4 additional books and bill you just $4.94 each in the U.S. or $5.49 each in Canada. That is a savings of at least 21% off the cover price. Shipping and handling is just 50¢ per book in the U.S. and 75¢ per book in Canada.* You may cancel at any time, but if you choose to continue, every month we'll send you 4 more books, which you may either purchase at the discount price or return to us and cancel your subscription.

*Terms and prices subject to change without notice. Prices do not include applicable taxes. Sales tax applicable in N.Y. Canadian residents will be charged applicable taxes. Offer not valid in Quebec. All orders subject to credit approval. Credit or debit balances in a customer's account(s) may be offset by any other outstanding balance owed by or to the customer. Offer available while quantities last. Books received may not be as shown. Please allow 4 to 6 weeks for delivery.

If offer card is missing write to: The Reader Service, P.O. Box 1867, Buffalo, NY 14240-1867 or visit www.ReaderService.com

BUSINESS REPLY MAIL

FIRST-CLASS MAIL   PERMIT NO. 717   BUFFALO, NY

POSTAGE WILL BE PAID BY ADDRESSEE

THE READER SERVICE

PO BOX 1867

BUFFALO NY 14240-9952

NO POSTAGE
NECESSARY
IF MAILED
IN THE
UNITED STATES

pushed away from the table. "I'm going to do some praying. Right now I just feel like giving up the dream. Maybe I was wrong. Singing is not for me."

Chapter Six

"You have company," Margaret announced from the doorway of Desiree's bedroom. Her mouth twitched with amusement. "He's a nice-looking man, I have to tell you."

Looking up from her laptop computer, Desiree asked, "Who is it, Mama?" She hadn't been expecting anyone.

Margaret strolled into the room and whispered, "I think it's that Bradley Rhodes. I heard he was a fine looker."

"What is he doing here?" Desiree wondered aloud. She wanted to believe that he'd sought her out of simple interest but she knew better.

"Go on out there and find out."

"Mama, why are you so excited? The man hates me."

"He wouldn't be here if that was true."

Desiree shook her head. "I'm sure it's not what you're thinking. Mama, Bradley and I… It just wouldn't work."

"I'm here to tell you, chile. That man is interested in you. He wouldn't be here in this house otherwise."

"He probably came to tell me that he's not going to work with me anymore."

Margaret shook her head no. "I don't believe that for a minute."

Desiree nodded. "I'm sure of it. Bradley doesn't want to give me any more lessons." Her bottom lip trembled as she rose to her feet.

"I think you should hear him out before you decide the worst," Margaret stated.

"Bradley and I just don't work well together. I'm not going to give up, though—I'll just find another teacher."

"You won't know what he wants until you go out there and talk to him. Now go."

Desiree nodded. "I'd better go get this over with."

"I'll be back here if you need me."

Desiree gave her mother a brave smile. She vowed not to break down in tears when Bradley gave her the news. With each step she took, Desiree kept reminding herself that not working with him would be best. He was a temperamental man, blunt to the point of rudeness. They would never get along, no matter how handsome he was.

She found Bradley standing in front of the fireplace looking at the photographs on the mantel when she rounded the corner, entering the living room.

He turned around to face Desiree.

She lowered her eyes to avoid his gaze. "I'm sorry for keeping you waiting for so long."

"I thought maybe you were still mad at me."

"It would be a waste of my time."

Bradley's eyebrows raised in surprise over her comment.

Desiree met his gaze this time. "I know why you came. You don't want to be my teacher anymore, right?"

He broke into a grin. "That's not it at all. I've come to apologize. I'm sorry for the way things ended."

She could hardly believe her ears. Surely she'd misunderstood the words that had come out of the great Bradley Rhodes's mouth.

"Did you hear me?"

"I think so," she responded slowly. "It sounded like you apologized." Desiree leaned against the back of her father's favorite leather recliner.

"I did. Last night I did some thinking and realized that maybe I was too hard on you on Tuesday. We've really gotten off to a bad start and for that, I'm sorry."

Desiree broke into a smile. "I owe you an apology, as well."

"For what?"

"I usually don't throw tantrums, Bradley. All my life I've wanted nothing more than to sing."

He nodded in understanding.

"I was a bit overzealous and I'm sorry."

"Desiree, from what I heard Tuesday night, there are a few things you need to really work on. One is learning to sing on pitch, and your range. This has to do with chord strengthening and smoothing out the bridges. Your vocal cords must be stretched and strengthened. Before you can work on this, however, you have to know what it all means."

"You're right, because I have no clue what you're talking about." Desiree paused a heartbeat before adding, "Do you think I have a chance?"

"Singing on pitch once your breaks are smoothed out is very easy. There are only a few reasons why people can't sing on pitch. One is that they don't allow themselves to absorb or hear the tones before doing scale work, or they haven't done any scale work at all."

"It's a lot of work, I see."

"If you're not willing to continue the lessons, I'll understand and you don't have to worry. I won't kick you out of the choir, but it might be better if Alton or Nina works with you."

Shaking her head, Desiree replied, "I'd like to keep working with you."

Bradley seemed surprised.

"You're supposed to be the best," Desiree elaborated further. "I'm more than willing to pay you for your time."

Shaking his head no, Bradley stated, "Keep your money."

"You're sure? I don't want you to think I'm taking advantage of you. I know you work with professionals all the time and I'm sure they pay for your services."

"I don't need your money. You don't have to pay me."

"Thank you so much, Bradley." Desiree couldn't get over how nice he was acting. She couldn't help but wonder what had come over him. *Thank You, Jesus,* she cried silently.

"Have you eaten?"

Oh, my goodness. Is he asking me on a date? she wondered. "No, I haven't," Desiree replied.

"I was thinking about grabbing a bite to eat before our lesson tonight. Would you like to join me?"

"I'd love to have dinner with you. Just give me a few minutes to freshen up and I'll be ready."

Bradley took a seat on the sofa while Desiree strolled off to her bedroom.

Margaret was in her room waiting for her.

"Mama, Bradley and I talked. Everything is fine now. He even apologized."

"I told you Desi Mae, that man has an interest in you," Margaret insisted. She picked up a comb off the dresser and handed it to her daughter. "He wouldn't have come over here just to do some apologizin'. If that's all he wanted, he would've done it when he saw you at church on Sunday."

After combing through her hair, Desiree touched up her makeup. "It's not a date or anything, Mama. We're just having dinner. It's probably Bradley's way of trying to make up for being so mean to me."

Shaking her head, Margaret murmured, "I don't know why y'all think your parents don't know nothing. I've already walked the road you're on. Darlin', I may not hear like I used to, but I'm not blind. Bradley Rhodes is interested in you."

Desiree did a final check in her mirror before grabbing her purse. "I really thought he was here to tell me he was quitting."

"I never thought so," Margaret said in a loud whisper. "After you leave, I think I'm gonna take me a long hot bath and just relax. Your father should be coming home in another hour or so. He's picking up some chicken dinners for us."

"Sounds like you two are going to have a quiet evening."

Margaret nodded. "We are. Your dad's been workin' real hard lately—they're shorthanded at the factory. I thought we'd have a light supper and then go on up to bed."

"That sounds nice, Mama."

Desiree introduced Margaret to Bradley, who was as

charming as ever. She stood there watching him work his charm on her mother.

After a moment, Margaret gestured toward the front door. "Y'all have a nice time tonight."

"It's nice meeting you," Bradley said on his way out.

Outside, he held the door open for Desiree.

"Thank you," she murmured softly as she climbed inside a Nissan Pathfinder.

"Is this a new car?" Desiree inquired. "It's nice."

"No, this is mine. I had it shipped here about a week ago. The other car I'd been driving was a rental."

They continued to chat as Bradley drove them over to a restaurant on Main Street. And, still being the perfect gentleman, he even opened doors for Desiree and escorted her safely to the front entrance of Romano's Italian Restaurant, where they were seated almost immediately.

While they waited for the waiter to take their food order, Bradley lapsed for the first time into a story about Indigo.

Desiree burst into laughter. Bradley was a lot of fun when he allowed himself to relax, she silently acknowledged. There was something warm and enchanting in his humor.

"What's so funny?"

A flash of merriment crossed her face. "You are. I can't believe you did that."

"What else could I do? We were onstage in the middle of a song. I couldn't just leave."

"I know. But to have the speakers fall over while you're singing. How humiliating for you, Bradley." Desiree brought her hand up to stifle her giggles.

His laugh was marvelous, catching and had her totally enchanted. "It was no joke, but I got through it. I was never happier to leave New York."

"You poor thing," Desiree murmured. She enjoyed seeing this side of him. Bradley didn't seem so much like a stick-in-the-mud. She was actually having a wonderful time with him.

Over dinner, Desiree gave Bradley an overview of Summerset. "The town is named after George Rutherford Summerset. His axel broke on the way to Shreveport, so he settled here and raised his family. It's a wonderful place to live…"

Desiree reached for her glass of water and took a sip. "Our deputy mayor is African-American and so is the sheriff… Oh, you're going to enjoy the Annual Harvest Celebration. We have a parade, music—the highlight is the gospel concert and the county fair."

"Where is it held?"

"On the college campus. Have you seen Summerset Junior College yet?"

Bradley shook his head no.

"It's just outside of town. Their music department is outstanding. My friend Grace—she was the old music director for church—used to be part of it."

"I've heard a lot about Grace. She sounds like she was a nice lady. Heard about her husband, too." Bradley finished off his pasta before asking, "Have room for dessert?"

Smiling, Desiree nodded. "I have a terrible addiction to the chocolate mousse cake here. I can't leave without having a slice."

Bradley's tender gaze met hers. "I guess I'll just have to try it for myself then."

Desiree's heart did a flip in response.

* * *

"So what are your plans for this weekend?" Bradley inquired after parking his car in front of Desiree's childhood home.

"Well, I close on my town house tomorrow evening and then I'm moving this weekend."

"Congratulations on your new home." He turned up his smile a notch. "Do you need any help with moving?"

Desiree couldn't keep the surprise out of her voice. "You'd help me move?"

Bradley nodded. "Why not? Looks like I'm going to be looking for a place myself—I'm going to need some help moving."

Desiree laughed. "So you help me and I help you—is that it?"

His eyes brightened with pleasure. "I think it's the perfect plan."

"I do, too," she confessed.

"Alton told me that you recently moved back home."

Nodding, Desiree replied, "Yeah. I attended college in Dallas and was recruited by Texas National Bank for their management-training program. The corporate offices are based in Dallas but I got a promotion about four months ago and so I'm the assistant manager at the Summerset branch."

"Congratulations again."

Desiree saw that he was watching her intently, his gaze bold. Bradley's eyes continued to travel over her face; something intense flaring through his entrancement.

For a moment she thought he was going to kiss her and Desiree's insides jangled with excitement.

"What is it?" Bradley questioned.

"N-nothing," she managed to reply. "I'd better go on

in. I've got a long day tomorrow." Desiree's pulse skittered alarmingly. "I'll see you on Saturday."

Bradley surveyed her face. "You sure you're okay?"

"I am." Desiree clenched her trembling hands into fists. She was acting like a schoolgirl. "I'm just tired, I guess."

"I'll let you go." Bradley opened his door and got out. He strolled around the car to assist Desiree.

She was touched when he escorted her safely to the front door.

"Bradley, I had a nice time tonight." Desiree could hear the faint ringing of a telephone coming from within her parents' house. Considering the hour, it was probably for her.

"I had a good time myself. Thank you for having dinner with me. It can get lonely at times."

"I know. That's how I felt when I first moved to Dallas."

They talked for a few minutes more before Desiree unlocked her front door and went inside. She watched Bradley drive away from the picture window in the living room.

It had been hard drawing the evening with Bradley to a close.

Alton handed the television remote to Nina who said, "I just got off the phone with Mrs. Coleman. Desiree and Bradley had dinner together tonight. Can you believe that? I can't believe she'll actually make it through an entire meal without wanting to kill him."

"I told you that Bradley is one of the good guys. You just have to get to know him, Nina. Give him a chance."

"He's your friend. Not mine." Nina surfed through several channels, looking for something interesting to watch on television. She and Alton both enjoyed the *Law and Order* spin-offs.

"I want him to be our friend, sweetheart."

Nina settled back against the cushions of the leather sofa. "Okay. I'll give him another chance, but Bradley Rhodes had better not blow it. I'll see how he acts this weekend when we're helping Desiree move."

She handed the remote back to Alton. "*Without a Trace* is coming on after this show. I think it's *CSI*— we missed the first half."

Alton wrapped his arm around her. "We're going to have a good time, Nina. You'll see."

"Humph."

"Hey, wouldn't it be something if Bradley and Desiree really hit it off?" Alton questioned in the middle of the first commercial break.

"Don't tell me you're actually playing matchmaker?"

"I'm not. I'm just saying—"

Nina interrupted him by saying, "Humph, I really think Desiree can do better."

"She'll be good for Bradley."

"Let's just change the subject," Nina suggested. "I'm not completely sold on them as a couple. I can't even see them being friends."

"You're not going to give my man a break, are you?"

She laughed. "You can relax, honey. I'm not going to interfere with whatever Desiree wants. If she wants Bradley, then that's between them."

Chapter Seven

On the way to the church, they passed the Dairy Queen. Bradley made a mental note to stop there after the lesson to grab a chili cheese dog. He'd become addicted to them since his move to Summerset.

At the church, Bradley got out and opened the door for Desiree. Together they walked into the church.

"Believe it or not, Bradley, I have tried to practice my singing," Desiree announced as she laid her purse and car keys on the front pew.

Bradley sat down in front of the piano. "Really?" he questioned as he thumbed through a stack of sheet music. "Show me what you do."

When she was done, he said, "I think I know what you've been doing. Watching too much television. We're going to start with something simple. What you've seen are some of the more complicated techniques and exercises." He picked up a piece of paper. "We're going to try this today. I brought along the tape if you'd like to hear it."

Desiree nodded. She took the paper from him and scanned the lyrics. "I know this song."

"I thought you might. Now remember, you don't have to overpower your singing. The exercises you just did will massage and loosen your vocal cords. As we move forward, you'll learn how to hit the same pitch both powerfully and gently, but with very little effort."

Encouraged by his words, Desiree murmured, "Okay. I'll give it my best."

Bradley sat down in front of the piano. He could hear Desiree humming softly. He began to play and nodded when he wanted her to start singing.

"Much better," Bradley murmured when she finished. "You did great, Desiree. Let's try it one more time, okay?"

She nodded.

Two hours later, Desiree handed the sheet music back to Bradley, saying, "This session was wonderful. I never realized singing was such hard work."

"It's worth it, though. Don't you think?"

Desiree nodded. "Oh, yeah. I love it."

"Why do you love it so much?" Bradley wanted to know. "Why is this so important to you?"

"I'm not doing this for fame. I just love singing and I want to do it for God."

"Okay…" He waited for her to continue. When she didn't, he asked, "Is that it?"

Desiree broke into laughter. "All my life I've wanted to sing, Bradley. It was my dream. I promised God that if He gave me a talent for singing, I would do it only for His glory. I believe that He honors faith and I have that mustard seed faith that He will give me the desires of my heart. Well, singing is one of them."

"What's the other?"

"Marriage and a family."

"You don't want much, do you?"

"I don't need much, Bradley. I'm twenty-seven years old. I have a great job and now I have a chance to do something I have a heart to do. I have God's favor and I'm so blessed. I'm happy."

Bradley was quiet.

"What do you want for yourself?" Desiree inquired.

"I want to manage some of the greatest singers in the music industry. I want to be back on top one more time."

"What else do you want, Bradley?"

"That's it," he responded. "I don't need anything else. I just want to be back on top. Only this time, I don't intend to take it for granted. Before, I didn't even appreciate what I had. When I got burned out, I just walked away." Bradley shook his head. "That was so stupid."

"I don't think it was stupid. Maybe you needed a break from everything at the time."

"Perhaps. I just didn't think I'd be forgotten so easily."

"Is that why you decided to get into gospel music?"

Bradley was mildly surprised. "How do you know about that?"

Grinning, Desiree replied, "I did some research on you."

"I see."

"What happened? You only recorded one album. I have to warn you that I'm on the lookout for it, by the way."

"My album bombed, so I walked away a second time. If you want a copy of the album, I can give it to you."

Bradley gave a derisive laugh. "I have plenty. Anyway, that's when I started my management company."

"Bradley, you definitely weren't forgotten. Everyone was so excited when they found out you were going to be our music director. Even I was."

He broke into a smile. "Then I opened my mouth."

Desiree smiled back. "But it's gotten better. Look at us now—at least we're talking and being civil to one another. This is a blessing in itself."

They both laughed.

After gathering up his things, Bradley said, "Let's get out of here. They're having something tonight at the church."

"The Men's Bible Study."

Bradley nodded. "That's right." Shrugging, he added, "I couldn't remember what it was. My memory's fading, I think."

He walked her to her car. "I won't forget that I'm helping you move Saturday, though."

"Thanks for taking time out of your weekend to help me like this. I really appreciate it, Bradley."

"I don't mind. It's not like I had something planned. It gives us a chance to get to know us better."

"You want to know me better?" Desiree teased.

Bradley gazed into her eyes. "I do. You are very interesting, Desiree."

"And you, as well," she said. Desiree unlocked her car and climbed inside. She started her car before confirming, "I'll see you Saturday."

He nodded and waved as she drove away.

Bradley carried a cardboard box into Desiree's new town house and gently set it down in the kitchen. Wiping his brow with a paper towel, he asked, "Is this everything for the kitchen?"

"I think so." Desiree's eyes scanned the boxes arranged haphazardly around her kitchen. "They're all here. There were only three of them. The other boxes contain the china my gram gave me before she died."

Alton entered the town house carrying a box with Nina on his heels. In her hands she carried a smaller box.

"Where do you want this one?" he asked. "It's not labeled."

Desiree pointed toward the second bedroom. "In there." She followed Bradley toward the front door and outside.

"You have a nice place," he said.

"I like it. Actually, I love my new town house. I considered buying a house, but then I decided I could always sell this place if I ever needed something bigger. This is all I need for right now."

After all the boxes were inside the town house, Nina and Desiree began to unpack her bed linens while Alton and Bradley set up her bed.

"This place is beautiful, Desiree. I love it," Nina said.

"I do, too. When I saw it, I just fell in love with the open floor plan and the view."

"I can truly see why. The builder did a great job of duplicating the old world charm of homes that were built almost a century ago in Summerset." Nina's eyes bounced around, admiring the interior of the house.

Desiree agreed. "It adds to the nostalgic charm of Summerset. But modern enough for me."

"Who knows, I may buy one of these for myself."

"You should, Nina. They have so many different styles to choose from."

"I picked up a packet a while ago. They have one that I love. It has a huge living room—"

"Perfect for a baby grand piano, huh?"

Laughing, Nina nodded. "Just planning ahead."

"No harm in that."

They burst into laughter.

"Why are you two in giggles?" Bradley questioned as he and Alton entered the room.

This sent them into more laughter.

"So you like her, don't you?" Alton inquired when they were alone near the rented U-Haul truck.

"I do," Bradley confessed. "She's an incredible woman."

Alton grinned. "But a handful."

"That, too."

"I think she'd make some man a wonderful wife. Desiree is not the type of woman you play around with, Bradley. She's the marrying kind."

"I realize that."

"Don't break her heart. If you have no plans of getting hitched, just leave her alone. Be her friend and nothing more."

"I hear you."

"Better me than Nina or Desiree's mama. Those are two women you don't want to mess with."

"I wouldn't do that to Desiree. She's a sweetheart. Besides, I'm more concerned about incurring her wrath. She might be tiny, but as you said earlier, quite a handful. I have a feeling she'd come after me with everything she's got."

They burst into laughter.

"How are things going between you and Nina?" Bradley asked as they headed back into the building.

"Great. In fact, I'm planning to ask her to marry me but I want to wait for just the right moment."

"Congratulations."

"Thanks, man." Alton tossed a look over his shoulder to see if Nina or Desiree were within earshot. "So do you think you'll be happy living here in Summerset? It's nothing like Los Angeles."

Bradley gave a slight shrug. "I don't know. I'll tell you in a couple of months. I grew up in a small town in Georgia, so I don't think it'll be that much of an adjustment. Although I think Brunswick might be a little bigger than Summerset."

When Desiree strode toward them, Alton broke into a grin. "Somehow I think you're going to end up staying here."

"Maybe. Maybe not. If things go the way I want, I could end up almost anywhere."

Alton grew quiet.

"You don't have to worry," Bradley reassured him. "I'm not planning to just pack up without notice. I'm just talking long-term goals—nothing immediate."

"What's the ultimate goal, if you don't mind me asking?"

"I plan to get back into managing musicians. Building careers."

"Speaking of which, how are the singing lessons coming along with Desiree?"

"She did much better on Thursday. I have to admit that she's not as bad as I originally thought. Like you said, she'll improve more and more with each lesson."

"Don't forget the most important part, Bradley. Desiree really has a heart for singing to glorify God. I just don't believe He would give her that dream and not provide her with the means to achieve it."

Bradley nodded in agreement. He hadn't even considered that truth until now.

Chapter Eight

Bradley and Desiree spent the rest of the summer getting to know one another. She'd helped him find a three-bedroom house to rent until he decided whether or not he would be staying in Summerset indefinitely.

Desiree secretly prayed he would because she was beginning to develop feelings for Bradley. Feelings that seemed to be reciprocal, she was sure of that much.

The telephone rang, interrupting her thoughts.

"Desiree Coleman speaking."

"It's Bradley. Did I catch you at a bad time?"

"No, not at all," she replied quickly. The sound of his deep baritone voice wrapped around her like a warm blanket. Leaning back in her chair, she inquired, "How are you?"

"I'm fine. What's your schedule like for tonight?"

"I'm free. What's up?"

"Nothing. Just wanted to take you to dinner, if you're interested."

"I would love to have dinner with you."

They continued to talk for a few minutes more, making arrangements.

When she hung up, Desiree exhaled a long sigh of contentment. She enjoyed spending time with Bradley, although there were those times when he would suddenly become silent and moody. During those times, he liked to be alone, he'd explained once when she'd assumed it was because of something she'd done. Desiree came to realize that this was just another facet of his personality. From some of their conversation, she discerned that Bradley was dealing with some pain from the past.

That evening, Desiree changed clothes three times before deciding to wear a black pantsuit. She had just finished running her fingers through her curls to fluff up her hair when the doorbell rang.

"Bradley's here," she heard her father call up the stairs.

"I'll be right down." Desiree sent up a quick prayer for Bradley. "Heavenly Father, I thank You for this day. I come before You asking Your guidance for Bradley. He is a man filled with pain. Please help him and fill him with the joy he once had for You...."

Her mother knocked softly before sticking her head inside. "Don't keep the young man waiting, Desi Mae."

"I'm coming."

"Darling, you look beautiful," Margaret complimented as they walked toward the staircase.

Bradley did a double take when she descended the stairway and echoed her mother's words.

"You look beautiful."

Desiree broke into a big grin as she reached the bottom of the stairs. "Thanks."

He took her by the hand. "We should leave. Our reservations are for seven-thirty. I know you don't like being out too late during the workweek."

"That's so thoughtful, Bradley, thanks."

Once they were in the car, he announced, "I like you a lot, Desiree. I like the way this feels between us."

"I do, too," she confessed.

"We make good friends, don't you think?"

Desiree nodded.

Bradley stunned her by abruptly changing the direction of their conversation. "There's a gospel concert in Dallas on Friday night. Alton and I were thinking about going—what do you think of making it a foursome?"

Desiree was surprised. When she found her voice, she said, "I would love to go. I know Nina will feel the same way. This is going to be so much fun."

"We can get two hotel rooms. Alton and I will share one room and you and Nina will have the other one."

Desiree agreed. "Works for me."

Bradley had made reservations for them at Nellie's Restaurant, so there wasn't a long wait for them after their arrival.

Shortly after being seated, the waiter appeared to take their drink orders.

"I'll have a glass of iced tea, please," she stated.

"I'll take tea also," Bradley said when his turn came. They gave their food order and talked while they waited for their meals to arrive.

Bradley reached across the table to take her hand. "Desiree, I want to see how far this goes. I—"

Desiree interrupted by saying, "You want to be my boyfriend. My man."

His smile broadened in approval. "Yeah, I want to be your boyfriend."

"It's official, then. We're a couple now." Desiree held up her glass. "Here's to us."

Bradley tapped his glass to hers. "You never cease to amaze me."

"Never boring, huh?"

He laughed.

After dinner they decided to take a walk through the downtown district.

Bradley embraced her. "Why are you so quiet?"

She looked up at him, studying his face. "I'm just thinking about us."

"What about us?"

"I thought you were such a horrible man when I first met you, but getting to know you these past three months—you're really sweet and very caring. You're nothing like I first imagined."

His dark brown eyes narrowed speculatively. "Not even on my worst day?"

Desiree shook her head. "Not even then."

Bradley wrapped an arm around her. "You bring out the best in me, sweetheart."

"I don't know if I'd say that." She grinned.

He stopped walking. "I mean it. Desiree, you really have made me a much better man. I know I'm moody, rude and I can be selfish, but you've motivated me to push past all my issues to find a part of me that I'd long forgotten."

"You're a good man, Bradley." His handsome face was kindled with a warm masculine beauty enhanced by dark eyes and his many secret expressions. It was the mystery in Bradley's eyes that beckoned to her irresistibly.

Although Desiree wasn't ready to share this with him, she was falling in love with Bradley.

The Friday before Labor Day, Nina, Alton, Desiree and Bradley piled into his Pathfinder and drove to Dallas.

Each time Desiree entered the city nicknamed the Big D, she was immediately awed by its billowing skyscrapers, modern architecture and wonderful shopping malls. For her, it was a great place to live during her college years but now she preferred living in Summerset and just coming into Dallas for weekend getaways.

They arrived into the city around noon and had lunch.

"So what are we going to do until it's time for the concert tonight?" Alton asked.

Nina picked up her water glass and took a sip. "I'd like to do some shopping. I haven't been to the Galleria in months."

"Me, too," Desiree chimed in. "That mall has some wonderful stores."

Bradley groaned. "Shopping? I hate shopping."

"You don't have to go," Nina returned. "You and Alton can stay in the hotel. I'm glad you have us staying near the Galleria."

"I had a feeling you ladies would want to do some shopping," Bradley teased. "Just make sure you're back in time for the concert. We want to get there early."

"We will be," Desiree promised. "I'm not going to miss tonight for anything in the world. I've been looking forward to this concert all week. I can't wait to hear Michael James sing. His songs really minister to me."

Alton and Nina began to chatter animatedly about him, but Bradley didn't utter a word.

Desiree eyed him. He was in one of his moods, she decided.

Four hours later, Desiree and Nina strolled into the lobby of their hotel carrying shopping bags from nearly all of the boutiques.

On the elevator, Nina said, "Girl, I'm going to need another job just to pay off my credit card bill. I lost my mind once we saw all those stores."

"You bought some really cute clothes."

"So did you—only you are so much better with money. I have to keep reminding myself that I am a kindergarten teacher. I don't make a whole lot of money."

"The sales were incredible, Nina. I don't think you wasted money—you've got some great clothes."

"I guess. To tell the truth, I really needed some new stuff. When I get home, I'll clean out my closet and donate all the clothes I can't wear anymore to the women's shelter." Nina gave a short laugh. "I'm never going to be a size five again—I need to get used to it."

The elevator stopped on the eighth floor.

Desiree checked her watch as they headed to their room. "We'd better get a move on. We don't want to be late. Bradley will never let us live it down."

One hour later, the men knocked on their door.

Nina ran to answer it. "We're almost ready," she said.

Bradley glanced down at his watch. "Uh-huh."

"I heard that," Desiree stated from across the room. "I'm just putting on my lipstick. That's all."

"Uh-huh," he muttered, causing Alton and Nina to burst into laughter.

Desiree picked up her purse off the nearby desk and joined them by the door. "See, I'm ready."

"You ladies look beautiful," Alton complimented.

Bradley agreed.

Nina and Desiree responded in kind. The foursome left the hotel room and headed to the elevator.

While they waited, Nina gave a short overview of their shopping spree.

"I just know you didn't even buy me anything," Alton teased.

"Yes, I did," Nina countered. "I bought you a tie."

They burst into laughter.

The elevator car arrived, and its doors opened sluggishly. Bradley and Alton waited for Desiree and Nina to step inside before joining them.

Bradley reached over and took Desiree's hand as they rode down to the lobby.

Nina gave Alton a gentle nudge and smiled.

Desiree noticed Bradley's mood seemed to change as soon as they arrived at the Majestic Theatre. He had become quiet and sullen.

They were seated in the first row on the main floor, not too far from the stage—which delighted Desiree.

When Michael James took the stage, she immediately stood up and clapped her hands. He was one of her favorite gospel singers. Although she still had a long way to go, Desiree was proud of how far she'd come with her own singing.

Desiree glanced over at Bradley, who was still sitting down, a scowl on his face.

She dropped down beside him. "I don't understand what's going on with you, Bradley. Why are you in such a rotten mood?" she whispered.

"Just drop it, Desiree," he whispered back. "I don't want to go into it right now." Bradley got up and stalked down the aisle and through the exit doors.

Desiree nudged Nina and said, "We'll be right back." Getting up, she walked briskly behind him.

When they were in the lobby area, Desiree confronted him. "Actually, I think now is the perfect time to talk about what's bothering you, Bradley. We're supposed to be here having a good time. I don't want your mood swings to interfere with that."

"Just go back inside with your friends. I'm fine."

"I don't agree."

"Desiree, I know how much you like Michael. Go on back inside. I'll be there shortly."

"I came here with you, Bradley. You can't just dismiss me like this. I won't stand for it."

"Desiree, just stop hounding me," he snapped. "I've already said I don't want to go into this right now. Leave it alone."

Her eyes flashed in fury. "Don't you go raising your voice at me, Mr. Rhodes. I am not your enemy." Glaring at him, Desiree folded her arms across her chest. "You definitely need to change your attitude."

"You're absolutely right," he admitted sheepishly. "I'm sorry. You don't deserve this."

"I'm really not trying to be nosy, Bradley. I just care about you. I care a lot. Plus, I thought we were friends."

He brushed his fingers across her cheek. "We are more than friends—you know that, sweetheart."

"Then please don't shut me out."

Bradley sighed softly. "I thought I was beyond caring anymore. Michael James is who he is because of me, Desiree. I found him working as a janitor in South Carolina. I heard him singing when I went to use the bathroom in some hotel back there. I worked with him—paid for his clothes, his demo...."

"Then he left you," Desiree interjected. "Is that why you're so upset?"

"Wouldn't you be?"

"Tell me something, Bradley. Why do you do this—you know, help singers and choirs like you do if it upsets you so much? Is it just for the money?"

"Money is a big part of it," he confessed. "But I like the challenge that comes with it, too. I don't just work with choirs for the sake of working with them—I'm looking for that next great singing sensation."

"I'm not sure I understand."

"Veronica…I wanted to make her a star."

Comprehension dawned, prompting Desiree to reply, "That's why you agreed to come to Summerset. You came for Veronica."

"I did," Bradley confessed. "She had that special something. I felt like my luck was changing."

"I see."

"Did you know her?"

Desiree nodded.

"Tell me about her. What was she like?"

"Veronica wasn't just a fabulous singer. She was a really nice person, too. She didn't have a big ego or anything like that. She just wanted to glorify God with her talent. I miss her terribly because she was a good friend."

"I assumed as much. I regret never having the chance to meet her."

"Bradley, I hate to tell you this, but I think she would've disappointed you. She didn't want record deals and concerts, things like that. Veronica was a small-town girl who just wanted to sing for the Lord."

"I might have convinced her otherwise."

"I doubt it. You may get mad with me for saying this, but I think you've lost yourself somewhere in this. I don't think you're doing this for God, Bradley." Desiree paused for a second before adding, "You have your own agenda."

"What are you talking about?"

"This should be totally about God. Only what you do for Him will last, Bradley."

"Yeah," he muttered. "Desiree, music is my life. When I was out there doing secular music, God convicted my heart. It's because of Him that I gave up performing. But I didn't sign on to be a nobody. I love being on top. I want to be on top again—it's not like I'm managing secular performers. All of my people sing gospel. Yet I'm still hitting these setbacks. When I was in the secular world, I didn't have these problems."

"It sounds to me like you're a bit reluctant to give God your all."

"Excuse me?"

"I mean it. Bradley, you should put God first in this. Maybe that's why things are going the way they are."

"Don't preach to me, Desiree. I'm not in the mood."

"Why do you insist on being such a jerk at times?"

Bradley broke into a short bark of laughter. "Now I'm a jerk?"

Desiree didn't back down. Lifting her chin in a defiant manner, she responded, "Yes, you are. A big one at that." Desiree pointed to the doors leading back to their seats. "I'm going inside. Are you coming with me?"

He gave her a slight smile and nodded.

After the concert, they stopped to have dessert before returning to the hotel.

"What happened to you, Bradley?" Nina wanted to know. "You disappeared on us in the middle of Michael's performance and you missed the first part of Rizen's."

He stole a peek at Desiree before responding. "I needed to get some air."

"Oh. Well, you missed it. You could really feel the Holy Spirit moving around the room."

Desiree concentrated on her cheesecake. She knew Bradley was trying to keep the bitterness he felt toward Michael James at bay. She'd also discovered that he once managed the group Common, as well. They'd performed after Michael. Reaching out, Desiree took his hand in hers.

Nina seemed to sense something going on but kept her comments to herself; however, Desiree didn't miss the curious glances that passed between her friend and Alton.

Later when she and Nina were in their hotel room getting ready for bed, Nina asked, "What's up with Bradley?"

Climbing into bed, Desiree plumped up her pillows. "He's moody, Nina. But tonight was more than that. He used to manage Common and Michael James. He feels used after the way they treated him."

"I didn't know that. What did they do?"

"They fired him. He made them stars and they fired him. Moved on to the big boys, I guess."

Nina wrapped a scarf around her head. "That's too bad. I guess I can understand how hard tonight must have been for him. I'm surprised he wanted to come in the first place. Why do you think he suggested we come?"

Shrugging her shoulders, Desiree replied, "He was backstage talking to someone—I think it was a friend of his. Maybe he came to see him."

"I guess," Nina muttered.

Desiree was still awake long after Nina had fallen

asleep. She was worried about Bradley. "Dear Lord, I want to help him...just show me what I need to do. What I need to say..."

"Bradley, you okay?"

He glanced over his shoulder to look at Alton. "I'm fine. Why do you ask?"

"It just seemed like...like you were bothered by something."

"I used to manage both Common and Michael James," Bradley began. He gave Alton a brief summary of his time with them.

"That's cold, man. I had no idea."

Bradley agreed. "No, it wasn't right, but look how well they're doing and look where I am. In Summerset, Texas. Something just doesn't seem right, if you ask me." Bradley made his way over to his bed and sat down on the edge to remove his shoes. "I have to find a way to make this up to Desiree. I think I kind of spoiled the evening for her."

"What about flowers?" Alton suggested.

"Flowers," Bradley repeated as he stood up. "You think I should buy her flowers."

"Don't you? You just said that you ruined her evening. Women like getting flowers, you know." Picking up the remote, Alton began surfing television channels.

As if to make his point, he stopped and pointed. "See. Women love flowers."

Bradley eyed the television a moment, watching a romantic commercial, before saying, "I hope this is not where you get your ideas for your relationship with Nina."

"I'm telling you, Desiree loves flowers. Get her some flowers and she'll forget all about last night."

Walking briskly across the room carrying his overnight bag, Bradley tossed a glance over his shoulder and replied, "Flowers, huh? I'll give it some thought."

He entered the bathroom and showered quickly. Bradley was tired and couldn't wait to get into bed. His mind traveled to Desiree and he couldn't help but wonder how she was feeling. He'd wanted their time together in Dallas to be special but then he had gone and ruined it.

After he toweled himself dry and put on pajamas, Bradley considered calling Desiree but after stealing a glance at the clock on the nightstand, he changed his mind. Climbing into bed, Bradley fell asleep almost immediately.

The next morning, Bradley was up early. He told Alton, "I've got to go out for something. I'll be back before we meet Desiree and Nina."

He left the hotel in search of flowers and returned forty-five minutes later. With a dozen roses in hand, Bradley took the elevator up to the room where Nina and Desiree were staying.

Desiree opened the door, wearing a tangerine-colored dress with silver accessories. Bradley surveyed her from head to toe, smiling in approval. She looked stunning.

"What are the flowers for?"

"What do you think? I bought them for you," Bradley announced. "I'm sorry for being a jerk last night as you so eloquently put it."

Grinning, Desiree reached for the yellow roses. "They're beautiful. Thank you, Bradley."

Nina joined them. "Oh, my goodness," she exclaimed. "They're beautiful."

Desiree embraced Bradley. "Thank you. I love them."

"I'm glad." Looking over Desiree's head, he said to Nina, "We should call Alton and have him meet us in the lobby for brunch."

She nodded. "I just got off the phone with him. He should be on his way down there now."

"Then we should be leaving. You two have everything packed?"

"We do," the women answered in unison.

Desiree sniffed her rose bouquet before setting the vase down on the dresser. She met his gaze and smiled.

They took the elevator down to the lobby where they found Alton waiting for them. As soon as Bradley had a moment alone with Alton, he said, "You were right. The flowers were a hit."

Chapter Nine

On Sunday, the adult choir had the day off, so Desiree and Nina sat together in the congregation, four rows from the front.

The youth choir was singing an original song written by Bradley which moved Desiree to tears, it was so beautiful. She closed her eyes, impressing each word upon her memory.

She'd observed Bradley on several occasions as he rehearsed with the youth and found he was totally a different person with them. It was clear he genuinely loved children—especially toddlers and babies—and they responded to him, as well. On more than one occasion she found Bradley in the back of the church singing to one of the little girls or trying to bring a smile to a little boy.

Just before he took his seat, Bradley stole a peek at Desiree and smiled.

She smiled back. Every day her feelings for him

deepened and intensified. Despite the maddening hint of arrogance surrounding him at times, Bradley projected an energy and power that drew her.

Pastor French's voice intruded her thoughts making Desiree suddenly feel guilty. She turned her attention to his sermon.

After church Bradley and Desiree went to her parents' home for dinner. They sat around the table talking and laughing over a meal of fried chicken, macaroni and cheese, collard greens and corn bread.

Margaret served slices of sweet potato pie for dessert.

Later, they all gathered in the family room.

"I rented a couple of movies," Desiree announced. "And y'all don't have to worry. I didn't get any love stories."

"What did you get, then?" her father inquired.

"Thrillers. I know how much you like them. Bradley likes them, too." Desiree walked over to the entertainment unit and started the first movie.

"I'll make some popcorn for us in case we feel like snacking," Margaret announced.

"I'll go with you," Barton said.

"Thanks, sweetheart," Bradley whispered when she sank down beside him.

Desiree gave a tiny shrug. "I don't mind, really. I like to make people smile."

Bradley's gaze was as soft as a caress. "You certainly make me smile."

Drawn in, Desiree leaned forward, lifting her lips to his.

Margaret cleared her throat noisily. "The movie has started," she murmured with a laugh.

A blush like a shadow ran over Desiree's cheeks. She buried her burning face against Bradley's shoulder.

* * *

Three hours later the movie ended, bringing Bradley to his feet. "I'm going to get out of here, so you all can relax. Mrs. Coleman, thank you for inviting me to have dinner with you all. I don't get much home cooking, so I really appreciate it whenever I can get some. Everything was delicious."

While he talked to Barton and Margaret, Desiree strolled off to the kitchen, returning a few minutes later carrying two covered bowls containing leftovers.

She handed the bowls to him before turning around to embrace her mother. "Thanks, Mama. I'll see you on Tuesday. We're having lunch, remember?"

Next she hugged her father. "Bye, Daddy. I love you. I love you both."

Bradley watched as she blew a kiss to them before walking out the front door. Desiree was very close to her parents. He and his parents had been close like that, as well. Seeing them together like this served as a poignant reminder of all he missed.

He followed her out to the car.

"Thank you," Desiree murmured as she climbed into the car.

Bradley went around to the driver's side and joined her. "What are you thanking me for?"

"For being such a charming man. My parents are really crazy about you. They like you a lot."

"I like them, too."

They continued to discuss her parents until they reached her town house. Bradley escorted Desiree safely to her home. They stood in the foyer holding hands.

Bradley bent his head to kiss Desiree.

Standing on tiptoe, she inhaled his masculine scent as his kiss left her mouth savoring every sensation.

He reluctantly pulled away from her. "I'd better go."

Desiree nodded. "Okay. I'll see you Tuesday evening."

Bradley took her face into his hand and held it gently. His heart was hammering foolishly, his breathing uneven. "I…I'm crazy about you, Desiree."

"I'm crazy about you, too."

Bradley knew they shared an intense physical awareness of each other, but both were committed to celibacy. It was one of their very first conversations when they decided to take their friendship to the next level.

He kissed her again before leaving.

Bradley drove home, his mind clouded with thoughts of Desiree. He was in love with Desiree. He'd almost confessed as much to her earlier but chickened out. He had never felt so deeply for a woman in his life and it unnerved him.

Later at home, Bradley changed into a pair of sweats and reached for his Bible, removing the thin layer of dust. It had been months since he'd picked it up to read or study the Word.

He closed his eyes and began to pray. *Heavenly Father, thank You for Your grace and Your mercy. I know it's been a while. I have no excuse and I ask for Your forgiveness. Father God, I have been so angry about everything. I just thought that when I gave up the secular music, You were going to make me a star.* Bradley paused a moment before continuing, *Instead I'm here in Summerset, Texas…* He shook his head. *I'm sorry, Father. I'll do whatever You want. I'm not sure why You brought me here, but I will stay here until You call me to do something else.*

Bradley continued to pray in earnest. When he finished, he opened his Bible and began to read, stopping every now and then to take notes.

An hour passed before Bradley closed his Bible and turned on the television. For the first time in a long while, he felt at peace.T .C. Holloway was on television.

Bradley settled back against the leather cushions of his sofa to listen to his friend.

"In my morning devotion," T.C. was saying, "I came across this verse in Proverbs. 'Lying lips are an abomination to the Lord; but they that deal truly are his delight.' God wants his children to be real. So much of what is happening in our churches and in the lives of God's people becomes fake. It is more show than glow...."

Bradley sat up and leaned forward.

"When Satan encouraged Christ to add some excitement to his wilderness experience, Christ chose the glow over the show. He chose to live by every word that proceeded from the mouth of God."

Guilt poured over Bradley as he continued to listen to T.C.

"I'm going to leave you all with this—are you real, or just show? Only the Word of God can make you glow."

For the rest of the evening, Bradley considered T.C.'s words.

Chapter Ten

"What are we doing here?" Nina asked when Alton parked his car in front of Desiree's town house. "She's not here, baby. She went to her parents' house."

"We're not here to see Desiree."

"Then why are we here?" she asked a second time while following Alton to the sales office.

"We're here to look at the model and the floor plans. When we get married, we're going to need a place to live. I know how much you love it here."

Nina stopped walking. "Are you serious?"

Alton pushed his glasses away from his nose. "I'm very serious, honey."

Nina held up her hand. "Just so you know, I'm still waiting for you to ask me to marry you proper."

He laughed. "I hear you. Now come on and let's buy us a house. I already know which one I want. I need to see if you agree."

"Hmm, you've already picked one, huh?"

"I have my favorite. I think it's the same one you're going to pick."

"We'll see."

Alton insisted they check out the model before speaking to the sales agent. He led her to the steps leading into the town house.

"What's going on with you, Alton? You're acting kind of strange."

"How do you like this floor plan?"

"I love it." She glanced over at him. "This is the one you chose?"

He nodded.

"I really like the idea of having a morning room but I can't quite visualize it."

"They have one available with the morning room. Want to see it?"

"Yes, of course."

Alton introduced Nina to the sales agent who immediately turned over a key to one of the homes.

Nina was suspicious. "She acted like she knew you well. Just how many times have you been out here?"

"Jealous?"

"No. Just curious."

Unlocking the door, Alton held it open for Nina to enter. She glanced down at the hardwood floors and broke into a smile. Her eyes traveled from room to room, trying to absorb everything.

"This house is stunning. The owner and I have a lot of the same tastes. The walls are painted vivid colors— you know how much I hate white walls. The hardwood floors…I love it."

Alton led her upstairs. "We're saving the master bedroom for last," he announced as he led her from one room to another.

When they walked into the master bedroom, Nina gasped.

She turned to face Alton. "I don't think we should be in here. Somebody has already moved in—at least partially." Nina looked over her shoulder at the beautiful four-poster bed with the leather-and-suede comforter in an emerald color. The room itself was decorated exquisitely in emerald and cream with splashes of burgundy.

On the bed lay a bouquet of red roses. Alton walked over and picked up the flowers.

"You'd better put them back," Nina warned. "We don't know if the owners are coming back anytime soon. Let's get out of here." She headed for the door.

"Honey, it's okay. These are for you."

Nina stopped walking. She turned around. "Those are for me? You brought me flowers?"

Alton nodded and hand them to her.

Smiling, Nina sniffed, inhaling the sweet fragrance of the red roses. Her eyes traveled once more to the bed and noticed a tiny gift box lying in the middle.

"What's that?" she asked with her heart racing.

"Pick it up."

Nina did as she was told. She screamed when she opened the box. "I can't believe it."

Alton turned her around to face him. "Honey, I love you so much and I don't want to spend another moment without you being my wife. I know you want a big wedding and all, but I have to tell you—I want to marry you today. I can't wait no more." He paused a second before saying, "Nina, will you marry me? This house that we're standing in is ours." Alton gestured toward the bed. "That's our bed over there. This is our home."

Tears streamed down Nina's face. "I love you, Alton Stone." Wrapping her arms around him, she added, "I don't care nothing about a wedding. I just want to be your wife. We can get married tomorrow morning and move into this house tomorrow evening."

Alton laughed. "There's a three-day waiting period."

"The point is that I want to get married as soon as possible. I want to be with you."

Two weeks after the impromptu marriage of Alton and Nina, the month of October burst in, changing the leaves of the trees to vivid colors of gold, orange and red. It was less than seven weeks away from the Annual Harvest Celebration and the air in Summerset was electrified by the excitement of the upcoming event. Bradley was proud of how well Desiree was progressing with her singing lessons. They continued to practice every Tuesday and Thursday.

For Bradley, seeing a visual transition from summer to fall was something he'd missed while living in Los Angeles. He liked to take early morning walks just to enjoy the scenery. It was also a time that he chose to meditate on what he'd studied in the Bible before his stroll.

When he returned home, Bradley headed to his piano. Putting on a set of headphones, he decided to devote the next couple of hours to his music. He'd been inspired by his walk and wanted to get the lyrics floating around in his head on paper.

Ten minutes after twelve, Bradley removed the headphones and got up from the piano.

His cellular phone rang, jarring him from his thoughts. He answered it. "Hello."

"Bradley, I'm so sorry for just getting back to you.

I just finished my tour in Japan—I'm actually at the airport now. I heard the tape and you're right. That Veronica girl has a beautiful voice."

"Kandi—" This was the last person he'd expected to hear from.

"Bradley, you there?"

"I'm here, Kandi. Thanks for getting back to me. I—"

She interrupted him. "Hon, they're calling me. I have to go, but I'm going to be in Dallas next week. Let's get together."

"Sure."

"I'll call you later. Love ya."

Kandi was gone.

I didn't have a chance to tell her about Veronica. Bradley vowed to tell her when she called him back. Her call reminded him of everything he'd dreamed of—managing top singing acts. Maybe God had finally answered his prayer.

Later that evening, Kandi called him back and wanted to meet with him at the end of the week. Bradley decided to hold off until he saw her in person to inform Kandi of Veronica's death. He didn't want to risk her changing her mind about coming to Summerset. Although Desiree's singing was rapidly improving, she wasn't a Veronica.

Three days later, Bradley was seated in the lobby of the elegant Hubbard Hotel. He picked up a newspaper to read while waiting on Kandi to come downstairs. Because of their past history, he opted to meet in the restaurant instead of her suite. Bradley didn't want to give his ex-girlfriend the wrong idea.

"Hey, what are you doing here?"

Surprise flowed through Bradley when he looked up into the face of Desiree. *What is she doing here?* he wondered to himself.

"Are you meeting someone?" Desiree inquired.

Bradley nodded and answered, "I'm meeting an old friend. What are you doing here?"

"I had a workshop and luncheon in the Crystal Room. I'm on my way back to the bank now." Smiling down at him, Desiree asked, "How long will you be here?"

To her, Bradley seemed a bit nervous about "meeting an old friend." She noted the way he kept glancing over his shoulder. "You okay?"

He nodded. "I'm fine."

Desiree surveyed his face. "You sure?"

"Yeah, I'm okay." He laid down the newspaper and rose to his feet. Together, they walked to the lobby entrance. "I'll give you a call later, sweetheart."

"Okay. Have fun." She couldn't put her finger on it, but Desiree believed that Bradley was trying to hide something from her—but what? It just didn't make sense.

"Bradley..."

"It wouldn't look good for the boss to be late. We'll talk later, okay?" He didn't want to mention anything about Kandi or his plans right now. Bradley didn't want to get her hopes up.

"Okay," Desiree mumbled in response. Something definitely wasn't right.

She headed to her car, her mind plagued with suspicion. Why was Bradley trying to rush her off? What was going on with him?

Desiree climbed into her car and sat there for a moment. She had to find out what was going on with Bradley.

She got out of her car and walked back into the hotel lobby in time to see Bradley and a slender woman head into the restaurant. Although her dark sunglasses hid her features from curious onlookers, Desiree knew exactly who she was.

She turned on her heel and headed back to her car.

Kandi Tate was there to see Bradley. Desiree knew it like she knew her own hand. She was sure of it.

Chapter Eleven

"I can't believe Bradley Rhodes. How could he do this to me?" Desiree exclaimed into the telephone. "He's involved with that Kandi Tate. I just know it."

"You are really upset."

"We're close enough to be in a committed relationship. At least on my part, anyway." Desiree sighed softly. "Nina, I'm in love with him."

"Before you go jumping the gun, why don't you just go to Bradley and ask him about her?"

Her throat ached with defeat. "Why should I have to do that? Why didn't he just tell me he was meeting with a woman? I thought he was meeting a guy."

"This is why you have to talk to him, Desiree."

"All I want to know is where I stand with the man."

"I'm not a big Bradley Rhodes fan, but I know he cares deeply for you," Nina stated.

"I don't know…." A tear slipped down her face.

"He cares for you, Desiree. I'm sure Bradley's meeting with Kandi Tate—now, you're sure it was her? I mean *the* Kandi Tate. The gospel singer?"

There was a heavy feeling in her stomach. "Yeah. It was her, Nina. I'm sure of it."

"Well, he has to know Kandi from the old days. Maybe it was just business between her and Bradley. You know, a completely innocent meeting."

"I thought about that, but Nina, you should've seen the way he was acting. Bradley looked so guilty when he saw me in that lobby." Tears blinded her eyes and choked her voice. "He couldn't get me out of there fast enough."

"Well, I have to tell you, girlfriend, that I really think this was just a business meeting or just two old friends getting together."

Desiree wiped her face with a tissue. "So you don't think he could've been involved with Kandi at one time?"

"I guess he could have," Nina admitted. "You should get off this phone with me and give Bradley a call. Just talk to him."

When Desiree hung up, she considered Nina's words. Maybe her friend was right. She picked up the phone, then changed her mind.

She decided to see if she heard anything from Bradley.

Bradley sat in his family room dazed. Over lunch, Kandi had asked him to become her manager. This was a complete dream come true for him. An award-winning singer wanted to be represented by his management company. Kandi had also made it clear that she was more than interested in renewing their relationship, but Bradley quickly informed her that he was seeing someone.

He'd half expected Kandi to rescind her first offer at hearing that but she hadn't. She had always been a good businesswoman.

The ringing of his doorbell drew him out of his reverie. Bradley got up and headed to the front door. Opening it, he found Desiree standing there.

"I'm sorry for coming over here unannounced, but I needed to talk to you. Can I come in?"

"Sure." Bradley stepped out of the way to allow Desiree entrance. "Honey, what's wrong? You look upset."

Glaring at him, Desiree threw down her purse. "I am. I am very upset with you, Bradley."

Baffled, Bradley asked, "What's wrong with you?"

"I saw you with Kandi Tate today. Why didn't you tell me that you were meeting with her? Why was it such a big secret?"

"It wasn't a secret, baby."

"You didn't tell me you were meeting with her." She stormed over to the window and stared out. "I guess you have something to hide."

Bradley crossed the room to stand beside her. He turned her so that she was facing him. "Desiree, you don't have anything to worry about. Sweetheart, I care a great deal about you. Kandi and I...we're just friends—nothing more. I told you I was meeting a friend. She wants me to manage her, so see, you don't have any reason to be jealous. The only woman I'm interested in... is you." Bradley moved closer to her. He bent down to place a kiss on her lips.

"Wow," Desiree murmured.

Bradley laughed. "You are so cute."

"I'm sorry for jumping the conclusions. I just feel awful."

"I should've been more open with you, I guess. She and I are just friends. Longtime friends."

"So you two were never involved?"

"I didn't say that."

Desiree gasped and backed away from him.

"Hey! It was a long long time ago," Bradley quickly explained. He pulled her to him, trapping her in his arms. "There is nothing between Kandi and me. I told her all about you and how much I love you."

"You did?"

He nodded. "I don't want another woman—just you."

As if to prove it, Bradley lowered his lips to hers.

Later seated together on the sofa, Desiree commented, "This went a whole lot better than I thought it would. I came over here expecting you to blast me and tell me to mind my own business."

He chucked. "I'm glad I'm not that predictable."

Chapter Twelve

"Bradley, I'm not going to sing," Desiree announced on the way to rehearsal. The gospel concert was only three weeks away. She had given it a lot of thought and wasn't sure she was quite ready.

He glanced over at her. "Why not?"

"I'm a little nervous," she admitted. "I don't want to mess things up for everyone. They're all looking forward to performing."

"There you go again, putting everyone else above your own dreams. Sweetheart, you've worked very hard for this. Just as hard as the other choir members." Reaching over, Bradley took her hand in his. "Desiree, you're ready."

"You really think so?"

He nodded. "You should know by now that I wouldn't say it if I didn't mean it."

His words made her smile. "You're certainly right about that."

"I expect to see you in the choir stand when we get to the church. Don't make me carry you up there."

"You wouldn't dare."

"Oh, yes, I would. I'm not going to let you throw away your dream. I know that you'd be the same way when it came to me."

"Yeah, I would," Desiree acknowledged.

Bradley struggled with whether or not now was the time to tell her that Kandi's job offer meant his leaving Summerset. No, he decided quickly. Desiree was already nervous about singing for the concert. He wasn't sure how she would take the news and didn't want to risk upsetting her further.

They arrived at the church and parked. Bradley got out and ran around the truck to open the door for Desiree.

They walked hand in hand toward the white building.

"You're suddenly very quiet," Desiree observed. "What are you thinking about?"

"How much I love you."

"Oh, Bradley, I love you, too."

Inside the church a few of the choir members were seated along the first pew, talking and laughing. They greeted the couple as they entered.

While he went to set up the sheet music and turn on the sound system, Desiree sat down beside a woman named Lenora.

"I saw your mother at the store yesterday. She sure is looking good."

Nodding, Desiree smiled. "Yeah. She is doing so well since the surgery. It's truly a blessing and I just thank God for it."

Nina and Alton arrived a few minutes later. Another ten minutes passed before Bradley called them to the choir stand.

After only one song, the other choir members applauded Desiree and commented on her improved singing.

"Oh, Desiree, you sound so good."

She smiled at the woman standing beside her. "Thank you, Gladys. I'm working real hard on it."

The rest of the rehearsal ran smoothly. Afterward, Bradley took her bowling.

Nina and Alton met them there.

"Tonight, I think we really sounded great," Nina announced. "We're going to have everyone shouting all over Summerset Junior College. I am so excited."

"I'm real proud of you all." Bradley picked up a bowling ball.

Desiree cheered when he made a strike. "That's my man," she bragged. "Okay, Alton, let's see what you can do."

When Bradley left her town house, Desiree still felt as if Bradley had something he was hiding. Over the past month, he'd seemed different and distant.

Every now and then her insecurities would rise and she wondered if he was interested in someone else. A couple of times, she'd considered questioning him, but didn't follow through.

"Bradley, I wish you'd talk to me," she whispered in the silent room. "I feel like you're hiding something from me. What is it?"

The night of the concert arrived with a chilly blast. Desiree didn't know whether she was shivering from the cold air or nervousness.

"You okay, sweetheart?" Bradley inquired. He wrapped an arm around her.

"I'm f-fine. Just a little nervous."

Bradley gave Desiree a reassuring smile. "Honey, you're going to do great. Try to remember to sing with that choir and not above them."

"I will," she promised.

It was time for them to go on.

Onstage, Bradley winked and gave her a thumbs-up. Desiree awarded him a smile. The music started.

Ignoring her trembling fingers and legs, Desiree fervently tried to remember everything she'd learned over the course of her singing lessons. It had all come down to this and she didn't want to let anybody down.

Nina leaned forward to whisper, "Relax, honey. It's going to be okay."

Desiree gave a slight nod. She took several calming breaths and exhaled slowly.

Bradley raised his arm. It was time for them to sing.

Closing her eyes, Desiree allowed the lyrics to minister to her—soon the audience vanished; the other choir members were gone. She was on a great cloud pouring out her song before God. Her heart filled with love for her heavenly Father and overflowed onto her words.

The choir finished their first song. The next one was one written by Bradley and was a favorite of Desiree's.

The choir received several standing ovations before they were ushered off the stage.

Afterward, Bradley and Desiree escaped from everyone to change into sweaters, jeans and cowboy boots in two of the public restrooms. When Nina and Alton changed into more casual wear, the foursome strolled around the campus, stopping here and there to play some of the carnival games.

"I had such a wonderful time tonight," Desiree stated.

"So did I," Nina chimed. "Everyone is talking about how well we did."

"I have to admit that you all even surprised me," Bradley confessed. "The Peaceful Rest choir was definitely at its best tonight. Now I want you all to sound just like that in February for the competition."

"We will, as long as you're directing us, Bradley." Nina hugged the huge doll Alton won for her to her body.

Desiree glimpsed an array of emotions wash over Bradley's face. Curious, she watched him for a moment.

Bradley met her gaze and smiled.

Desiree returned his smile, but deep down she was even more convinced that he was hiding something. She looked past Bradley and pointed. "There's Pastor French and his wife. Sister Lilli Belle looks great in her leather outfit."

Following her gaze, Nina agreed. "Yeah, she sho' working that suit. I like that."

Desiree laughed.

Nina pulled her away from the men and whispered, "It looks like you and Bradley are really hitting it off. It's so obvious that he adores you."

"I know he cares about me." Desiree stole a peek at Bradley before saying, "But I still think he's keeping something from me. I can't put my finger on it—I just have this feeling."

"You think he's seeing someone else?"

"No, I'm pretty sure he's not cheating on me. It's something else, but what?"

Nina embraced her. "I don't think you have anything to worry about. Bradley loves you, Desiree."

"I hope you're right."

Chapter Thirteen

The next day, Desiree decided to confront him. "Bradley, there's something bothering me and I think we should talk about it."

"You're right," he admitted. "There is something I need to tell you. I hope you'll be happy for me. It's great news, actually."

Her heart in her throat, Desiree asked, "What is it?"

"I told you that Kandi Tate wants me to be her manager."

"Right."

He sat down beside her. "Well, there's more. Honey, I need to ask you something."

"What is it?" she asked a second time. Bradley was suddenly acting very nervous and it made her uneasy.

"Will you marry me?"

Desiree's mouth dropped open in shock. "W-what d-did you ask me?"

"I just asked you to marry me. I want you to be my wife. We can get married here in Summerset of course, then…"

Desiree was quiet while Bradley continued to rattle on with his plans for the two of them.

"…we can move back to Los Angeles after the wedding. Kandi's going to be back on the road, so we may have to delay our honeymoon. And—"

Desiree cut in. "You're taking the job, then?"

"Of course. Why wouldn't I? This is all I've dreamed about."

"I see."

"Desiree, I don't get it. I thought you'd be happy for me."

"What about the choir? What about the competition coming up in February? You're going to just walk out on them?"

"The choir is more than ready for this competition. Alton can take over as Music Director."

"How can you do this to us?"

"I'm not doing anything to you," Bradley retorted. "Don't you want to get married? You'll go with me to Los Angeles."

"What about my job?"

"Desiree, you won't need that job. If you want to work in a bank, they have plenty of them in L.A. A bank is a bank."

Bradley kissed her hand. "Honey, I thought you'd be happy for me."

"I am happy for you. But I also thought you'd be more supportive of Peaceful Rest Church. I can't believe you'd walk out on us like that."

"I'm not walking out on anyone. Desiree, I love you

and I just want to give you a wonderful life. I want us to be happy."

"I am happy. I don't need to be in the limelight—these are your dreams. Not mine."

"Okay," Bradley acknowledged. "These are my dreams. I've never lied about that. This is very important to me."

"I understand that, Bradley. Really, I do. What I don't understand is why it just can't wait until after the competition."

"Kandi wants me to get started as soon as possible. She's already waited a couple of months—"

Desiree interrupted him. "You've known about this for a couple of months? Why are you just now telling me about it?"

"I didn't want to upset you while we were preparing for the concert."

"Bradley, I can't believe you. How can you say you love me and then turn around and treat me like this?"

"Desiree, don't make this about you because it's not. It has nothing to do with you. This is the desire of my heart."

She didn't respond.

"I'm sorry. I didn't mean to snap at you like that." He let out a long sigh. "You know, I just realized that you never answered me. Will you marry me, Desiree?"

A tear rolled down her cheek. Desiree met his gaze and shook her head. "I'm sorry, Bradley. I can't. I can't marry you."

He was stunned speechless.

"This is your dream and I think you should follow your heart. I love you and I wish you well."

"I don't understand. Why did you turn down my proposal? You say you love me."

"I do love you, Bradley, but you and I want very different things. Loyalty means something to you only when you're the one who has been betrayed. For me, loyalty is a two-way street."

"You won't marry me because I'm leaving Peaceful Rest Church." He shook his head. "I don't believe this."

"It's more than that, Bradley, and you know it. You expect me to give up everything because you don't deem it important—it's all about you." Her eyes filled with water and her voice broke. "I r-refuse to l-live that way."

Desiree wiped the tears running down her face on her sleeve. "Bradley, I need some time alone. Could you please leave?"

He reached for her. "Sweetheart…"

Shaking her head, Desiree moved out of his reach. "Please, Bradley, we can talk later. Right now, I just need to be by myself."

Bradley stood up. "I didn't expect things to turn out this way. I really thought you'd be happy for me."

"When do you have to leave?"

"In a couple of days, but I'll be back around Christmas. Kandi's having a big party News Year's Eve and wants to…" Bradley's voice died when he saw the stricken look on Desiree's face. "I don't want to leave you," he confessed. "I don't want to lose you, Desiree. You mean too much to me."

"Follow your heart, Bradley. If you don't, you'll regret it."

"What about you?"

"I have to follow mine," she murmured, her heart breaking.

Bradley was up at the crack of dawn. He'd spent a restless night contemplating his situation. He loved Desiree more than he'd ever imagined.

Heavenly Father, I need Your help, he prayed. *I don't know what to do anymore...*

When he was done, Bradley lay on his bed playing T.C.'s sermon over and over again in his head. "Am I for real or for show?" he whispered. He went over his reasons for coming to Summerset in the first place. Bradley had to acknowledge that his motives weren't pure—hadn't been in a long time.

Until now he hadn't really considered that the ensuing results were the consequences of his actions. He'd let his selfishness and bitterness color his attitude, which carried over into his work. Sadly he admitted he hadn't really been a nice guy in a real long time. He was blessed that Desiree could see through it all. She loved him unconditionally.

"How can I hurt her like that?" His heart was heavy because of the way he'd treated Desiree and the choir members, but what pained him most was the way he'd allowed his ego to separate him from God.

Bradley's eyes grew wet. "I've always known You were my strength and that if I trusted You, You would make all things right. I just didn't trust You enough, heavenly Father. I know that I should rejoice in the privilege of serving You...." His voice broke. "I know that I am exactly where You want me to be right now. I know that—I wasn't ready to accept it before bu—"

The telephone rang, cutting him off.

Bradley picked up the receiver. "Hello."

"It's Kandi."

"Hi, I was just about to call you."

"I have something to tell you all," Desiree began after everyone had gathered in the choir stand. She stole a glance over at Alton and gave a sad smile.

Nina was immediately at her side. "Let me tell them," she whispered.

"I have to do it." Desiree cleared her throat. "Bradley—"

"I'm here," a voice uttered from behind her.

She turned around to face him. "Bradley, what are you doing here?" Desiree asked in a low whisper.

Looking into her eyes, he replied, "I wouldn't miss this for the world. This is where I belong."

"Bradley, are you sure?"

"I've never been more sure of anything in my life." He turned to the choir and said, "Okay, everybody, let's get started."

Smiling, Desiree walked up to the choir stand, joining the other members. As Bradley listened to them sing, he knew in his heart he'd made the right decision.

After the rehearsal, Desiree waited for Bradley beside his car.

"What happened to make you change your mind?"

"You and God. I think I knew from the moment I set foot in Summerset, Texas, that this was where I belonged—at least for the time being. I just didn't want to accept it because I wanted so much more. I love you so much, Desiree. Nothing is more important than spending the rest of my life with you."

"I'm so glad you didn't leave," Desiree confessed. "I kept looking for you to call me and tell me you weren't going, but when you didn't…"

"Desiree, I still want you to be my wife." Bradley pulled a tiny box out of his jacket pocket. He opened it to reveal a solitaire diamond ring. "Will you marry me, Desiree Coleman?"

"Yes. Yes, I will, Mr. Bradley Rhodes." She held out her hand.

Placing the ring on the ring finger of her left hand, Bradley grinned. Onlookers in the parking lot cheered and clapped.

Desiree burst into laughter. "This is going to be all over town in about fifteen minutes."

"Then we'd better head on over to your parents' house right now. I don't want them hearing about this from anybody else before we can tell them."

Desiree rushed over to her car and got in. Bradley followed her in his car the short distance to her childhood home.

Chapter Fourteen

The Peaceful Rest choir received a standing ovation after their performance.

"There's something I want to say," Bradley announced offstage after the choir took first place in the Statewide Gospel Competition for the fourth year in a row. "I want you to know just how proud I am of all of you. Y'all showed out." He laughed. "I've learned a lot from you and I want to say thanks for allowing me to take part in this historic moment. This has truly been a humbling time for me." His eyes traveled to Desiree and he smiled. "This will always be a special time in my life."

"Don't you have something else to tell them?" Alton pushed.

"Yeah, I do. Sorry." Bradley drew his attention back to the other people standing around him. "Kandi Tate has asked me to be her manager and I—"

"You're leaving," someone from the back interjected. "I knew it."

"Let him finish," Desiree replied. "Just hear him out."

"It's easy for you. You're going to be married to the man. First Grace leaves and now Bradley," a woman beside Desiree huffed.

"I'm not leaving," Bradley announced. "When I first came to Peaceful Rest Church, it was because I wanted to manage Veronica—I didn't know she'd died until after I arrived. I was looking for the next rising star to put me back on top. But it wasn't until I met you all and Desiree that I realized I'd been called to Summerset by God. This is where I belong—at least for the moment. As for Kandi, even though I didn't take the job, the choir will still be working with her."

"What are you talking about?" Inez asked.

"You all will be going to Dallas in a couple of months to record Kandi's new album. She wants the Peaceful Rest adult choir to accompany her."

"You're kidding," someone stated. "*The* Kandi Tate wants us to sing with her?"

Bradley nodded. "We've got a lot of work ahead of us, but I have every confidence that you all will rise to the challenge." He reached out and embraced Desiree. "I have one more announcement. My fiancée and I have set a wedding date. We're getting married in July. The twenty-second of July."

They were soon surrounded by choir members and other well-wishers who heard the announcement.

Desiree wrapped an arm around Bradley. *I love you,* she mouthed.

"I am so blessed to have you in my life," he murmured loud enough for her to hear.

"Why are you being so quiet?" Desiree asked Bradley later when they were sitting in the lobby of the Omni Austin's hotel waiting for Nina and Alton to come down.

"I was just trying to figure out how I got so turned around. I stopped singing secular music because it no longer fulfilled me. Eventually I told myself that it was because I wanted to sing and write music that glorified God—that's when things just got crazy. The truth was that I missed the excitement of being on top. I figured gospel music was another way to get there. It was about the show and not the glow."

"Excuse me?"

Bradley went on to explain. "I was listening to my friend on television—he used to be pastor at Peaceful Rest …"

"Reverend Holloway?"

He nodded. "He talked about how Aaron had a show, but Moses had a glow. Moses glowed because he was having communion with God. He was hearing and receiving God's Word. He even compared this to marriage. When we get married and if we're not having a devotional life together, our marriage is in danger of becoming a show without a glow. Do you understand what I'm saying?"

"I do."

"I was about the show and I thought because I was doing it in God's name, that I was going to have everything I wanted. Listening to T.C. put me on the path to figuring things out. I was guilty of the very same things I accused all those singers I worked with. I had my own agenda which didn't line up with God's."

"I think we've all been there. We're human."

"I know and I'm not beating myself up over this—I'm just saying that I've changed in a lot of ways. I'm finally on the right track, so to speak. Once I decided to stop looking for the light of the sun and start looking for the light of the Son of God, I feel such peace now. I haven't felt this way in a long time. This is my ministry. I know that for sure. Everything I do going forward will be for the glory of His kingdom. Like Chronicles 5:13 says, 'Indeed it came to pass when the trumpeters and singers were as one, to make one sound to be heard in praising and thanking the Lord and when they lifted up their voice with the trumpets and cymbals and instruments of music and praised the Lord saying "For He is good, For His mercy endures forever," that the house, the house of the Lord was filled with a cloud.'"

Taking Bradley's hand in hers, Desiree replied, "Amen."

* * * * *

HEART SONGS

Felicia Mason

Chapter One

As she glanced around the room at the classmates she graduated with twenty-five years ago, Carys Chappelle Shaw had to give herself credit for not only staying in shape, but also in touch with both reality and the evolution of fashion.

More than one head of impossibly black or red hair moved in front of her line of vision. Pounds and wrinkles and hard times showed on the faces and frames of some of the people she used to know. Carys was one of the few who still looked naturally like the Camden College yearbook image from all those years ago when they were undergrads at the North Carolina college.

Without consciously realizing it, she searched the crowd, looking for one particular face, one smile. After her third scan through, she sighed just a little—but not on the outside where it would show.

Maybe he wasn't coming.

Or, maybe the picture she'd seen of him was an old one and like at least three other male classmates she'd spied tonight, he'd gone bald and gained a hundred pounds. That fate had claimed the former all-star football player and self-proclaimed ladies' man of the class. Joe Holmes was scouting for wife number five and asked Carys, half jokingly, if she'd be interested.

"We could merge our business empires, beautiful. Me and you. We can fly to Las Vegas tonight."

Because she knew he was teasing, they laughed together before he moved on, flirting nonstop with more of their fellow alumni.

Merge their business interests, indeed. Everyone in this room thought she was flush with cash, including the fund-raising-obsessed Camden College president, Dr. Buford Brooks, who'd been all grins the moment she hit the door. Carys had no intention of correcting all their assumptions. She was rich, just not the way anyone figured.

Returning to the college after all these years seemed strange to her. She'd been in touch, though, mostly via substantial checks to pet departments and specific fund-raising efforts—all sent under the Chappelle name. But she felt as if at any moment, a sorority sister would bounce in front of her and propose a trip to the mall, the movie theater or a neighboring college. They'd pack eight in a car and head off for an adventure.

Carys smiled.

Those were the days. Days when the future was a distant shore far beyond even the imagination, and happiness was the only conceivable fate for those who lived charmed lives. Time had, of course, done its number on that way of thinking.

Now, all she could do was wonder just what had happened to twenty-five years of her life—a quarter of a century gone by in two blinks of eyelashes carefully thickened with a Parisian mascara.

"If you don't smile, Carys Chappelle, Dr. Brooks and everyone else is going to think your family is pulling its money for that new medical-arts building we've been hearing about."

She recognized the voice near her ear, and a smile blossomed on her face. Her heart hammered in her throat. "I-is that really you?"

"Turn around and see," he said.

Willing her heart to stop beating so wildly, she carefully placed her soda glass on a covered tray and turned slowly toward the man.

She let out a delighted squeal. And then they were hugging each other. Laughing together. Rejoicing.

He clasped her around the waist and Carys reveled in his touch. This is why she'd come back. Why she'd been standing in a corner instead of being the social butterfly she'd been most of the evening, as well as while in college, and during the intervening years.

"T. C. Holloway. You're a sight for sore eyes."

"And you're as beautiful as ever. More so."

Carys thrilled at the words, even more grateful that she'd never slacked off on gym time, pedicures, manicures and the attendant pampering of a well-kept woman. It took work to make a forty-seven-year-old look not a day over thirty-five. Thank goodness Carl always insisted on that.

"You always knew how to flatter a woman."

"It's not flattery," Thornton said. "I only speak the truth."

A delicate tapping of a fork tine on crystal stemware halted her next words. The two hundred or so people gathered in the ballroom for the alumni reception all faced the front of the room where a man in dress whites stood next to a woman in a too-snug blue sequined cocktail dress.

"May we have your attention," she said, a lilt in her voice.

As the room quieted down, Carys glanced at T.C. He'd filled out a bit in the years since they'd graduated, but not an ounce of fat showed on him. The blue suit that she'd immediately pegged as Armani fit him the way the designer intended for his clothing to flatter the male physique.

She noted the French-cut sleeves and elegant cufflinks at his wrist. And if she weren't mistaken, she got a fleeting glance at a top-of-the-line Rolex on his left wrist.

Carys smiled to herself as she faced the podium.

T. C. Holloway had done all right for himself.

"I see a few people we want to bring up here and re-introduce to you. Everyone remembers the captain of the football team. Come on up here, Joe."

Joe Holmes, the former football player who'd acquired one hundred or so pounds in the intervening years, owned a mini-chain of used-car lots. Carys knew because along with his proposal to head to a Las Vegas wedding chapel, he'd pressed into her hand a flexible plastic key chain with the Trust Joe logo on it and invited her to stop in for test drive. Carys didn't think that she'd be trading in her luxury vehicles anytime soon—especially not for a used whoop-dee. But she applauded as Joe heaved himself up the steps and gave a booming welcome to all.

Thornton Holloway wasn't given to speechlessness. As a matter of fact, he earned a living and provided for his family by exploiting not only his intellectual knowledge, but his skill at breaking down those complex thoughts into concepts and sound bites easily digested by the masses, everyone from children to seniors.

But none of the degrees he held, none of the experiences he'd had in the years since graduating from college prepared him for coming face-to-face with Carys Chappelle.

He'd come a long way from his days growing up in Texas. His family had been so proud when he'd graduated with an associate's degree from Summerset Junior College. Even then his calling to ministry was evident in the work he did at Peaceful Rest Church, the congregation that to this day he considered his home church. On a scholarship and lots of prayers from the members, he'd transferred to Camden College where he discovered a whole new world, a world a country boy at first found baffling. But it was here on this campus in North Carolina where he'd honed his speaking skills—and where he'd fallen in love with Carys Chappelle.

A part of him hoped that Carys would be at the class reunion. He wanted her to see that he'd overcome the debilitating deficiencies that plagued him when they were undergrads. He wanted to see if she'd be as beautiful in the flesh as she was in his memory.

The answer to that—an overwhelming and resounding yes!—sent his senses into overload, short-circuiting every rational thought in his head. He hadn't given any consideration to what their first meeting might be like. Throwing herself into his arms, she'd taken charge of the moment and him by surprise. What didn't come as a surprise, though, was how wonderful she felt in his arms—as if she'd always belonged there. When he looked in her eyes, his entire world seem to slip off its axis.

Feeling as if he suddenly needed an anchor in a tumultuous sea, he reached for a drink from the tray of a passing waiter. Belatedly, he realized it was champagne, and put the flute back on a draped tray set aside for discarded glasses and plates.

He needed something to safeguard his hands. If he didn't watch it, he'd wind up putting them around Carys Chappelle's waist again. Thornton jammed his hands in the pockets of his trousers.

Joe Holmes completed his welcoming remarks and passed the microphone back to Anita, the former head cheerleader, who gave an overview of the weekend's activities.

"But before we jump right in," she said, "I think it would be appropriate if one of our own got us started on the right foot. T.C., would you lead us in a prayer?"

He nodded, knowing Carys's eyes were on him.

"Ladies and gentlemen, friends and classmates," Anita said, imbuing each word with bouncy enthusiasm. "After the invocation from our own Reverend Doctor Thornton Holloway—we all knew him as T.C.," she added on a conspiratorial aside, as if they'd been close back then, "we have a few icebreakers I think you'll enjoy."

Thornton excused himself from Carys and made his way to the front. He then gave thanks for allowing the class to be together one more time, for getting travelers safely to their destinations and for keeping watch over those who wanted to but couldn't be in attendance for the weekend. "Thank you, Lord, for abundant blessings, boundless grace and new mercies everlasting."

Muffled "Amens" went around the ballroom. Then the festivities commenced in earnest.

Prizes were awarded for everything from the class member who'd traveled the farthest distance to the ones married the longest and the most—a prize Joe claimed. Thornton returned to the spot he'd last been standing in with Carys but she'd disappeared. A search of the ballroom revealed not even a hint of the dove-gray silk wrap dress she wore.

It was just as well, he figured. The scent of her perfume, something light but evocative—just like the woman—still played havoc on his senses. He'd been alone all these years. There was no sense in getting worked up over an unattainable woman.

Carys came out of the ladies' room with one of her old sorority sisters. They lived about an hour apart and had stayed in touch by phone calls and getting together for lunch every now and then. Lynn's running commentary on just about every person they'd graduated with kept Carys entertained.

"And would you just look at that," Lynn said, tapping one long manicured nail against her cheek and speaking just loud enough for Carys to hear. "Who could have guessed that T. C. Holloway would turn out like that? Remember those Farmer Jack flannel shirts he used to wear? He walked around campus looking like something out of The Grapes of Wrath."

Carys had to smile as she followed her friend's gaze toward Thornton. Lynn might still be a world-class gossip, but American literature remained her passion.

"Mercy, look at that man."

Carys lifted an eyebrow at the tone and glanced at Lynn.

The look earned her a nudge from her friend. "Don't jump all prissy and refined on me now, Carys. Back in the day, you liked a nice piece of eye candy just like the rest of us."

"Yes," Carys said. "But that was back in the day when we were young and immature."

Lynn rolled her eyes, but she kept that interested gaze on Thornton who stood talking with two other people. He'd never been exceptionally tall, probably stood about five feet ten or eleven. But instead of being lean, wiry and almost emaciated, the way he was in college, he had filled-out. Clean-shaven, the caramel color of his skin remained smooth. The sculpted fade of his haircut and the touch of gray at his temples gave him a wise look that Carys found both comforting and appealing. His face and his bearing imbued confidence and invited people to confide in him.

"The brother is working that suit," Lynn muttered.

Carys had to agree with that. Overall, the package was a very handsome distraction—just the sort she didn't need or want.

At just that moment, he lifted his head, saw her and smiled. Carys smiled back.

"Mercy," Lynn said, fanning herself. "I need to go find my husband. Quick. See you later, girl."

Chuckling to herself at Lynn, Carys began to work the room, making her way toward Thornton, who looked to be doing the same thing. Their steps had an easy grace, both maneuvering in such a way that only an astute observer would notice they had a mission in mind. By the time they met up again, in the middle of the ballroom, they'd both greeted and chatted with several classmates who'd stopped them along the way.

"So, where are you staying this weekend?" she asked him.

"Across town at the Omni."

"I knew I should have made a reservation there."

He smiled. "Are you flirting with me, Carys Chappelle?"

She tucked a stray strand of hair behind her ear. "It's Carys Shaw now," she said. "And maybe I am."

Chapter Two

Thornton didn't know what to make of the woman standing in front of him. For so long all those years ago he'd dreamed—big time—of just this sort of moment with her when she'd focus that six-hundred-watt smile on him.

The only problem was they weren't nineteen-or twenty-one-year-olds flirting for the first time. And, she was married. The huge diamond on her ring finger and her correction on her last name told him that.

Why, then, was he wishing like crazy that he'd been the man he was now with the Carys Chappelle she'd been then?

"Would you like to join me for coffee?" she said in invitation. "The lobby bar at my hotel is open late."

"I don't drink coffee so late."

Even as the words came out of his mouth, Thornton felt like a complete idiot.

Where was the great Thornton Charles Holloway—
the man who held a doctorate from Harvard, pastored a
church with more than 3,500 people and made regular
appearances on television and the radio? Standing here
now next to Carys Chappelle Shaw he couldn't seem to
string together a coherent sentence.

How pathetic was that?

"Some things never change," he muttered to himself.

She touched the sleeve of his jacket. "I beg your
pardon?"

He looked at her hand, wondering if she felt the energy between them, a charge that apparently hadn't di-
minished. Then his gaze met hers.

Thornton cleared his throat. It was time to get out
of the deep water in which he had no business being.
Riptides and undertows threatened to take him down.
And this time, he wouldn't have youth and inexperi-
ence to blame.

"I'd love to, Carys. But I can't tonight."

She looked truly disappointed and he felt even more
pathetic than he'd been as a shy country boy almost
thirty years ago when they'd first met. Though on the
outside, he knew he exuded the confident aura of a successful executive, the epitome of a big-time preacher,
the veneer threatened to peel away in front of Carys.

"Well, maybe I'll see you at some of the events this
weekend." She made the statement sound like a question.

Thornton wanted to put his arms around her slim
waist and never let her go. But the civilized man in him
simply nodded. "I'll look forward to that."

She cocked her head and regarded him. Considering.
"What?"

"I was just thinking about Chapter Five of your last book."

She'd read his books? Thornton was stunned. Flattered. Flabbergasted.

Then it dawned on him to just what she referred. Chapter Five of his most recent book was about Christian couples reclaiming the magic that existed in their early relationship.

Thornton cleared his throat again. Then he asked, "What made you think of that?"

She smiled. "Oh, I was thinking of that night we walked together on the waterfront."

His heart dropped into his gut. She remembered that night?

"I always wondered what might have become of us if I'd made a different decision that evening."

Thornton opened his mouth, but no words came out. He tried again. "I…"

"Shh," she said, putting a slim finger across his lips. "Don't. It was a long time ago."

He nodded. In real time, it had been a moment from the distant past. But in his mind's eye, that moment stood as real as this one.…

Near one o'clock in the morning, the night air on campus carried a nip. T.C. left the confines of the dormitory room he shared with two other guys for a walk on the lakefront. They were up laughing, talking and playing a game. T.C. needed quiet to think—to sort out his life and his options. He needed to make a decision soon: grad school or the job. The offer on the table was for a lot of money. And not just for a country boy who felt a need to contribute to the family coffers back home. It was a lot of money period—thirty thousand dollars to start. All he had to do was say yes, sign on the dotted line and pack his bags for Chicago and his first job out of college.

The only problem was the tug on his heart saying Washington, D.C., and seminary. Though the money would help considerably, both his parents told him to go to God for the answer. He'd been doing just that, praying constantly and getting zippo by way of a response on the direction he should take.

As he walked along the shoreline, he came upon one of the benches strategically placed near the lake. A woman sat on one, her hands clutching the rim of the bench, her head bent. Drawing nearer, he heard her crying.

"Excuse me? Can I help you? Is something wrong?"

She looked up, blinked. "Oh. T.C. It's you."

"Carys? What are you doing out here in the middle of the night?"

He shrugged out of the sweater he'd donned to ward off the chill and draped it around her bare shoulders. The thin bands of a light tank top were thrown into contrast by her soft dark skin.

T.C. glanced away, ashamed that he'd noticed.

He'd always liked her—had fallen head over heels in love with her truth be told. But all from a distance. Carys Chappelle was light-years out of his league. She was always friendly, though, and that was enough.

She inched over, silently inviting him to sit next to her. Like a marble statue in a formal garden he remained rooted to the spot where he stood, not trusting himself to do anything else.

"What's wrong, Carys?"

"It's Nate," she said.

T.C. knew she'd been dating Nate Wade, another

one of the college's old-money legacies. Nate's family owned furniture stores—a lot of them. They probably had as much or more money than the Chappelles. Everyone expected Carys and Nate to announce their engagement at any moment. The merging of those two powerful African-American families would make headlines in the society pages.

"What's wrong with him?"

"He wants to, you know…" She shrugged. "We're almost engaged so he says there's no need to wait."

For a moment he didn't know what she meant. Then the lightbulb went on. Oh. That.

He cleared his throat, shifted his weight from one foot to the other.

What was he supposed to tell her?

Now, as he dressed for bed in his hotel room and powered up his laptop to get a little work done, Thornton thought about the boy he'd been then, trying to comfort a woman he cared about.

There in the moonlight with Carys Chappelle, his next course of action had seemed evident, as clear and bright as the near full moon shining down on them.

He'd reached for her hand.

It was late. Almost as late as it had been that one very special night so long ago.

Carys stood at the bank of windows in her suite. Her view from the hotel looked out over a man-made lake that reminded her of the one at Camden College. In her mind's eye she was seeing that spot on campus where she'd first lost her heart to T. C. Holloway.

Carys smiled. The thought of her fumbling now embarrassed her, but in that distant hazy way that didn't make her self-conscious.

A moment later, though, her smile faded as she pulled the drapes together, closing out the reminiscences.

She'd made him uncomfortable tonight and that hadn't been her intent. Not at all.

Carys sighed, the sound laced with regret and seasoned with a pinch of remorse. Something about that man always made her lose her perspective, her maturity and apparently her morals, as well. Like some brazen hussy, she'd thrown herself at him tonight.

Shame coursed through her.

She realized she was just as bad as her friend Lynn. No, worse. Lynn dearly loved her husband of twenty-two years. Despite the suggestive nature of her talk, Lynn wouldn't do anything to jeopardize her marriage or someone else's.

Thornton didn't seem to have his wife with him at the reception, but the bios of his books clearly said he lived with his family in Richmond, Virginia. They were probably sharing a laugh right now as he regaled her with tales of the poor little rich girl who'd tried to hit on him.

Carys went to the king-size bed in the hotel room. She sat at the foot of the bed and slipped off her shoes, dropping one high-heeled mule while holding the other. Evidently, she hadn't learned much in the time since graduation. She'd made the same mistake tonight with T.C. that she'd made twenty-five years ago.

Chapter Three

She didn't see him the next day at breakfast and only briefly spied him from across the room during the class meeting where pledges were turned in. Thornton didn't return her cheerful wave. Before Carys could make her way over to apologize for her behavior, he'd disappeared with the university chaplain.

It served her right that he was avoiding her. Maybe after the way she'd acted last night he regretted not bringing his wife along to the reunion. Her presence could stave off unwelcome advances.

Members of the twenty-five-year class and other alumni who'd returned for the weekend filled the seats in a small auditorium near the music department. The room barely held two hundred; its primary purpose was a gathering place for musicians waiting to go into the larger theater in the academic building. But during the school year, senior-thesis recitals and master classes with visiting professionals served as the primary audiences within its walls.

As people chattered all around her, Carys slipped into one of the seats on the left side, not too far back, but not so close that she'd be conspicuous if she decided to leave. Carys didn't hear the echoes of long-ago concertos and tuned out the voices of classmates who for a few hours this weekend wanted to return to their carefree days of yesteryear.

Despite the comfortable bed at the hotel, she hadn't slept well. To compensate, she'd worked out in the hotel's exercise room early in the morning and spent a few minutes in the sauna in an attempt to rejuvenate her body.

According to the program she'd been handed at the door, T.C. would deliver the message. Maybe listening to him preach could get her spirit rejuvenated. She sure needed it.

She had a lot to be thankful for, namely two terrific children and a grandchild she doted on. She had a fine home—two actually: her primary residence, an architectural wonder in an affluent Northern Virginia enclave of doctors, lawyers and high-level Washington, D.C., politicos; and the other, a waterfront retreat on the Outer Banks in North Carolina that earned hefty rental fees when she and the kids weren't in residence.

Carl had left the homes to the children who immediately after his death signed both pieces of property over to their mother who should have been his heir in the first place.

As the service started, Carys thought about the life she'd spent with Carl. He'd died as he lived—and no one the wiser. It was best that way.

She'd been a good wife to him. She knew because

he always told her so, showering her with gifts of privilege, worthy of their station in life. He withheld the
one thing she wanted however, and that, Carys knew,
was her own fault.

She stared at her hands. She still kept her fingernails
fairly short, rounded in a classic style, today's polish
an elegant but understated pearlescent pink. Keeping
them short had become habit, like so many other things
through the years. Though she would have preferred to
try out the long acrylic nails that were so popular with
a lot of women, they didn't fit in with the image Carl
wanted projected. But the very large emerald-cut diamond and equally glittering anniversary band on her
ring finger did. The rings had been one of his most ex-
travagant gifts, marking their twentieth wedding anniversary. Never mind the fact that Carys would have
preferred gemstones or a simple gold band. He'd presented her with what a successful cardiologist's wife
should have on her finger and that was that.

Carys closed her eyes for a moment. Despite her
gripes, she'd grown to care for Carl—even if they hadn't
been head over heels in love. Some people would say
she had nothing to complain about. They'd shared a
good life together.

But now what?

The program progressed and as the names of the
deceased were called out, Carys found her eyes moist.
When Nate Wade's name was read off the roll, someone, she didn't turn around to see who, patted her on
the shoulder. Maybe it was her imagination, but she felt
the heat of pitying stares before someone coughed and
she shifted in her seat.

As the service leader began a communal prayer of
remembrance for classmates, friends and fellow alumni

who'd passed on to glory, Carys couldn't help but feel deprived and more than a little sorry for herself. For many, this weekend and place held fond and pleasant memories. But for others, like Carys, it brought home the painful truth of being truly, truly alone.

Back when she'd been young and full of dreams that included fairy tales and happily-ever-after endings, she'd daydreamed about T.C. and what it might be like to grow old with him. In the haze known as youthful fancy, she imagined sitting with him, maybe on a front-porch swing watching fireflies chase the tops of wildflowers as the fragrance of magnolias and gardenias on a warm Southern night soothed her into a light doze, cuddled safely and securely in T.C.'s arms.

Of course, in Carys's real world, people didn't have front porches. And if they did, they were the result of an architect's whimsy—they surely weren't used for anything except decoration. Her mother's friends always had something catty and clever to say about people who sat on their front porches watching the world go by. The ladies always laughed at the comments, but to young Carys, the words always seemed cruel, as if they were making fun of people who couldn't do any better financially or defend themselves.

To Carys's way of thinking, it would be really nice to sit on a front-porch swing with T.C. and watch the world go by. But in the world in which she lived as a child and as an adult, outdoor entertaining—and there was a lot of it both then and now—was done poolside at her parents' or on one of the decks off the Georgian-style executive home that Dr. and Mrs. Carlton Shaw and Family called home.

She couldn't say what, exactly, triggered the despair. One moment she sat in the small auditorium with her

classmates and friends, and in the next she found herself overwhelmed with emotion, conflicting ones, but
strong feelings nonetheless about so many things—
what she'd done with her life since graduating college,
where the time went, lost chances, regrets and, over-
laying it all, just how much she missed the comfort of
Carl's presence.

But it was way too late to holler "Do over" and re-
make her life.

Denise Henderson, who used to be a Resident Ad-
viser in the dorm Carys lived in during her junior year,
slipped onto the piano stool behind the service leader,
placed her hands on the keyboard and began playing
the opening bars of "'Tis So Sweet."

"Father God, we come to you today with bowed
heads and humble hearts."

Carys's gaze flew up and to the podium where
T.C. stood. Lost in her thoughts, she hadn't even seen
him approach. Today, his suit was a charcoal double-
breasted one. It, like the one yesterday, fit as if tailored just for him. He held the sides of the lectern as
he prayed.

Standing there, the evidence of his calling showing
in his demeanor, T. C. Holloway looked just as good
as he did twenty-five years ago when they'd graduated.
No, Carys thought, *make that better than he looked at
that time.* He'd been all gangly young man then. She
remembered enjoying the way his rich tenor complemented her soprano when they sang in the college's
gospel choir. They could sing in harmony without even
making an effort to do so.

Thornton concluded the prayer and segued straight
into a hymn. On the piano, Denise didn't miss a beat.
Thornton turned toward Carys and held out a hand as

he sang. She well knew the lyrics. They'd sung them together in the college chapel as soloists in the choir.

She smiled, rose from her seat and walked to the front of the auditorium, her voice lifted in song as if the songwriter wrote the hymn especially for the two of them to sing in harmony.

Thornton held her hand and Carys sang with a joy and liberation she hadn't experienced in a long, long time. When at last, the notes on the piano faded away and applause sounded all around them, Thornton hugged her. Then he held one of her hands high.

"Carys Shaw, everyone," he said by way of quasi-introduction and acclamation.

Beaming and in a far better mood than when she'd entered the auditorium, Carys returned to her seat.

"The preaching moment is here," Thornton said. "I promise I won't keep you as long as I keep my people at New Providence."

"That's okay, Brother Holloway," Joe called out from a seat in the last row. "This is the only church some of these heathens will have all year."

Good-natured laughter greeted that comment.

Knowing it was probably true, Thornton had taken special care preparing the message and meditating on the Scripture.

"This is a reunion, so I don't expect you to have your Bibles with you. But if you do, please turn with me to Psalms 106 and rise for the reading of the Lord's Word."

He read from the first six verses about God's mercy enduring forever, despite the sins and iniquities of people who knew better. After everyone was seated, he began to expand on the text.

"The living God we serve is a God of second chances," Thornton said. "We know that to be true because we're all still sitting here today, right here in this service dedicated to those who've gone on. The Bible cites many occasions where God gave people second chances. Examples of how miracles were worked in the lives of a bunch of people who lived a long time ago. But God's infinite mercy is with us today. Still. This book," he said, holding the Bible high, "is relevant to our times.

"Think back for a moment. Flip through that mental photo album to the snapshots of your life while here on campus or maybe at some later point. Did you ever do something stupid? I mean really stupid."

People in the auditorium laughed and nodded.

"Did you ever do something you full well knew you shouldn't be doing? And it doesn't matter if you're one of those people who never misses a Sunday at church or if you're a C-M-E saint." That earned him more chuckles, mainly from those who were Christmas-Mother's Day-and-Easter churchgoers.

"You probably sent up a prayer or two that went something like this. 'Lord, if you just get me out of this mess I promise that I will…' And here's where we start making deals with God. Can I get a witness?"

Several "Amens" filled the auditorium and a few people raised their hands in testimony.

"You know the kind of deals I'm talking about," Thornton said. "They go something like 'I'll go to church every Sunday, Lord.' Or 'I'll pay my tithes.' Or 'Lord, I'll give You all of my next paycheck if You just get me out of this bind right now.' Or 'If You'll just get him out of this hospital bed, Lord, I'll never speak another ill word about this trifling husband You gave me.'"

People in the Camden College reunion classes hooted at that one.

"We try to bargain and negotiate with God as if we

had any power at all. But you know what?" Thornton said. "God is a mighty good God. He sees through those deals we try to make—good intentions that never see the light of fulfillment. Everybody here knows where that road paved with good intentions leads.

"Despite everything we do, time and again God grants us new mercies, new opportunities to live right, to live just and to give him the praise."

"Preach, pastor!" was called out from somewhere. And an amen corner had taken up residence at Thornton's right.

Carys listened to him, her eyes wide as she sat riveted.

"Too often, though, just as soon as that valley of experience is over, just as soon as the Lord delivers us out of the wilderness, we forget from whence we've come. Just as soon as the tight place gets a little oxygen or those bills are paid or that miracle got worked right in front of your eyes, we are like—" he slapped his hands together "—gone!"

He paused for a moment, making eye contact with several of the people in the audience. "We forget all about God until the next time when we stand before Him begging and pleading and trying to cop a plea bargain before Judgment Day."

Carys realized T.C. had been born to preach. She understood the appeal of his books because she'd read them. Listening to him, though—that was another dimension altogether. He struck a balance between mainline theology and street-corner jive that connected with people. But more than that, he'd hit her on the street where she lived. It was as if T.C. had been inside her head, inside her house.

"God isn't concerned about deals," Thornton said.

"He wants our whole hearts. The new mercies He grants for each of us over and over and over again is all the proof we need that His mercy does endure forever."

How many times had she made deals with God? Insane deals, impossible bargains.

The biggest one concerned Carl. Before she could follow through, he'd died, leaving her adrift and alone and feeling incredibly guilty.

They'd grown apart in the last years of their marriage, but the understanding they'd reached the night he proposed stood between them until the day he died.

He'd left no financial need unmet. And in her own right, Carys had far more money than she'd ever be able to spend. But money couldn't fill the hollow emptiness in her, the secret longing for something more, something of value that would stand the test of both time and personal regrets.

In the middle of Thornton's sermon, Carys found herself crying. It was as if a reservoir of emotion flooded her after a long drought, overflowing the banks of her parched soul, tearing down the walls of her resistance.

As he continued, she reached for her purse intending to find a hankie. But an older woman, maybe about seventy, passed a tissue to her. Carys nodded her thanks and tried to get herself together.

Still sniffling, she listened as T.C. concluded and offered the invitation.

With a pang of both longing and regret, Carys realized she'd missed the nondenominational services she used to attend while in college. But as Carl's medical practice and clientele list grew ever more exclusive, he insisted they become members of a church that catered to the social set comprised of his patients and their friends.

Though her husband didn't know it, Carys maintained her ties with a church she'd found, one that nourished her spirit and operated an outreach ministry to members who'd moved to other areas. Sometimes that covert faith was all that kept her going.

After attending church with Carl and the children, services that always left her vaguely wanting more, Carys spent an hour or so "napping" each Sunday. Only the children knew that mom's naps frequently involved a Bible and a handkerchief to dry the tears she dared not let her husband see.

Now as she watched T.C., all of those things came to mind. Lost opportunities. Abandoned dreams. And most of all, wasted time.

She hadn't realized until just now how much she needed new mercy in her own life…or how much that dream of the front-porch swing had sustained her through the years.

Chapter Four

Thornton found himself in a quandary. Why had Carys cried through the entire sermon? For the first time that he could remember in a long while, he'd been distracted in the pulpit. And it was all because of Carys. Twenty-five years may have passed since graduation, and they'd lived separate lives; yet Carys Chappelle still had the power to make him forget what he wanted to say.

Focusing on the moment, Thornton offered the invitation. "The Lord wants you just the way you are," he told the assembled group. "There's no need to dress up, put on airs or get yourself together before you come. Won't you come to Him now, just as you are?"

He started singing the familiar hymn "Just As I Am." Thornton held out his hands, inviting people to step forward. As his gaze scanned the audience, it connected with Carys's. She was standing, singing along with him.

Thornton smiled at her lilting soprano blending with his tenor. He motioned for her to join him.

A moment later, they stood together at the podium—like old times—each singing from the heart the hymn that Carys had always cherished. The hymn had a special meaning for Thornton, as well. The Peaceful Rest Church choir was singing that song as the invitation when Thornton came forward, giving his heart and his life to the Lord. For many years Peaceful Rest's choir sang straight from the hymnbook. He liked those hymns. A lot. Thornton closed his eyes for a moment, reveling in sweet communion with God.

Carys slipped her hand into his. Thornton looked at her and smiled. Together they completed the verses of the beloved hymn.

"It's been a long time since I heard that hymn," Carys told him later. They were walking across campus to the lot where their cars were parked. "What made you sing that?"

"You did," Thornton told her.

"Me?"

He nodded. "I saw you sitting there and I thought about all those Friday night Vespers services and those Sunday mornings in the chapel. We used to sing and sing and sing. You always loved that song."

"And got teased for liking the oldies," Carys said.

Thornton chuckled. "I remember that. We were all busy adding intricate hand clapping to the latest gospel tune burning up the radio airwaves, and little Carys Chappelle wanted to sing some dried-up hymn from the national songbook." He glanced over at her. "For the record, I always preferred the hymns, as well. Still do."

"I miss those old songs," Carys said. "My church doesn't utilize the hymnbooks very much."

"Mine, either, though my home church back in Texas did all the time. The director of choirs at the church I pastor writes much of what is sung. He's very talented and music is important in a ministry. In some cases, it's what brings people to church."

Carys nodded, remembering how a song could lift her heart, soothe her troubled spirit or mirror the joy she felt deep inside.

They paused for a car to pass on a side street. Thornton steered Carys to the inside walkway as they moved from street to paved sidewalk. She felt his hand at the small of her back. The innocuous connection fueled within her a longing that brought tears to her eyes again.

She tried to wipe them away, but T.C. noticed.

He paused, took her hand in his. "Carys, what's wrong?"

She shook her head. "Nothing."

Carys knew she was acting like an idiot, a weepy, silly idiot. She couldn't very well explain to him that she'd teared up for the umpteenth time today simply because he'd guided her along the sidewalk. But that's just what had happened. His hand at her back was one of the thousand little courtesies that she missed.

"Can I buy you a cup of coffee?"

She nodded.

So instead of heading to their cars, Thornton led her to the campus student center where they ordered coffees and settled at a table away from the heavy flow of student and alumni traffic.

"Why were you crying in service?"

She should have expected the question. The answer,

though, well, that was a tough one. "I've been through a lot in the last few years."

"Want to talk about it?"

She shook her head. "Let's talk about you."

Thornton smiled. "My life is an open book. You know all the backstory. I gave my life to God at Peaceful Rest Church. I came out of Summerset Junior College with an associate's degree, transferred here, got the B.A. Then kept going to school until somebody called me Doctor and put a bunch of letters after my name."

Carys bit back a grin. "Not the résumé. What's been going on with T.C. the man?"

He leaned back in his chair. "T.C.," he said, as if trying the nickname on for size. "No one has called me that for years."

"Would you prefer I call you Thornton?"

He shook his head. "No, Carys. To you, I'll always just be T.C., a country boy."

"You're a long way from the country today."

Reflective, he nodded. "Yes, I suppose so."

"How many children do you have?" she asked him.

"Just one. A beautiful daughter, Lydia. She's responsible for this," he said, touching the gray hair at his temples.

Carys laughed. "I have two and a grandchild. But my kids never gave me problems."

"You must have raised them right."

"I'd like to think so," she said.

"Lydia is a good kid. Sassy. Bright. She takes after her mother. This year, she's a sophomore at the University of Richmond. But she lives on campus, thank goodness."

"And your wife?"

"She died about twelve years ago."

Carys reached for his hand, squeezed it. "I didn't know that, Thornton. I'm so sorry. It must have been difficult for you raising a daughter by yourself."

He nodded. "But I had plenty of help. My mother moved in about four months after Deborah died. I'd just been called to pastor New Providence. It was devastating, and I was having a real hard time adjusting."

"But you never remarried?"

He shook his head. "I've thought about it a time or two. But it was never right. What about you?"

"Get remarried? I don't think so. It's taken me this long to adjust to being a widow. I've always had a rebellious streak. I just didn't realize how suppressed it was until independence was thrust on me."

"How did you lose your husband?"

She told him about Carlton's heart attack, the years they spent together. Carys pulled from her purse photos of her children and granddaughter.

"You barely look old enough to have adult children, let alone a grandchild."

Carys laughed, the sound musical. "Well, bless your heart, T.C. Unfortunately, you and everyone else here knows just how old I am. This is our twenty-fifth reunion year."

They both fell silent for a moment. Carys stirred her coffee with a plastic stirrer that featured Camden's logo on the top. "Where did all of that time go?"

"I think we're all asking the same question this weekend," Thornton said.

"It's not just about reflecting on the past," Carys said. "Regret is mixed up in it, too."

"What do you regret?"

Before Carys could answer, a man's voice boomed over them.

"Well, look who's here. Just like old times, chatting up one of the prettiest girls in the room."

Carys and Thornton looked up to see a couple standing at their table.

Thornton's face broke into a wide grin as he jumped up. "Roscoe Baker! You old reprobate. What are you doing here?"

Thornton and his old buddy clasped hands then shared a bear hug.

"Phyllis?" Carys asked the woman.

The woman's eyes grew wide and a moment later schoolgirl-style squealing echoed in the food court as the two women hugged each other.

Thornton pulled two additional chairs over and the four eventually sat down.

"Carys, this is an old pal of mine from my junior college days at Summerset. He's a good ol' Texas boy, Roscoe Baker."

"And this," Carys said after shaking Roscoe's hand, "is Phyllis Taylor. We lived in the same hall in our freshman and junior years."

"What are you doing here, man?" Thornton asked.

Roscoe draped an arm across Phyllis's shoulder. "The wife's twenty-fifth. Couldn't miss that."

Thornton looked at Phyllis. "You married him?"

She nodded. "Twenty years next month."

"You have my sympathy." Thornton said it with a straight face, but couldn't maintain the somber look. He and Roscoe chuckled.

"Men," Phyllis said, shaking her head at Carys. "So, I didn't know you two hooked up."

"We ran into each other at the opening reception," Carys said, understanding what Phyllis meant and deliberately answering the unspoken question another way. "I hadn't seen T.C. in years."

Phyllis glanced between them. She quickly shielded a vaguely disappointed look. "You know, I always thought you two—"

"So where do you guys live?" Thornton asked as they all settled at the table.

Carys saw Phyllis lift a brow at the quickly changed subject.

"My daughter and I live in Richmond," Thornton said.

Roscoe nudged his wife. "Watch what you say around this one, Phyl. He's posing as a big-time preacher these days."

Phyllis rolled her eyes at her husband. "He's the one who needs to find some church," she said, indicating Roscoe. "I, on the other hand, have two of your books. I wish I'd known you'd be here. I could have gotten an autograph."

"Don't go pestering the man, honey. We're right outside Dallas," Roscoe said, answering the initial question.

"So you did go home," Thornton said to his old friend.

"Family duty called."

"You wouldn't know it to look at him, Carys, but that's a bonafide cowboy sitting across from you."

"I gave up the spurs a long time ago. Now I'm an innkeeper."

Phyllis waved a hand. "Pay him no mind," she said, leaning forward, her elbows on the table. "We run a small chain of dude ranches. We get a lot of tourist business."

While the couples continued to talk, the noise level

in the food court area grew louder as more and more returning alumni found their way to the campus student center.

Several people drifted to the table where Thornton and Carys seemed to be holding court. Stories were swapped about the good old days and then over the sound system that had been piping easy-listening jazz throughout the center, someone recognized a tune that had been a favorite during their college years.

A woman who'd been a lead alto in the gospel choir started humming, then picked up the lyrics. Someone else joined in and before long, they were all harmonizing.

"Remember when we did that arrangement of 'Just A Closer Walk with Thee'?" someone asked.

"Oh, man. That song just does something to me," Phyllis said.

Thornton, who'd been one of the campus choir's student directors, stood up. "Where are my altos?"

Several women in the group of about twelve rose their hands.

"And the sopranos?"

"Sopranos in the house," Carys said on a laugh as she got up and joined three other women who sang that part.

"Men, do we have any bass or is everybody tenor?"

"I can handle it if you show me the way," Roscoe said, deliberately deepening his voice.

"All right, now. On my count," Thornton said as he tapped out the beat to the jazzed-up arrangement of the standard hymn.

When he lifted his arms and cued the altos it was as if years fell away from each person present. They were no longer middle-aged parents or grandparents back for a weekend to relive their youth. They were young—at heart and in spirit.

As the impromptu choir sang, people in the student center gathered around them until an audience of about seventy people formed a U around the original table where Carys and Thornton had been sitting.

Following Thornton's direction, the choir brought the song to a close. Applause rippled through the food court area and several people high-fived each other.

"Just like old times!" somebody called out.

"I think that sounded better than old times," Carys said.

Joe Holmes, the former football star, came up and slapped Thornton on the back. "Ya'll ought to do a concert before we leave."

"What a great idea!" Phyllis said. "T.C., you want to direct?"

He glanced at Carys. "Well, I don't think…"

She nodded. "We could sing at the banquet."

"Yeah," Phyllis added. "They said they wanted the classes to participate in the program."

Under the force of bobbing heads and enthusiastic smiles, Thornton relented and the Alumni Gospel Choir was born.

"All right," he said. "Who's up for doing a miniconcert, maybe just two or three numbers?"

All of the hands shot up. Thornton laughed. "Well, it looks like we have an alumni choir."

"Do we have to rehearse today? I'm headed out on a tour soon," somebody called out.

"Rehearse right now," Joe said. "This ain't the Kennedy Center or Carnegie Hall."

Applause greeted that suggestion. Thornton looked at his so-called choir, spotted Alatrice who used to bring the house down with her deeply moving rendition of Negro spirituals. "Alatrice, Roscoe and Carys."

The two women, knowing exactly what he was thinking, grinned and came forward.

"Now wait a minute," Roscoe said, holding his hands up to stave off being volunteered for something. "I didn't even go to this college. Don't put me in the middle of this."

"Come on, man. Be a sport," Thornton said. "I can do the tenor part. We need a bass. Besides, you know how to do this. Remember when Brother Jefferson at Peaceful Rest used to testify about growing up a share-cropper? Then he'd break into that deep voice singing about troubled times."

Roscoe grinned. Then he did an imitation of the old deacon, lowering his head and stomping his foot while the onlookers smiled.

"We had a deacon like that at our church," some-one said.

"Can we count on you?" Thornton asked him.

In answer, Roscoe sang a verse. The impromptu choir applauded.

A moment later, Thornton tapped off a slow, steady beat. "All right, follow my lead."

Foot tapping filled the room and the four led the choir in a soul-stirring medley of spirituals.

Later, with the choir's plan in place and arrangements made for one more "rehearsal," Carys and Thornton finally made it to their initial destination, the parking lot.

"The class picnics will be starting soon," Thornton said. "Were you planning to go?"

"My sorority is sponsoring it."

"That's too bad," Thornton said.

She raised an eyebrow. "That the sorority is in charge?"

A smile tilted his mouth. "No, that you're not available."

Their gazes met and held. Carys's breath caught. Was she supposed to infer another meaning to his comment? Whether intentional or not, she'd picked up on something besides a conversation about the alumni reunion picnic.

"About last night…" she started.

Thornton reached for her hand. "It was my fault," he said. He traced the hairline of her face, tucking in a stray curl. "Let's really catch up."

Carys closed her eyes for a moment, reveling in his gentle touch. Then the reality of the moment caught up with her. She was a widow with a grandchild. He was one of the nation's most prominent preachers. What they'd shared twenty-five years ago couldn't be replicated now. Could it?

"Catch up on what?" she asked him.

"How I let the woman I loved get away from me."

Chapter Five

Thornton wasn't sure who was more surprised at his words, Carys or himself. They'd sprung from a place deep inside, a place that recognized though he'd loved his wife with all his being, he still had room there for this lovely woman, someone he'd never really stopped loving.

He realized that the atmosphere, being on the campus again, reliving old memories, finding Carys widowed—and therefore available?—all contributed to the complexity of emotions ricocheting through him. He wasn't the gangly kid he'd been all those years ago. He could ask a woman out without getting tongue-tied and sweaty palms.

At least he hoped that was the case.

Instead of playing coy with him, Carys laughed. Which confused him.

"T.C., you sly dog. It's always the quiet ones."

His confusion must have shown on his face.

"All right," she said. "I'll play hooky with you from the picnic if you promise to tell me who the mystery woman was."

Thornton's brow furrowed. "Mystery woman?"

She nodded. "The one you loved and let get away."

Was she serious or pulling his leg?

Not too much later, they settled in at a booth at a restaurant near the campus.

"You were that woman, Carys," he told her. "I think I fell for you the moment I saw you."

Stunned, Carys stared at him. A thousand different thoughts rushed through her head, chief among them the what-ifs. What if she'd been strong enough to defy her parents and marry T.C. or someone like him? What might the last two decades have been like? What if, what if, what if?

"You never let on," she said, her tone almost accusing. "You never said anything."

"What was I supposed to say? I had little to offer a woman like you."

"What do you mean, a woman like me?"

He reached for sweetener to add to his iced tea. "You were wealthy, a campus queen. I was a country boy who'd transferred in from a junior college few people around here had ever even heard of. I didn't run with the right cliques. Stood no chance of even being accepted into them."

"But you were the sweetest guy I knew. I could always come to you with my problems."

Thornton nodded. "Even then I think my calling as a counselor and minister was evident, though I didn't know it."

Considering who she'd been at that time, Carys nodded. "You know, you're probably right. I wouldn't have been receptive to you then. I was too afraid of rocking the boat in my family. That's why I married Carl."

"Tell me about him."

Carys took a deep breath and leaned back. She closed her eyes for a moment. "There's not much to tell. He was a man like my father. A surgeon. Prominent. Wealthy. Domineering."

"He hurt you?"

She shook her head. "No. In our relationship, I did the hurting."

"What do you mean?"

"I didn't love him," she said. "Not the way I should have." She picked up her fork and moved lettuce and a cherry tomato around on her plate. "That's the only thing he ever wanted from me—for me to be in love with him. I never gave him my heart."

Thornton's gaze met hers. "Why?"

Carys's eyes filled with tears. "I don't know. It just wasn't in me, I suppose."

He reached in his jacket pocket, pulled out a handkerchief and pressed it into her hand. "I didn't mean to make you cry."

She shook her head. "You didn't." But she wiped at her eyes anyway. "I've been nothing but a leaky faucet since the moment I got here. Too many memories, I guess. Being here, seeing everybody again gives me too many moments to wonder what-if. Twenty-five years, T.C. It's been twenty-five years. Where did the time go?"

"It went into raising your kids, into living each moment to the best of your ability at any given time," he said. "There's no reason to look back with regret."

"What about you?" Carys asked as she folded his handkerchief. "Is there anything you regret about the time spent since graduating?"

He shook his head. "Every step of the way, for better or for worse, led me here. I can't regret that."

Carys smiled. "You're still a philosopher."

"No, just a realist."

Their server appeared at the table and refilled their iced tea glasses. "Can I take these away?" Neither had put a dent on the large salads before them. "Would you like a couple of boxes?"

After looking to Carys who shook her head, Thornton said, "No, but thank you."

"You know what I would like, though?" Carys said.

"What's that?"

"Dessert."

The server laughed. "You barely touched your meal, but you want dessert? I like your style! The house specialty is a hot fudge double-brownie sundae made especially for sharing."

"Up to you," Thornton said.

"Sounds decadent," Carys said. "We'll take it."

While they waited for the brownie to bake, Carys asked him about his ministry.

"Shortly after I was called to be senior pastor at New Providence, my wife died. Talk about being adrift and without a raft. My new church family was incredibly supportive, but there I was with this baby girl and no idea how to raise her."

"What'd you do?"

"Hollered for Mama," Thornton said on a laugh. "My mother came to live with me, to take care of Lydia while I worked and ministered. Before long, I'd established a pattern, a way of coping with both the grief and my loneliness."

"That's the hardest part," Carys said. "The being alone. But it's also the most liberating, at least in my opinion. Why didn't you ever remarry?"

He shrugged. "I didn't have time. My ministry took off. The church grew from two hundred members to twelve hundred, then a couple of thousand. Today, there are about four thousand members. We do three services every Sunday and offer support ministries to both members and people in the community."

"And you write books."

Thornton smiled. "And lead seminars and maintain a full travel schedule."

"I guess that doesn't leave time for much else."

"And that is exactly what my problem is," he told her. "I keep my calendar jammed so I don't have to face the truth."

"What truth?"

"That I've tried to fill the emptiness with busyness."

Shaking her head slightly, Carys must have looked as bemused as she felt.

"What?" he inquired.

"None of it shows," she said. "I saw you on television once. I've read your books. You must do a lot of hiding behind facades."

"I don't hide my emotions," Thornton said. "At least I don't think so. Whenever I'm going through something, it comes out. The Lord works on preachers just like he works on everybody else. I have my own issues. Like most people, some are private. Others are public."

"Well, it's pretty easy to see when I'm an emotional wreck," Carys said. "It shows here," she said, lightly touching the area near her eyes. "And here," she said as she placed a hand over her heart. "I used to carry a song in my heart."

"What's there now?"

She smiled and it was like old times, baring her heart and boyfriend troubles to T.C. "Before I arrived on campus this weekend there was nothing but a hollow emptiness there, like a bass drum cylinder without the membrane to give it sound."

"And now?"

She smiled at him. "Now I hear humming, like the gently swelling melody of a forgotten love song."

Both the moment and her words carried an expectant note. The voices of other diners and the muted clink of silver on china faded to nothing when Thornton gazed into her eyes.

He leaned forward. So did she.

His hand covered hers. Carys's gaze dipped to the joining, then returned to his face.

"Carys."

"Yes, T.C.?"

"I've missed you so much."

She smiled. "I've missed you, too."

"Carys?"

"Yes?"

"Do you know what I want to do?"

"Yes," she said.

"Do you mind?"

"Stop talking, T.C."

When his lips covered hers, it was like a soft rain on a spring day, like coming home after a long absence. The kiss was meant to be.

She lifted her hand, caressed his face. He captured her hand and squeezed it.

"I didn't have the nerve to kiss you when I was

nineteen going on twenty. I've always wondered what I missed out on."

"And now that you know?"

He grinned. "Better than expected."

Her answering laugh eased the tension a bit. "You're a mess, T.C."

"And you're still as beautiful as the day I met you."

Three tables away, two women craned their necks trying to see what was happening at Carys and Thornton's table.

"I'm telling you, that is Pastor Holloway over there."

"Move over some. Let me see. If he's kissing on someone, it ought to be Melva."

"Well, unless Melva has lost about thirty pounds, put some extensions in her hair and started looking and dressing like she's headed to a country club, I'd say that's not her."

"Ooh, where's my cell phone?" the other woman said as she reached for her purse. "Just wait till I tell Gloria about this."

"Well, I think it's nice," her companion said.

"You think it's nice that he's stepping out on Melva?"

The woman chuckled, but the sound wasn't amused. "No, I think it's nice that we finally have some proof that Dr. Thornton Holloway is human like all the rest of us."

Kissing T.C.—Thornton—had seemed so right, their time together had been filled with laughter and light and had ended with a kiss that held sweet promise.

Now, however, Carys felt conflicted. She'd hoped that attending the reunion would enable her to disengage from some of the emptiness she'd been feeling lately.

But instead of getting her head and her act together, she was making herself more confused. She'd hoped that in returning to the place where she'd made decisions that affected her entire life, she might find a new clarity, a new beginning for this second part of her life. What she'd stumbled into, though, were all of the not quite forgotten fragments of her youth. A youth spent subjugating her own dreams while being the obedient young woman and wife.

She was forty-seven years old. Wasn't that old enough to start living for herself?

"I hope that dreamy look in your eyes was put there by a man. Maybe T. C. Holloway?"

Lynn's remark jerked Carys out of her reverie. The sorority sisters were at a tea with the younger members of the organization. Having had a full lunch with Thornton, one that consisted primarily of a rich chocolate brownie and homemade vanilla ice cream, Carys didn't touch the finger sandwiches or petit fours, but did sip at a cup of tea.

She reached for that cup now. "Don't be ridiculous."

"Um-hmm," Lynn said with a knowing smirk. "I didn't see you at the picnic."

Carys glanced at her friend, then looked to her left and right to make sure no one was listening. "All right," she whispered. "T.C. and I left and had lunch together. No big deal."

"No big deal?" Lynn's voice carried so loud that several people turned toward them.

"Shh," Carys shushed her.

Lynn leaned toward Carys, her voice low. "No big deal? You two were made for each other."

Carys rolled her eyes as Lynn turned her attention to the speaker. "Shh."

She was trying to sort out her burgeoning, not to mention complicated, feelings about T.C. There had always been an attraction between them. She didn't need or want Lynn to point out something that now, in hindsight, seemed so obvious. But she wouldn't trade the journey she'd ultimately taken—at least not most of it. She'd had a decent life, a pampered life. And she also had two terrific kids who'd never caused her any of the heartache that some of her friends' children caused them.

The only problem with Carys was Carys—her perception of what she'd spent the time since college doing. And perception, she knew, was just as, if not more powerful than, reality.

Carl had been gone for more than a year now. She knew women whose husbands were barely in the grave before they'd started dating again with remarriage the goal and as soon as possible.

For Carys, it wasn't so much a matter of time as it was degree. She'd spent two decades of her life being Mrs. Carlton Shaw. And before that she'd been Carys Chappelle, daughter of Dr. and Mrs. Chappelle. For her entire life she'd accepted and worn labels put on by other people. For the first time, she felt as if she were finally—at long, long last—coming into her own.

She was enjoying just being Carys.

Then T.C. showed up wreaking havoc in her carefully controlled and modulated world.

She wasn't naive enough to think that a few songs and a kiss during a weekend fraught with reminiscences of how it used to be and what might have been equated with a long-term future or walking down the aisle with T.C. But just being here, thrust into an environment that made her question her own independence, was enough to send Carys running home to her big empty house.

What might it be like to live in a small one- or two-bedroom apartment? A condo that she'd picked out all by herself just for herself or maybe even a town house with an extensive flower garden that she maintained—without the assistance of professional landscapers?

Those were the types of thoughts that had crowded her mind in recent months. Now, though, she found herself questioning even those desires. A favorite Scripture from her college days came to mind: "Delight thyself also in the Lord, and He shall give thee the desires of thine heart."

What did her heart desire? To sing a new song? One of joy and peace and everlasting love? Or did she, at least for now, need to continue on the lonesome and sometimes wretched road with her soul crying out for mercy, for sustenance?

Carys closed her eyes for a moment, praying a jumbled prayer, not quite sure what, exactly, she sought entreaty for from the Lord.

"Carys?"

Her eyes popped open. "What?"

"Get up there," Lynn prompted. "They're trying to honor you."

She glanced around. "Honor me? For what?"

"A service award," Lynn said. "Go on."

Slowly, the faces of the women around her registered on Carys—sorority sisters of all ages, from newly pledged undergrads to sorors in the emeritus class who'd graduated from the college more than fifty years ago. Many of those faces looked expectedly upon her now.

"Go on," Lynn urged.

Putting aside her thoughts of Thornton, Carys rose

to applause from the group. The sound swelled, carrying her to the podium where the presiding soror waited.

This was something she knew how to do—put on the gracious public face she'd learned to wear as the wife of a prominent surgeon. A moment later, though, a genuine smile emerged when she was presented with the sorority's Alumna of the Year award.

"For your tireless support for and mentoring of young women," the senior sorority sister said.

Accepting the engraved plaque, Carys shook her head. "This doesn't belong to me," she told the ladies assembled for the tea. "It belongs to all of you, all of you who have ever taken a moment of your day to offer assistance to someone in need. That half an hour or hour you spent meant the world to someone. All I've done is make sure that the steps I take leave a path for someone to follow."

She then told them the story about a young single mom she'd met who was working at a dry cleaner's and the young woman's struggle to succeed despite the odds stacked against her. "What she needed," Carys said, "was an opportunity." As she finished, she called out several of the volunteers she'd worked with throughout the year, highlighting each woman's work or sacrifice with a mentoring program that helped women like the one who worked at the dry cleaner's. "These are the ladies who should be receiving this award today," she said. "I'm honored to be standing here representing them."

After thanking the committee and assorted officials, Carys made her way back to her seat where she got a hug from Lynn.

"That was excellent," Lynn said, wiping her eyes. "Just excellent."

"Why are you crying?"

Lynn just shook her head.

Carys accepted congratulations from her tablemates, who also dabbed at their eyes. "What happened?"

Lynn laughed. "See, I told you all," she told the other six women. "She doesn't even realize she got the whole room choked up."

Carys glanced around, spying several women who discreetly touched tissues or hankies to their eyes. She then leaned toward Lynn. "What did I say?"

"My friend, you have no idea how many lives you touch just by being you."

After the tea, Carys found herself surrounded by people offering well wishes and congratulatory hugs. A young woman approached from the side.

"Mrs. Shaw?"

"Yes?"

The girl took both of Carys's hands in hers and pumped them in a double handshake. "I never thought I'd ever meet you. I got the impression, well, we all did, that the woman behind the Opportunity Fund was old or dead."

That earned her a laugh from Lynn and Carys. "Sometimes we feel like it," Lynn said.

"Speak for yourself," Carys said. "Where are you from?"

"Florida. A little town no one's ever heard of in the Panhandle. My name's Diana," she said. "And I just wanted to thank you. If it weren't for you, I wouldn't be here. There was no way my family could have afforded this college or any other one and my high school grades weren't good enough for me to earn any scholarship money."

"And how are your grades now?" Carys asked the student.

Diana beamed. "Dean's list every term."

"Good for you!"

"I'm a business major with a minor in ethics and philosophy. I want to be a lawyer."

"I like to keep up with the Opportunity Fund students, so will you let me know how you're doing and when it's time for you to graduate?"

The girl nodded. "I will."

After a hug, Carys turned back to Lynn who was watching her with undisguised glee.

"What?"

"I always wondered," Lynn said.

"Wondered what?"

"Just what you did with all that trust fund money. You started the Opportunity Fund didn't you?"

Carys shrugged. "Maybe." When she felt Lynn's gaze still on her, Carys huffed. "What else was I going to do with it?"

Lynn's answering grin was a reward. "Most people would have spent it on themselves or on expensive toys."

"I'm not most people," Carys said, wondering why she was feeling oddly picked upon.

As she tucked her arm in Carys's, Lynn told her, "You always did know how to get things done quietly and effectively, without turning on the spotlight."

Carys eyed her friend then looked at the plaque she'd been given by the sorority. "You're the one who ratted me out to the Alumni of the Year committee."

Lynn tried to look innocent. "I wouldn't know anything about that."

Chapter Six

Later that afternoon, Carys ran into Thornton at the college's museum and galleries. A special exhibit featuring the work of a celebrated artist who as also an alumna of the school was on display. Along with visitors and other returning alumni, they roamed the exhibition rooms. Carys and Thornton paused at a series illustrating families in worship.

Considering the first painting in the series, Thornton glanced at Carys. "Do you know the reason I never missed a Friday night chapel service?"

"Because you enjoyed the fellowship?"

Thornton shook his head. "Because there was always a chance I would hear you sing."

That made Carys laugh. "Well, you must have been sorely disappointed on many a Friday night since I spent most of my junior and senior year being a socialite. Looking back, I can see that my priorities were all mixed up. I was completely absorbed in Nate and parties."

"That's not true," Thornton said. "You were at Friday Fellowship more than a lot of people."

Conceding the point, Carys nodded. "I liked to sing."

"Past tense?"

"Well, there hasn't been a lot of opportunity lately."

"Are there a lot of soloists at your church?" he asked.

She shrugged. "Not anymore than I suppose any church has. Carl wasn't really big on me singing."

"Why?"

Carys stood there for a moment considering his question as she studied an image of a mother opening a hymnbook for a child. "I don't know," she said, her voice low, her tone contemplative. But soon came the realization that she did know, the reason obvious now that Carl was gone. She blinked and swallowed hard, determined not to shed another tear during the weekend of self-reflection.

Thornton reached for her hand. "What is it? Is something wrong?"

Carys shook her head. "Look at how reverent they are," she said, pointing out details in the painting. "Here in the faces, the eyes. And right there, look at the way the artist used light and shadow to highlight the sense of wonder and devotion in the girl's expression." Carys glanced over at Thornton. "Singing was something I loved." She said the words slowly, as if realizing for the first time how much music meant to her.

"Yes. I know." He reached in his suit jacket pocket and pulled out a freshly laundered handkerchief.

The edges of her mouth turned up. "You keep a steady supply of these just for me?"

He smiled. "Just in case." His concern, however, remained evident to her. "Carys?"

"I'm not going to start crying again." But she took a deep breath then faced the sorry truth about her years of marriage with Carl. "It was, I suppose, a sort of childish game we played. Carl's retribution."

"For what?"

The kindness and concern in Thornton's eyes seared her. She'd married a man she didn't love and paid for it every day of her marriage. Carl's request seemed so reasonable, especially given their children's hectic schedules and the myriad social and civic obligations that required the support or presence of Dr. and Mrs. Shaw.

Later on, Carl's refusal to let her sing in the choir had seemed puzzling, churlish even. Now, however, she understood. Too late, she understood. Boy, what a succession of revelations this weekend was presenting.

"We stayed together because it worked, like a habit you get used to," Carys told Thornton. "I loved singing, but Carl didn't want me to spend the time away from the children in order to attend choir rehearsals."

She shook her head as she realized the insidiousness of their constant game of polite one-upmanship. "I'm embarrassed now that I've figured it out," she told him.

"Would you rather talk about something else?"

"Yes," Carys said. It was too depressing to comprehend that Carl had withheld music from her the way she'd withheld her love from him. She'd cared for him, of course. But she'd never truly been deeply, madly or head-over-heels in love with her husband.

They continued their stroll through the exhibit, leaving the family-in-worship displays and heading to a permanent gallery where the vibrant colors of the abstract paintings looked as disjointed to Carys as she herself felt.

Yes, indeed, she thought. Changing the subject was a grand idea.

"Your sermon about new mercy has really had me thinking about how much mercy and grace have sustained me through the years," she told him. "How does that work?"

"How does mercy work?"

Carys smiled. "That part I understand. I mean putting a sermon together, a sermon that speaks to the hearts of so many individuals all at the same time? How do you know what people need to hear?"

"I don't," Thornton told her. "But the Holy Spirit does. I'm just the vessel God uses to get his message to his people. It's a lot like that painting back there," he said indicating the gallery they'd just left. "The artist had a vision, something she needed to bring to life on canvas. Artists don't know how their work will be received or if people will get it. They just paint. Some people will receive the message the way the artist envisioned. Others will misinterpret it. But it's not really a misinterpretation if they are bringing to their viewing of the painting their own experiences, then filtering that experience through the images on canvas until the piece has personal relevance."

Carys considered both the man and his words. "I've never heard a painting be compared to a sermon before. That's a different perspective. But I see what you mean. The mother and child piece we were looking at back there really touched me."

Thornton nodded. "Because you found personal relevance in the artist's statement."

Walking over to a large piece of sculpture in the abstract gallery, Carys sent a saucy smile over her shoulder. "This, on the other hand, doesn't do anything for me."

The six-foot tall sculpture featured tennis-ball sized globs of marble climbing up three sides.

Joining Carys, Thornton peered at the piece then read the small placard. "The artist is Pablo Diego Muñoz. He calls it 'Celebration.'"

"Hmm, more like abomination," Carys muttered as she rounded the art, looking for relevance. She couldn't find any.

"I'm sure he was following a vision," Thornton said. "It will speak to someone."

"If you say so," Carys answered while shaking her head. She strolled over to study the paintings in the room. When she felt Thornton beside her, she picked up their earlier thread of discussion. "How do you just, you know, pull words out of the air?"

He chuckled. "It's not quite like that, though it may seem like it sometimes. There's a lot of preparation that goes into a sermon."

"Like what?"

He raised an eyebrow. "You're really interested in this?"

"I'm interested in everything about you, T.C."

The air stilled between them. Carys held his gaze. Thornton didn't blink or flinch. After what seemed like forever, he smiled, breaking the tension, easing the moment.

"I think you're flirting with me."

It was Carys's turn to smile. "And if I am?"

"I like it."

He held his hand out to her. Carys clasped it and together they completed the circuit of exhibition rooms while Thornton told her how he prepared his messages.

Emerging from the museum, they stood together on the sidewalk. Thornton acknowledged several people who waved or greeted him.

"What are you doing this coming week?" he asked Carys.

She shrugged. "Not much. I need to make appointments to have the pool serviced and the decks treated." How pathetic was that? she wondered even as she told him. She'd lived her entire adult life as window dressing and had nothing to occupy her time except maintenance of the things beyond the view of the window.

"So nothing pressing?" Thornton said.

"No. Not really. Why do you ask?"

Thornton took her hand in his. "Spend the week with me."

"Excuse me?"

The tone, she knew, probably sounded as if it belonged to the regal and pampered princess she'd played while in college. But Carys didn't know what to make of his proposition. She was old enough and wise enough to know when she was being propositioned. That it came from Thornton Holloway— the Reverend Doctor Thornton Holloway—is what stunned her.

But Thornton didn't seem in the least bit fazed. "Stay here," he said. "Let's spend some time together."

"But…I… You… I can't do that."

"You just told me you had nothing urgent waiting at home. Why not spend a week of leisure with an old friend?"

Carys opened her mouth, closed it. Opened it again. "I know I ran a little wild and free back when we were in college, but that was then, T.C. I'm a different woman than I was then. And you, you're a preacher!"

He nodded. "Yes. And what does that have to do with anything?"

Carys shook her head as if to clear it. "You must practice some kind of newfangled religion. I'll have none of it, thank you very much. I have enough on my conscience already without adding a—" she circled her hand around, trying in vain to come up with a word to describe what he was proposing they spend the week doing "—without adding a…a dalliance to my list of sins."

"A dalliance?" For a moment Thornton looked genuinely confused. Then he let out a chuckle.

"That's not what I was talking about when I said we should spend the week together."

She eyed him, suspicion clouding her brow. "What then?"

He reached for her hand, placed it in his and closed his other palm over her hand. "Just what I said. Getting to know you again. I knew a girl named Carys Chappelle. I'd like to get acquainted with the woman Carys Shaw. I have another week of vacation. I'd planned to do nothing but kick back and relax the entire time. But seeing you, being with you this weekend made me realize I'd rather spend the time renewing our friendship."

"Friendship?"

Carys's thoughts about Thornton had been a little more than of the "just friends" variety. She wanted to believe that God had a reason for leading her here this weekend. Could it be so she could reconnect with T.C.?

"Friendship," Thornton repeated. "You could extend your stay at your hotel. We can go to the movies, pick strawberries…."

"Pick strawberries?"

He nodded. "I saw an ad in the newspaper at my hotel. If you don't like that idea, we could drive to the beach."

Shaking her head, Carys rejected that suggestion. "I didn't bring a bathing suit."

"That's why they have malls."

Carys looked at him, really looked at him. Thornton inspired in her a confidence she hadn't felt in a long time. He also stirred within her the hopes and dreams of a time gone by. Would it be so wrong to explore the feelings provoked by this reunion weekend?

In many ways, she figured, it would be a lot like going on a fishing expedition. If she caught something, fine. If not, she'd spend a little time out in the sun, enjoying the process and the progression of the day.

"It'll be like playing hooky from life," she said. "Like we've been doing all weekend."

Thornton smiled and nodded, agreeing with her. "Yes, like playing hooky from life."

Back in her hotel room, Carys made arrangements to stay an additional week, then called her children.

"That sounds great," Sharon said after Carys told her daughter her plans. "Hold on a sec while I tell Trey. He's over here for dinner."

Carys could hear Sharon filling her brother in on the news. A moment later, Trey, so called because he was Carlton Shaw III, picked up an extension.

"Hi, Mom. We were hoping you'd hook up with some friends and take a vacation."

Carys raised an elegantly arched brow. "Are you two saying I need to get a life?"

"Yes!" their voices echoed from the receiver.

"What if I'm hooking up with a man?"

"All the better," Trey said.

"Are you?" came Sharon's quiet entreaty.

Carys figured this was something she'd keep to herself for now. "I've run into some old friends."

"Well, good for you," Trey said. "Hey, sis, I think the steaks are burning. I want mine medium, not charred."

"And something's wrong with your hands?"

"Hey, I'm the dinner guest," Trey said.

Carys laughed at the byplay between her offspring. It had always been that way. Sharon, two years older, was cautious about some things but could give her brother what-for when the occasion warranted.

"Gotta go, Mom. Apparently, if I want to eat in this house, I also have to cook."

"You take care, Trey." After he clicked off the line, Carys asked her daughter, "Where's my baby?"

"We were out of salad dressing so Michael ran down to the grocery store, and you know where Daddy goes, his little girl is with him."

Carys smiled. She doted on the granddaughter who was her namesake. Following a few more minutes of chitchat and the advice from her daughter to "live it up," Carys said her goodbyes.

The ramifications and doubts began to assail Carys just as soon as she got off the telephone. She stared at the phone and then turned and looked unseeingly over her sitting room.

"What have I done?"

That night, with Thornton directing and solos presented from both Carys and Alatrice, the alumni choir brought down the house at the gala and banquet.

"For a group with half a rehearsal under our belts,

that wasn't bad," Phyllis said. She and Roscoe were at the same table as Carys and Thornton. Lynn and her husband were also there, along with two sisters from the emeritus class who rounded out the table of eight.

"I think it's time for the little girls' room," Lynn said.

Roscoe nudged Thornton and groaned. "Here we go, brothers. It's time for the dissection."

The men grumbled good-naturedly as they rose when the ladies did. Phyllis gave her husband a peck on the cheek. "We only talk about you because we love you."

As Carys, Lynn and Phyllis picked up their small handbags, one of the sisters peered at Thornton from across the table. "Aren't you that preacher from TV?"

Carys wondered how he'd respond, but Lynn and Phyllis both tugged her along.

"Let him do his fan thing. We need to talk to you," Lynn declared.

In the ladies' room, Carys didn't stand a chance against the dual onslaught of her college friends.

"So, what's the deal with you and T.C.? You two have been joined at the hip this weekend."

"And several people commented on the disappearing act you pulled at the picnic today."

"Must my life be under a microscope?" Carys asked on a long-suffering sigh.

"Yes," Lynn said.

"I thought we were beyond and above all that."

"Think again," Phyllis said, with a grin tossed in Lynn's direction.

Lynn pulled out a compact and touched up her makeup. "Go ahead now. We're waiting. Spill all the juicy details."

"There are no details," Carys said. "Juicy or otherwise."

The two antagonizers eyed each other. "You know he's always had a thing for you," Lynn said.

"That's right," Phyllis added. "Back when, a lot of us thought you should dump Nate and go with T.C."

"Yeah, right," Carys said. "As if anyone would have advocated I choose the shy and impoverished country boy over the captain of the football team and heir to a fortune."

"T.C. is rich now," Lynn pointed out as she applied lipstick to her mouth. "His church is big, not as large as some of the megachurches in D.C. or Dallas, but pretty big nonetheless, several thousand members. And he writes those books you're always reading."

"And your point would be...?"

"You're single," Phyllis said slowly as if explaining a quantum physics concept to a toddler. "He's single. You like each other. Always have. You do the math."

"There's no math to do," Carys said.

Even as she protested, though, Carys wondered why she was resisting this. It's not as if she were again twenty years old and concerned about what people might think. She was her own woman now. Right?

"I think you two are reading way more into this than the situation warrants," Carys added.

She unsnapped her handbag and plucked out a tube of coral lipstick that matched her dress.

"So you don't deny it?"

"Deny what?" Carys said as she jockeyed for a position in front of the mirror.

"That T. C. Holloway still has a thing for you."

"Aren't we a little old to be talking about 'having a thing for someone'?" Carys said, adding air quotes around her so-called friend's words.

"You might be old, sister," Lynn said. "But my best years are in front of me."

"That's right," Phyllis concurred. "I'm looking forward to fifty. I'll finally be a grown-up."

Both Lynn and Carys chuckled at that. But Carys wasn't yet embracing the idea of fifty. While it was still three years off, only now did she feel as if she were coming into her own. If fifty meant the downslide had started, she didn't like the idea of having wasted her youth.

But it wasn't wasted. She had two beautiful children. A delightful granddaughter. And for better or worse, she and Carl had made a comfortable home together.

Comfortable.

Dull. Predictable, even in its myriad complexities.

"We only get so many shots at happiness, Carys. It would be a shame to blow this one because you're afraid."

Carys blinked, wondering when Lynn had managed to turn so insightful. Normally, she could count on her friend to point out the lighter, more flirtatious side of life. Carys didn't even try to deny—to herself at least—that her feelings included a measure of trepidation. And her girlfriends didn't even know about the week she'd tentatively planned with Thornton.

"I'll try not to," she said.

"What's that saying about trying?" Phyllis asked.

"All right," Carys said on a huff. "If this is a golden opportunity…"

"For something wonderful with T.C.," Lynn interjected.

"For something wonderful with Thornton," Carys parroted. "I won't blow the opportunity."

"Opportunity for what?" Lynn pressed.

Carys looked at each girlfriend, then clasped their hands in hers. "For happiness," she said.

It was well after two in the morning by the time Carys got back to her hotel. After the banquet and festivities, a group of the reunion class members went to the waterfront to cast stones into the lake, a tradition begun at the college so long ago that no one knew exactly why it was done.

After sleeping in late the next morning, Thornton buzzed her suite at eleven. It had been a great reunion weekend she thought as she checked her lipstick before going downstairs. Saying goodbye to old friends and new ones was difficult. But they'd all keep in touch this time, Carys knew.

Carys, dressed in a summer Capri set and sandals, met him in the lobby. Thornton was also casually dressed in khaki slacks and a Polo shirt. "Are you ready for day one of our adventure?"

"As ready as I'm going to get."

Even to her own ears, Carys realized her words didn't carry much, if any, enthusiasm.

Thornton must have heard the hesitation. "You're having second thoughts about this aren't you?"

"No," Carys told him. "I'm way beyond second thoughts."

He took her hand in his and led her to one of the overstuffed sofas in the hotel lobby. A huge arrangement of exotic flowers scented the seating area.

Thornton nodded at a man reading a newspaper as they took their seats. "This was supposed to be fun, not stressful."

Clasping her hands together in her lap, Carys met his concerned gaze. "I've never done anything like this before. I don't think I really realized until an hour or so ago that this is probably the most spontaneous and impetuous thing I've done since graduating from college."

"Do I make you nervous or is it the situation?"

"Honestly?"

"I wouldn't have it any other way," he said.

"Well, it's both, then."

He contemplated that for a minute, then Thornton asked her about her children.

So they sat in the hotel lobby talking, neither realizing how much time had passed as Carys told him more about all the things she'd wanted to do and never found the time. He shared with her the trials of being a single father while pastoring a large congregation.

They laughed together about the headaches of coordinating play dates then later getting first young children and then teenagers to assorted practices and lessons.

"When Lydia turned sixteen, I was only too happy to get her a car for her birthday," Thornton confessed. "My mother said I was spoiling her, but let me tell you something, it was a relief not to have to shuttle that girl from cheering to piano and then her part-time job."

"Your daughter worked?"

Thornton nodded. "Sure. She needed to learn the value not only of a dollar but of hard work. I grew up without and wanted to make sure that didn't happen to my family. But I also didn't want to deprive her of the lessons she'd have to learn herself about stewardship and discipline. Lydia is a good kid. She makes me proud."

"It sounds like you did all right raising her by yourself."

Thornton chuckled. "That's not quite how it went.

With a church full of surrogate mothers and my own mother hovering nearby, there was little chance I'd veer too far off the home-training track."

"There's a term I haven't heard in ages—home training."

"At New Providence, we have a lot of outreach ministries. One that I work closely with is a youth ministry targeting at-risk kids in the community that the church serves. It's really easy to see which ones have had some home training by parents or mothers who spend time with their children. Everybody thinks those kids are the ones who'll be all right, but they, like the ones who have essentially raised themselves, also need positive role models and support to succeed."

Carys smiled.

"What?"

"You turned out exactly the way I thought you would."

"And how's that?" he asked her.

"Full of life, committed. Focused on service. You were all those things back when we were in school."

"Not really," Thornton said. "I was just a country boy who had a crush on an unattainable girl."

Carys's gaze met his.

"Yes, you. I had nothing to offer you then. If it hadn't been for scholarships and a lot of prayers, I never would have even been here. Getting a two-year associate's degree from Summerset was the furthest along in education anyone in my family had ever gone."

"And look at you now," Carys said.

Thornton shook his head. "I'm still the same man. You can put the country boy in tailored suits and wing tips, but you can't take the country out of him."

"You miss it, don't you?"

"Shh," Thornton said, putting a finger to his lips and glancing both ways. Laughter danced in his eyes. "If word got back to Lydia that I even joked about moving back to Summerset, I'd never hear the end of it. Mom and I used to take her there to visit relatives and she'd cry the entire time. And when she stopped crying all she did was complain about Grace's boring music. 'Daddy, did somebody die?' she asked me. I had to laugh, because Grace could make anything sound like a dirge."

Carys's stomach rumbled and her eyes widened. She placed a hand over her tummy. "I'm so embarrassed."

"Don't be," Thornton said. He glanced at his watch. "It's after four. We missed lunch."

Carys reached for his wrist. "It can't be that late. I just came downstairs."

"Time flies when you're spending it with someone you enjoy."

Carys nodded. "That's true."

"How about we go find a late lunch or an early dinner?"

"Sounds like a plan."

A few minutes later, they were strolling the downtown streets, considering restaurants and perusing menus posted outside to lure diners in.

"You know what I really want?" Carys said.

"What's that?"

"A big, juicy burger."

Thornton tapped the menu of the all-American restaurant they were standing in front of. "I think we've found our place."

Carys reached for his hand, entwined her fingers in his as they entered. "Yes. I think we have."

It wasn't until much later that Carys realized that moment had been a turning point. Finding her place in life meant more than learning to live single in a double world. For Carys, finding her place also meant learning to trust again, to put her hand in someone else's.

That night as she prepared for bed, she thanked God for allowing her to reconnect with Thornton.

At his hotel across town, Thornton stared out the window at the dark of the night. Like a calm river, contentment ran through him. Thornton smiled. Today had been a good day. Every day, every moment with Carys was good.

As he thought about the time they'd spent together in the last few days, he realized that the song playing in his heart had never ceased its melody. Carys's name was engraved on each note.

More than once over the next few days, Thornton and Carys were mistaken for husband and wife. The first couple of times, they corrected the person, be it waiter or usher. Then, it became something of a joke between them.

The maître d' at tonight's restaurant had come to the same conclusion.

"Maybe we just look like we belong together," Carys whispered as they were led to an intimate table for two.

After dinner, they enjoyed an elegant lemon torte and then coffee.

"I've been thinking about that," Thornton said. Soft candlelight illuminated the small dining room. A Haydn symphony accompanied the murmur of voices and the muted tinkle of silverware on china.

"About what?"

"How we make a good team."

"We do."

"Then let's make it permanent," he said.

Carys's dessert fork clattered on her plate. Her gaze met him. "Excuse me?"

"Marry me, Carys Shaw. I've always loved you. I love you still."

Carys glanced to her right and left. "Thornton, hush. You're embarrassing me."

"Is that a no?"

With not quite steady hands, she reached for her coffee. "You shouldn't play like that."

He stilled her hand. "I'm not. I've waited a long time for our timing to be right. It is right now."

"Thornton…"

"Hear me out," he said. He reached into the inside pocket of his suit jacket. "I have something for you."

Carys's eyes widened and she began to shake her head. "I can't, Thornton. I'm just not…"

"It's not a ring," he said, pulling out the long thin box.

He handed it to her.

Without breaking eye contact with him, Carys accepted the box. "What is it, then?"

"Open it and you'll see."

For a moment, they just stared at each other. Then, Carys, taking a deep breath, lifted the hinged lid on the black velvet box. Nestled inside was a strand of exquisite pearls. A small charm was attached to the center of the strand.

Chapter Seven

"That must have been some reunion," Lydia Holloway said as she snapped her fingers in front of her father's face. "Earth to Dad. Come in, Dad."

"Yes, baby?" He put down the newspaper he hadn't been reading.

"You know, I can be ignored up at school."

Thornton smiled. "I'm not ignoring you, daughter mine."

Lydia smiled. "So I can go?"

Thornton eyed his offspring. "I think the answer is no."

"You don't even know what the question was."

He laughed as he got up to top off his coffee. "True. But you've been running that scam on me for twenty years now. You always wait until I'm distracted, and then you pounce. I know how to smell a trap."

Lydia snapped her fingers again. "Curses. Foiled again."

"Why are you here tormenting me?" Thornton asked. "Don't I have an expensive hair or nail appointment to pay for?"

Lydia held out her right hand examining her fingernails. "Hey, that's not a bad idea. Can I take the platinum card and the convertible?"

"No. And no," Thornton said.

"Boy, I am really striking out today."

Thornton tugged on her ponytail as he passed by on the way to the kitchen counter. "That's what you get for trying to take advantage of your old man."

He refreshed her coffee then put the carafe back on the heating element of the coffeemaker.

"So you had a great time at the reunion, huh?"

He nodded as he leaned against the counter. "The best." He eyed her over the rim of his mug as he sipped. "You know how you're always encouraging me to, uh, date."

Lydia looked up, a slow grin spreading across her face. She was the spitting image of her mother, but had Thornton's dark, serious eyes. "Is that what you were up to? You sly fox."

"Hey, I'm still the father."

She hopped up, stood on tiptoe and pressed a kiss to his cheek. "Well, I think it's terrific."

He raised an eyebrow. "You do?"

"Sure. What's she like? When do I get to meet her?"

"Soon, I hope," Thornton said. "And she's wonderful. We were close friends in college."

"And she looks the same as she did when you guys were in school?"

"No," he said, shaking his head. "She looks even better."

"That must have been some reunion you and T.C. had," Lynn told Carys. Although they'd been home for almost a week, the two old friends had talked twice and decided to meet for lunch even though each had to drive an hour to meet in the spot midway between their homes.

"What makes you say that?"

"Hmm, could it be that silly grin that's been glued on your face?"

Carys tried to wipe away all expression from her features. "What grin?"

"That one," Lynn said, pointing to the edge of Carys's mouth where the telltale edges of a smile valiantly tried to break through. "The one that hasn't let up since you and Thornton got back together."

"Well, we didn't exactly get back together," Carys said by way of clarification. "There never was a together to begin with."

Lynn waved that comment away. "A mere technicality."

"I have something to show you," Carys said.

Lynn nibbled on a piece of celery while Carys reached into her tote bag. She pulled out a black jewelry case.

"What's that?"

"A gift from Thornton."

"Get out! What is it?"

Carys opened the case and showed Lynn the strand of pearls. Attached on a gold pendant was a small key.

"What's that?"

"It's a key that I gave Thornton years ago."

"A key to what?"

Carys's gaze met and held her friend's. "My heart. I told him to hold on to it in case Nate broke my heart."

"Oh," Lynn said, clutching her chest. "Oh, my. This changes everything. You know that, don't you?" She reached a hand out and touched the small gold key. "He kept it. All these years?"

Carys nodded.

"Wow," Lynn said. Still apparently not believing what she was seeing, her face scrunched up in concentration as she worked through the implications. "Men don't hold on to sentimental trinkets, unless they have a really strong significance. So, he's giving your heart back to you. What exactly does that mean?"

Carys took a deep breath. "He asked me to marry him, Lynn. Thornton wants me to marry him."

Lynn's mouth dropped open and she plopped back in her chair as if a strong wind had whipped over her. "Double wow." After a moment, she sat up quickly, leaning forward. "You said yes, right? Please tell me you said yes."

Carys touched the pearls. "He said it takes many years to make one perfect pearl. He's waited all this time hoping he might be able to recapture what he lost all those years ago."

Lynn reached for Carys's hand and closed it over both the box and Carys's fingers. "You did agree to marry him, right? Right?"

"I told him I'd think about it."

Lynn tossed her hands into the air. "Think about it! What's to think about? You're crazy about him. You've talked of nothing else since the reunion, after which,

I might add, you spent a week getting reacquainted with the man."

"Exactly," Carys said, before Lynn could really get ramped up. "One week in the middle of a lifetime. I'm supposed to just run into the arms of someone I haven't seen in twenty-five years and after the span of, what, ten days, just ride off into the sunset with him?"

"Yes! It would have been better had you flown to Vegas and made it official."

Carys narrowed a look at her friend. "He's a minister, Lynn. Flying to Las Vegas for a quickie ceremony at a drive-through wedding chapel isn't his, or my, idea of the way to start a life together."

"Aha!" Lynn said. "So you have been considering his proposal. By the way, there's nothing wrong with Vegas weddings. I got married in Las Vegas and we've been together for twenty-some years now."

Carys sighed.

Lynn reached for her hand. "Talk to me, sisterfriend. What's wrong?"

Carys met Lynn's gaze, read the true concern there despite the teasing. "I'm afraid," she said quietly. "All my life I've been somebody else's thing. The pretty accessory on the arm. I want to be my own person."

Lynn nodded. "I can understand that. But you are your own person. You always have been," Lynn said, sounding like a sage. "Apparently, I don't know what your definition of success is. By everyone else's measure, you've exceeded expectations in phenomenal ways."

Carys rolled her eyes.

"It's true," Lynn said. "For the last twenty-five years, since graduation, you have been one of the most independent and progressive women I've had the pleasure of knowing. You set the benchmark so high, the rest of us wonder where you get the energy."

Carys stared at the pearls, ran a finger along the smooth ridges of the strand. "I've just lived my life one day at a time."

"And you're like the army, doing more by nine than most people do all day. Do you have any idea how many lives you've touched doing philanthropic and civic work? That's why I nominated you for the chapter service award. You're a behind-the-scenes player, one who makes things happen."

Carys shook her head, denying both the words and the praise. She closed the box with the pearls and placed it back in her bag. "That was all just a part of being a doctor's wife and a stay-at-home mom."

"Oh, really?" Lynn then ticked off the names of several mutual acquaintances, women in the same financial and education bracket, who all had professional spouses. "Not a one of them lifts a finger to do anything except order dessert at lunch. So I don't want to hear anything about how unfulfilled you think you are. What is it you want to do, anyway?"

Carys sighed heavily. "I don't know. That's the problem. My entire life has been spent defined as somebody's daughter. His wife. Their mother. When do I just get to be me?"

Lynn met her friend's gaze. "Maybe when you stop picking up and parading around in the labels other people put on you."

Thornton and Carys stayed in touch via phone calls and email. Though he asked her many times to come to his church to visit, just once did he broach the topic of the proposal; and that one time was in a context he was sure she easily dismissed as casual conversation.

He didn't realize just how much he'd been thinking about her until he'd been caught woolgathering for the third or fourth time in the middle of a meeting with the music and praise team leaders.

"You all right, Reverend?"

Thornton nodded at the music director, then put a hand at the back of his neck and stretched a bit. "I've been thinking," he said. "I'd like to see some of the old music incorporated back into the service."

The musician nodded, making a note on his digital assistant. "How far back do you want me to go? Our first CD?"

Smiling, Thornton shook his head. "Further than that." He got up and went to the bookshelves lining one wall of his office. From a shelf at eye level he pulled a red volume stamped in faded gold Peaceful Rest Church. "These old songs."

The choir director took the hymn book and grinned at the praise team leader. "It's been a long time."

Thornton nodded. "Too long. Can you and Mac put together an arrangement of 'Just As I Am'?"

"Shouldn't be a problem," the choir director said.

"But make sure the traditional way the song is sung is included in the arrangement," Thornton requested. "I've heard that done before. Caleb, the head of the music department at the college where I began school, Summerset Junior College—the one near my home church in Texas, did that for a couple of hymns. The arrangements were terrific."

"Will do, Pastor. When do you want it prepared? We have several rehearsals scheduled this week, but I'll only see the mass choir once."

"As soon as it's ready."

The two looked at each other and grinned. "In other words," Mac said, "make this a priority."

Thornton chuckled. "You know me too well."

As the two left, Thornton considered the work still awaiting him. After being away for two weeks, it had really piled up. Just about every spare moment on his calendar had been filled with a meeting or appointment, and a seemingly never-ending stream of visitors showed up at his office door.

Though New Providence was large, he tried to remain accessible to church members by holding open office hours one full day each week and for a half day on Thursdays. A team of associate ministers generally handled other visitors. It was starting to look like he might need to take another vacation just to get away so he could get some work done.

His speaker phone buzzed. Thornton sighed. "Yes, Trina?"

"Pastor, Melva Kimberly would like to speak with you. She said there's an issue with the keynote speaker for the women's retreat."

Thornton sighed again. He doubted if Melva was having any sort of difficulty. Her problem was she was upset because he continued to rebuff her advances.

"Send her in," he told his secretary. "But you come, too. And stay. I need to give you some material."

A moment later, Melva Kimberly strutted into his office at the church. She tried to shut the door, but Trina was right behind her. Melva was a woman who routinely earned second and third glances. Today Melva had poured herself into a neon-blue suit with a miniskirt and high, high heels that played her long legs to the best advantage.

Thornton found himself comparing her to Carys, who dressed in understated but elegant clothing, which always complemented her features and her figure.

At one time, Thornton had considered dating Melva. She was strong, independent and a longtime member of the church. Lydia's aversion to her, not to mention his own—though he could never figure out why—always stopped him. Lydia called her "grasping." Thornton was careful to always have someone in the room when Melva wanted to see him.

The secretary took a seat, crossed her legs and held a notepad at the ready.

Melva cast a exasperated glance in Trina's direction, but the assistant just smiled.

"I'd like a few words with the pastor."

"Trina's here to take notes," he said. Thornton indicated a chair for Melva. "You said you wanted to speak with me about the women's retreat. How are things going?"

Visibly annoyed, Melva positioned herself so she stood just in front of Trina. Behind her back, the assistant made a moue. Thornton bit the inside of his mouth to keep from smiling. There was no love lost between these two women. And it was just as well.

Thornton knew that the last thing Melva Kimberly had on her mind today was the women's retreat. He'd ducked three of her calls in the time since he'd returned from vacation. Maybe it was time to change his personal cell phone number. Again.

"Well, yes," she said, answering his question.

She tried a bit of chitchat, but when it became clear that Thornton would not entertain any personal conversation, Melva sighed then mentioned a few details about the upcoming retreat. The meeting didn't last long.

Trina shut the door behind the woman. "I don't know why or how you put up with that."

"Trina…"

The assistant put her notepad on his desk. "You do know what she's been running around telling people?"

"If this is gossip, Trina, you know I don't have patience for it."

"It's not gossip," she said. "It's intelligence. There's a difference."

Thornton had to smile at that. He sat back in his chair, nodded at the assistant who'd worked closely with him for the last seven years. "All right. What's your intelligence?"

She peered at him for a moment. "You're not dating her, are you?"

"Wouldn't you know if I was?"

For a moment, Trina looked uncertain. Then she let out a loud guffaw. "That's for sure. Anyway, that woman had the nerve to tell three members of the pastor's aid society that when she's the first lady of New Providence, some things would change."

"She assumes a lot," Thornton muttered.

"I'll say. And…"

He groaned. "There's more?"

"Mac and his wife saw her at a bridal shop trying on veils."

Thornton brightened. "Maybe she's found a boyfriend."

"Uh-huh. Right." Trina got up and went over to a large golden pothos and picked at a few yellow leaves on the plant.

He wasn't quite sure when the Melva issue had gotten out of hand. He looked up one day and she had somehow ingratiated herself into his inner circle of deacons, advisers and church leaders who conducted the day-to-day operation of New Providence. The annual women's retreat was a huge affair, more than a thousand women attended each year. Granted, Melva had worked her way up the ranks starting as a retreat volunteer, but somehow she'd gotten the impression that he had a personal interest in her.

"Trina?"

She dropped the leaves in the trash and faced him.

"May I ask you a question?"

"Sure."

"I'd like an honest reply."

"Have I ever given you anything except honesty?"

"No," he said. "You've always been a straight shooter."

"So," she said. "What's on your mind?"

Thornton paced the area between his desk and a credenza. "Have I in some way led her on, or any other single women in the church?"

For a moment, Trina just looked at him. Then she heaved a heavy sigh. "The truth of it, Pastor?" When he nodded, Trina said, "Yes, you have."

Thornton closed his eyes. "How? When?"

Trina got up, walked to his dressing area and returned with a small mirror. She handed it to him.

"What's this for?"

"Look in it," she directed.

Thornton stared at his reflection. "All right. Now what?"

"What do you see?"

Looking at his own image, Thornton replied, "Middle-aged black man. Circles under his eyes from not enough sleep. Needs a haircut. Gray hair."

"Wrong," Trina said. She took the mirror from him and placed it on the desk.

Thornton looked genuinely confused. "That's not what I look like?"

"Nope."

He sat down in his chair, clasped his hands together. "All right. Tell me what I'm supposed to be seeing."

"Single. Educated. Attractive. Very attractive. The gray enhances the look," she added touching her temples. "Wealthy. Powerful. In other words, bait."

"Bait?"

"Do you have any idea what it takes to deflect the women who prance in here trying to get a half an hour with you? It's unbelievable. And to make matters worse," Trina added, "you're a nice man. Genuine. Honest."

"If I didn't know you were happily married," he said dryly, "I'd wonder if you'd joined Melva's camp."

"Your fan club is legion, Pastor. Hold on a sec. I have something to show you that I'll bet you've never seen before."

Trina disappeared into her own office for a moment. When she returned, she held a box and a glossy magazine in her hand.

"Remember when you were featured in Ebony as one of the fifty top preachers in the country?"

Thornton nodded, then pointed toward the magazine cover on his wall.

"Well, here's another magazine's take on it," she said handing him the other publication. "You also ranked in the top percentile in this."

"What is it?"

Trina opened the publication to the centerpiece spread: "Could You Be His First Lady?"

Horrified, Thornton stared at a photo of himself. "What is this?"

"It's an article telling women how to snare a preacher husband. Five of the nation's most eligible ministers are featured. You, Pastor, are number one on the list."

Thornton dropped the magazine. "You're joking? Who would buy something like this or read it? When did this come out?"

"No, I'm not joking," Trina said, answering the first question. "You'd be surprised who reads it. That was just published. It hit newsstands last week. And here's what's come in so far."

She then dumped the contents of the box onto the top of his desk. Keys, letters, photographs and two small teddy bears toppled out.

Thornton eyed the pile. "What is all that?"

"Fan mail," Trina told him. "From women who want to be Mrs. Reverend Doctor Thornton Charles Holloway."

Chapter Eight

Thornton had plenty of experience in stepping lightly through the myriad minefields associated with being a single father and pastor. This one beat them all, though.

He stared in disgust at the magazine, not so much irritated by what it said but the time it would take one of the staff members to devote to dealing with the flood of mail it would generate. If the responses Trina had were an early indication, it might go on for a while. He didn't even have to instruct her on what to do with the items. Trina was already handling the situation, making sure each person was sent one of New Providence's prayer ministry brochures and that the other items were donated or disposed of.

One thing Thornton had learned through the years was that he couldn't control what people said about him—in particular his personal life. He didn't have to like it, but he couldn't control it.

Despite what some people said or thought, he didn't think it was odd that he'd remained single all this time. Thornton knew and trusted God's plan for all aspects of his life—from Lydia's upbringing, to his own social agenda.

Spending the week with Carys yielded confirmation on something he'd known for many years. Though he'd loved his wife dearly and grieved after she'd died, the reason he had never remarried was simple: he'd never stopped loving Carys Chappelle.

He'd told her the truth about coming close to getting married a time or two. He'd thought about it, but in each case, the Lord placed a barrier in the way, something that prevented the relationship from developing or moving toward a long-term commitment. With Carys, though, every day was a new window of blessings opening to him.

During the week with her, he'd discovered that his feelings were genuine, not manufactured by loneliness or nostalgia. He'd suspected that her appeal might be tied up in the wistful longing and memory of his youth, that time and distance and perspective might counter the crush he'd had on her.

But this was no mere crush.

After a boat ride, two movies, three evenings watching the sun set beyond and a week of meals filled with laughter and good conversation, Thornton realized that the love in his heart was expanding, not receding.

So he'd given her the key, the very one that she'd given to him all those years ago on the waterfront. He remembered her words as if it were yesterday.

Hold on to this for me, T.C. I might ask for it back later, but right now you're my anchor in a rough sea.

Thornton chewed on that for a moment. An anchor in a rough sea.

His mind already running, Thornton opened his laptop computer and started writing the sermon he'd deliver during the Sunday services.

Midway through the call to worship for the eleven o'clock service, Thornton saw her. His mouth dropped open for a moment, then broke into a broad smile. Nodding, he acknowledged her presence. Carys beamed at him and Thornton knew that no matter what happened between them, he'd always cherish their friendship.

Carys was dressed in a soft lavender suit and wore a wide-brimmed hat that matched her outfit. She was sitting near the front, across the aisle from his mother and daughter.

"I'm pleased to see a special friend in the sanctuary this morning," he said later when he got up for pastoral observations. "She didn't stand during the greeting of visitors but I'd like for her to do so now." He smiled at Carys who rose as he introduced her. "We go back," Thornton said, "so far that I won't tell you how many years."

People in the congregation chuckled as heads strained to see the woman he'd singled out. Lydia was looking at Carys, but from the corner of his eyes Thornton saw his mother was focused on him. A gentle smile curved her lips as she nodded.

Carys was wearing a single strand of pearls. But Thornton's heart plummeted when he realized the key wasn't on the strand. *She probably has lots of pearls,* he told himself as he tried to concentrate on what he was saying.

"Carys has a voice you won't believe," he said. "Would you sing with me?"

When she stepped out into the aisle, Thornton came down and escorted her. Then with New Providence's two-hundred-voice choir backing them, Carys and Thornton sang "Just As I Am," Carys easily following Thornton's lead on the new arrangement of the hymn.

When they finished, praises went up throughout the congregation.

Thornton kissed her on the cheek and led her back to her seat. "Carys Shaw," he said to the congregation.

Carys waved, then turned to him as applause sounded from the upper level to the far corners of the large sanctuary. "Thornton, this belongs to you," she said in his ear as she pressed something into his hand.

Thornton looked down. Resting in his palm was the key. The one to her heart.

His eyes raked over her, searching for meaning. "Carys?"

She nodded. She hadn't planned to tell him in the middle of church, but the moment was the right one—now, when her heart soared and the love she had for this man filled her.

"Yes, Thornton. I'll marry you."

His eyes widened, and then he grinned. "You will?"

Carys nodded.

He closed his eyes for a moment, whispering a prayer of thanksgiving. Then he hugged her. "I love you, Carys Shaw."

"I love you, too."

When he returned to the pulpit, Thornton faced his congregation. "Carys and I used to sing together in the choir in college. You can hear why she was a soloist. Sometimes our lives take different turns. We all walk paths that seem fortuitous, but paths that are really ordained by God.

"After graduation, we went our separate ways, but the Lord saw to it that our paths were headed in the same direction. Sometimes we're blessed with second chances."

His solemn tone had every person riveted. Thornton heard a few gasps as the direction of his comments dawned on people.

"Through the years, a lot of you have asked me why I never got married. Well, you can stop asking. Carys has agreed to be my bride."

Hundreds of people jumped up cheering and applauding. Melva Kimberly and three of her friends got up and left. The moment belonged to Thornton and Carys, though, as the musicians riffed on a jazzy improvisation of "Here Comes the Bride." Thornton looked back and laughed, shaking his head, but when his gaze connected again with Carys's, his breath caught.

He'd waited a lifetime to claim her heart; now the music between them would be a love song to last forever.

* * * * *

A Brand-New Madaris Family Novel!

NEW YORK TIMES BESTSELLING AUTHOR

BRENDA JACKSON

COURTING JUSTICE

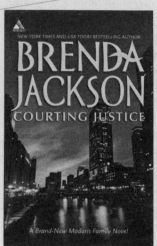

Winning a high-profile case
may have helped New York
attorney DeAngelo DiMeglio's
career, but it hasn't helped
him win the woman he loves.
Peyton Mahoney doesn't
want anything more than a
fling with DeAngelo. Until
another high-profile case
brings them to opposing
sides of the courtroom…and
then their sizzling attraction
can no longer be denied.

"Brenda Jackson is the queen of newly discovered love,
especially in her Madaris Family series."
—*BookPage* on *Inseparable*

Available now wherever books are sold.

Two classic Westmoreland novels in one volume!

NEW YORK TIMES BESTSELLING AUTHOR

BRENDA JACKSON

DREAMS OF FOREVER

In *Seduction, Westmoreland Style,* Montana horse breeder McKinnon Quinn is adamant about his "no women on my ranch" rule…but Casey Westmoreland makes it very tempting to break the rules.

Spencer's Forbidden Passion has millionaire Spencer Westmoreland and Chardonnay Russell entering a marriage of convenience…but Chardonnay wants what is strictly forbidden.

"Sexy and sizzling." —*Library Journal* on *Intimate Seduction*

Available July 2012 wherever books are sold.

REQUEST YOUR FREE BOOKS!

2 FREE NOVELS
PLUS 2 FREE GIFTS!

KIMANI™
ROMANCE

Love's ultimate destination!

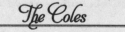